CELTIC MYTHOLOGY

OTHER TITLES BY PHILIP FREEMAN

The World of Saint Patrick

CELTIC MYTHOLOGY

Tales of Gods, Goddesses, and Heroes

PHILIP FREEMAN

Oxford University Press is a department of the University of Oxford. It furthers the University's objective of excellence in research, scholarship, and education by publishing worldwide. Oxford is a registered trade mark of Oxford University Press in the UK and certain other countries.

Published in the United States of America by Oxford University Press
198 Madison Avenue, New York, NY 10016, United States of America.

CIP data is on file at the Library of Congress
ISBN 978-0-19-046047-1

13

Printed by Sheridan Books, Inc., United States of America

CONTENTS

Introduction: Who Were the Celts? ix
Pronunciation Guide xvii

1. The Earliest Celtic Gods 1
2. The Book of Invasions 14
3. The Wooing of Étaín 29
4. Cú Chulainn and the Táin Bó Cuailnge 46
   The Discovery of the Táin 47
   The Conception of Conchobar 48
   The Curse of Macha 50
   The Exile of the Sons of Uisliu 52
   The Birth of Cú Chulainn 57
   The Boyhood Deeds of Cú Chulainn 61
   The Wooing of Emer 71
   The Death of Aife's Only Son 75
   The Táin Begins 77
   Single Combat 82
   Cú Chulainn and Ferdia 86
   The Final Battle 89

5. Tales from the Ulster Cycle 92
The Story of Mac Dá Thó's Pig 92
The Cattle Raid of Fróech 98
The Destruction of Dá Derga's Hostel 104
Athairne and Amairgen 115
Briccriu's Feast 116
The Intoxication of the Ulstermen 123
The Wasting Sickness of Cú Chulainn and the Only Jealousy of Emer 126
The Death of Cú Chulainn 133
6. Stories of the Irish Otherworld 137
The Adventure of Nera 137
The Adventure of Cormac 141
The Adventure of Conla 145
The Adventures of the Sons of Eochaid Mugmedón 147
The Voyage of Bran 149
7. Finn the Outlaw 153
The Boyhood Deeds of Finn 153
The Pursuit of Diarmuid and Gráinne 158
8. Welsh Mythology—The *Mabinogi* 165
Pwyll Prince of Dyfed 165
Branwen Daughter of Llyr 174
Manawydan Son of Llyr 180
Math Son of Mathonwy 185
9. Welsh Stories and Sagas 197
Lludd and Lleuelys 197
Gwion Bach and Taliesin 199
Culhwch and Olwen 205
10. Christian Mythology 213
Saint Patrick 214

Saint Brigid 224
Saint Brendan 231

Notes 241
Glossary 249
Bibliography 265
Index 267

INTRODUCTION: WHO WERE THE CELTS?

Over two thousand years ago, someone on the cold and windswept shores of the Atlantic Ocean sat down before a blazing fire and told a story. Long ago, this person said, there were two gods who were brothers, twins born together from the same womb of a great mother goddess of the sea. When these brothers grew up, they left the ocean behind and came to dwell among the people who lived near the sea.

There was much more to the story, but that is all that survives. The only reason we know even this bare outline is that the tale was passed on by word of mouth until a visitor from the Mediterranean world wrote it down. In time that document found its way to a Greek historian named Timaeus from the island of Sicily, who lived just after the age of Alexander the Great. He recorded the story as part of his monumental history of the world from legendary times until his own day. But all the volumes of Timaeus were lost over the centuries, so that his words are preserved only in a few quotations by later classical writers whose works did survive. One of these writers was another Greek named Diodorus, who three hundred years later briefly summarized the story of the twin gods he had read in Timaeus.

And thus the oldest myth of the Celtic people of ancient Europe has been preserved for us today by the merest chance.

Everyone today knows about the gods and heroes of the ancient Greeks, such as Zeus, Hera, and Hercules, and most have read of the Norse gods Odin, Thor, and Freya, but how many people have heard of the Gaulish god Lugus, or the magical Welsh queen Rhiannon, or the great Irish warrior Cú Chulainn? We still thrill to the story of the Trojan War, but the epic battles of the Irish *Táin Bó Cuailnge* are known only to a few. And yet those who have read the stories of Celtic myth and legend—among them writers like J. R. R. Tolkien and C. S. Lewis—have been deeply moved and influenced by these amazing tales, for there is nothing in the world quite like them. In these stories a mysterious and invisible realm of gods and spirits exists alongside and sometimes crosses over into our own human world, fierce women warriors battle with kings and heroes, and even the rules of time and space can be suspended.

But who were these Celts who told such tales, what sort of stories did they tell, and how have they survived? We know the Celts were one of the most feared and admired peoples of ancient Europe, inhabiting in Roman times the coastal lands from Spain, Britain, and Ireland across the continent to northern Italy and into eastern Europe and Asia Minor. They served as mercenary soldiers in the armies of Egyptian kings and fought for centuries against the expanding empire of Rome. Their druid priests taught of reincarnation and sacrificed human captives by burning them alive in wicker cages; their poets sang hauntingly beautiful songs of praise and satire. They were never a single nation but, rather, a vast collection of tribes sharing similar languages, religion, and mythology.

We first hear of a people called the *Keltoi* from Greek merchants and explorers who sailed to the western shores of the Mediterranean and Atlantic around 500 B.C.E. But soon these same Celts who lived in Gaul (modern France) were crossing the Alps and invading Italy and Greece. Writers such as the Greek historian Xenophon and the philosopher Aristotle describe them as matchless warriors who feared nothing and plunged sword-first into battle with joyous abandon, sometimes naked except for the gold torques they wore around their necks.

The Celtic warriors of northern Italy sacked the young city of Rome in 390 B.C.E. and demanded a ransom of gold before leaving the smoldering ruins behind them. Their descendants ventured into the Balkans and invaded Greece a century later. Some of these Celtic tribes even crossed into what is now Turkey and established kingdoms that would last for centuries in the mountainous heart of Asia Minor, becoming the Galatians to whom St. Paul would address one of his New Testament letters.

A curious and brave Greek philosopher named Posidonius visited the wild interior of Gaul at the beginning of the first century B.C.E. and wrote about the Celtic warriors who were his hosts. He records that they were a proud and brave people who loved fighting, riddles, and feasting. He was appalled to see the preserved heads that decorated the halls of their tribal chieftains serving as trophies of valiant enemies they had slain. He spoke of their devotion to the gods and their fondness for tales sung by their bards, though he preserved only a few hints of what these stories were.

Almost half a century after the visit of Posidonius, the Roman general Julius Caesar conquered the Celts of Gaul in a brutal war that left hundreds of thousands dead or enslaved. Caesar writes at length of his battles with the Gauls, but also briefly preserves some of our best descriptions of their gods and religion. And although the Romans took over Gaul and banned human sacrifice by the druids, they had little interest in changing native Celtic religion and culture. Bits and pieces of this religion and mythology survive in Greek and Roman stories, carved into stone monuments, or etched on lead tablets, though rarely anything that could be called a complete story. Sadly for us, the Celts of classical times did not record any of their own myths. Thus for the ancient Gauls, Galatians, and other Celtic peoples of continental Europe, we must be content with a few scattered references to their gods and a handful of short and possibly distorted myths that come to us from Greek and Roman visitors.

Caesar crossed the channel and attacked Britain twice during his first-century B.C.E. war in Gaul, but he left the conquest of the island to the Romans of the next century, beginning under the emperor Claudius. Years of bloody fighting by the legions pushed the Roman frontier all the way to Hadrian's Wall in northern Britain. The British Celts were eventually subdued and became a vital part of the empire, but their language, gods, and stories persisted under Roman rule until the Saxons and other Germanic tribes landed on their shores in the fifth century A.D. These new invaders were more thorough than the Romans. Celtic culture soon vanished from Britain except in the remote regions of Wales,

Cornwall, and for a time, in the native British kingdoms of the north. Others left Britain altogether and settled across the sea on the remote peninsula of Brittany in what is now northwestern France. But in all these Celtic enclaves, the ancient stories survived and evolved, most famously into the great Welsh tales of the Middle Ages, especially the collection known as the *Mabinogi*. The surviving medieval manuscripts in which these legends were written tell of magic and giants, of great kings such as the mighty Arthur, and of women and poets with supernatural powers. Although strongly influenced by European literature of the time, these Welsh stories are uniquely and wonderfully Celtic.

By the end of the fifth century A.D., only Ireland remained as a free land where the ancient ways of the Celts remained untouched by Rome. The classical world knew of Ireland only as a distant and savage island, supposedly full of cannibals and barbarians. In truth it was a rich and fertile land with an ancient and sophisticated culture. Kings, warriors, and druids formed an aristocracy that ruled over a land of prosperous farms where cattle were the measure of a family's wealth. Around these farms throughout the island were stone tombs and monuments far more ancient than the Celts that became a part of Irish mythology as entrances to the mysterious Otherworld.

Christianity reached Ireland by the early fifth century A.D., when Pope Celestine sent a bishop named Palladius to the distant island to minister to its people. A young Roman nobleman named Patrick, who had been captured in an Irish slave raid on Britain, escaped from captivity in Ireland during this time, but later returned as a missionary, bringing with him not only a new religion but also the art of writing, which could at last record ancient Irish myths on parchment. The monks of Ireland soon became famous scribes who wrote down both Christian tales and native Irish stories.

And what stories they were—gods and goddesses battling for control of the island in epic wars, heroes engaged in endless combat to win undying glory, voyages across the sea to magical islands, divine women who with the gift of their sexuality could establish or destroy the power of kings. Even early Christian saints such as Patrick, Brigid, and Brendan became part of Irish mythology.

For centuries the Irish and Welsh, along with the Scots, Cornish, and Bretons, preserved their traditional tales in their own languages as the English and French, through war and campaigns of cultural assimilation, tried to force them to abandon their heritage. But fortunately for all of us they did not prevail, so that when we ask who the Celts were, we should really ask who they *are*—for the Celtic people with their unique languages and cultures still survive. On the west coast of Ireland, in Welsh towns and villages, in the hills and islands of western Scotland, and on the farms of Brittany, visitors today can still hear the ancient tales of the Celts told and sung in their native languages. In music and stories, the mythology of the Celts lives on for all of us.

In writing any book on mythology, an author first has to decide what a myth is. The ancient Greeks thought of a *mythos* simply as a spoken story. But ask a random person today what a myth is and they will probably say it's a story that isn't true. Even scholars of mythology can rarely agree on what exactly a myth is. My definition for this book is simple—a myth is a traditional tale about gods and heroes.

One problem about our written sources for Celtic mythology is that many of the authors who recorded them were far removed from the original tales, if not plainly hostile to them. The Christian scribe who wrote down one version of the Irish epic *Táin Bó Cuailnge* includes on the last page a warning to his readers:

> *I, however, who have copied this history—or more accurately this fable—give no credence to various incidents narrated here. Some things in this story are feats of devilish deception, others are poetic figments, a few are probable, others improbable, and even more invented for the delight of fools.*

The earlier Greek and Roman authors who wrote about the Celts had their own prejudices that could distort the stories they were recording. To many of them the Celts were wild barbarians who threatened to destroy civilization; to others they were romantic figures of primal innocence. The later medieval stories, like the tales of Norse mythology, were all recorded by Christians who viewed an earlier pre-Christian world through the lens of their own beliefs and experiences. In many cases we can see beneath the classical and Christian biases to the original Celtic tale, but the recovery of a "pure" myth isn't always possible or even desirable. The best mythology of every culture is a rich blend of many influences—and the remarkable stories of the Celts are no exception.

It has been my privilege to teach courses on Celtic literature and mythology to university and college students for many years. It's always a thrill to stand before my students on the first day of class and talk about the stories we will be reading that semester. There's such excitement among people young and old about the traditional stories of Ireland, Wales, and the rest of the Celtic world that I can't imagine a more enjoyable project than writing this book to introduce readers everywhere to these tales.

I owe an enormous debt of gratitude to my own professors at Harvard University who patiently taught me the languages and myths of the Celts, but I also must thank the many friends in Ireland and Wales who have shared so many stories with me over the years and made the mythology of the Celts come alive before my eyes. I hope in my own small way I can do the same for everyone who reads this book.

PRONUNCIATION GUIDE

The ancient Celtic languages of Roman times are pronounced very much as they look (e.g., *E-po-na*), but the medieval languages of Ireland and Wales can confound even the most dedicated students of mythology. The following is a brief guide to a few of the more important features of the languages. A more extensive guide to the pronunciation of medieval Irish words and names is found in Carson, *The Táin*, xxvii–xxx. For Welsh, see Ford, *The Mabinogi and Other Medieval Welsh Tales*, 195–196.

Gaulish

Anyone who has studied a little Latin in school will have no trouble with the ancient Celtic words and names recorded in Greek and Roman authors. Like Latin, almost all the consonants and vowels are pronounced as they appear on the page and no letters are silent; *c* is always hard (*k*, not *s* or *ch*), as is *g* (as in *go*, never *j*). For example:

Lugus	*LU-gus*
Teutates	*teu-TA-tes*
Matrona	*ma-TRO-na*

Welsh

Medieval Welsh is related to Gaulish, but its spelling and pronunciation underwent radical changes in the early Middle Ages; *g* is always pronounced hard, *w* can be a consonant or a vowel (short as in *put* or long as in *tool*), *y* is a vowel (short as in *in* or long as in *screen*), *ch* as in German *ich* or Scottish *loch*, and *ll* (represented below by *LL*) is found in few other languages of the world—try pronouncing it by making a regular *l* sound without vibrating your throat:

Lleu	*LLai*
Pwyll	*pwiLL*
Culhwch	*KIL-huch*
Mabinogi	*mab-in-O-gee*

Irish

Like its linguistic cousin Welsh, medieval Irish evolved rapidly soon after the Roman era. Long vowels are marked by an accent (e.g., *cú*) and *ch* is pronounced in the back of the throat as in Welsh. Consonants standing between vowels are usually softened, so that for example *t* becomes *d* and *d* becomes the sound of the final consonant in English *bathe* (shown below as *dh*):

Ailill	*A-lil*
Cathbad	*CATH-badh*
Cú Chulainn	ku CHU-lan
Medb	*medhv*
Táin Bó Cuailnge	*tan bow KUAL-nya*

CELTIC MYTHOLOGY

1

THE EARLIEST CELTIC GODS

THE GODS OF THE ANCIENT Celts are a mystery. Even when we know their names—and we know quite a few—we seldom can say for certain what their powers were, how they were worshiped, or what stories were told about them. Julius Caesar devotes one brief paragraph of the long history of his war in Gaul to the gods of that land, but that short description is by far the best written evidence we have of ancient Celtic religion. A few other Greek and Roman writers mention the gods of the Celts and many of their names are found in local inscriptions or in tribal names, but compared to what we know about the gods of Mount Olympus, our knowledge of Celtic divinities is sorely lacking.

We know that the greatest of the gods of ancient Gaul was Mercury—so says Caesar. But in his description of the deities of the people he conquered, Caesar substitutes the names of similar Roman gods rather than use their native Celtic names. Caesar adds that there were images of this Mercury throughout Gaul, that he was the inventor of all the arts, and that he was a guide for every journey, as well as the most influential god in trade and business.

The Roman Mercury was a god of movement, not only of goods and people but also of words and ideas. He guided the souls of mortals to the land of the dead and moved on the boundaries of life in every aspect. It might seem strange that Caesar would choose him as the closest counterpart to the chief god among the Gauls instead of Jupiter, but his choice reveals something important about Celtic religion. The Celts were polytheists who believed in many gods, like the ancient Greeks and Romans, but their greatest god was not a white-bearded king of the heavens casting thunderbolts down to earth. The Celtic Mercury was a craftsman, an inventor, a traveler, and a guide for all in need.

Caesar's claim about the numerous images of this god are confirmed by archeologists who have unearthed many statues and sculptures of Mercury in Gaul. Usually he is portrayed as a young man in the classical mode, with his trademark caduceus staff, sometimes accompanied by a cornucopia-bearing goddess named Rosmerta. But nowhere in all of Gaul does an inscription tell us what the Celts themselves called Caesar's Mercury.

And yet we may be able to discover his true name. One clue comes from Caesar's own description of Gaulish Mercury as the inventor of all the arts. In medieval Ireland, there is a young and handsome god we will meet later who is described in Irish as *samildánach* ("skilled in all arts"). His name is Lug, which means "the shining one." He is the most honored and versatile of the Irish gods, and he is the divine father of Cú Chulainn, the greatest hero of Irish legend. Linguistics can tell us that if such a god existed among the Gauls, his name would be Lugus—and it happens that there is evidence for a god with this very name not only in Gaul but also throughout the ancient Celtic world. Numerous towns throughout western and eastern Europe were named for him, such as Lugudunum ("fortress of Lugus"), which became modern Lyon, France, as well as Luguvalium, modern Carlisle in southern Scotland. By no coincidence, ancient Lyon celebrated a great annual festival for Lugus on August 1, the same day the Irish danced at their celebration of Lughnasa in honor of their god Lug.

The ancient god Lugus also appears in Celtic Spain on a dedication by a guild of shoemakers. Here, as in a similar inscription in Switzerland, his name is found in the plural as Lugoves—probably because Celtic gods from Gaul to Ireland often manifested themselves as one god in three parts, like the Christian Trinity. Intriguingly, the later Welsh version of Lugus is a magical character named Lleu, who in one story puts aside his noble rank and works as a humble maker of shoes. Another inscription carved in stone on a mountaintop in Spain honors Lugus as tribal god at what seems to be a place of pilgrimage.

Caesar next says that the Gauls worship Apollo, Mars, Jupiter, and Minerva, who rule over the same areas of human life and the world as they do in Roman religion. Apollo, he says, drives away disease, Mars is the god of war, Jupiter reigns over the sky, and Minerva is devoted to crafts. Again, we don't know for certain what the Gauls called these gods, but we can learn something about them from the descriptive names given to them, from their depiction in ancient Celtic art, and from similarities to characters in later Irish and Welsh mythology.

In classical mythology, Apollo is a young god of healing, prophesy, poetry, and music. Disease in the Greek world was often seen as the result of impurity, and so shrines of Apollo were centers of purification rituals. Likewise in Gaul, natural springs were cultic centers of this god who could heal all manner of infirmities. The Celtic Apollo has more than a dozen descriptive titles attached to his name in surviving inscriptions, such as Belenus, Cunomaglus, and Grannus. Apollo Belenus is widely attested at therapeutic hot springs in Austria, northern Italy, and southern Gaul, as well as Britain. The root *bel-*, meaning "brilliant," is found also in the Irish Mayday festival of Beltaine ("brilliant fire"). Apollo Cunomaglus ("hound lord") appears in Britain as a young hunter god, while Apollo Grannus was such a well-known healing god that his cult spread beyond the Celtic world and was invoked by the Roman emperor Caracalla. Other of the many names and manifestations of Gaulish Apollo are Borvo ("the boiling one"—probably from his association with hot springs), accompanied by a consort Damona, and Maponos ("the divine youth"), invoked in a magical tablet unearthed in France that was written in the native Gaulish language in the first century A.D. Maponos was especially popular in northern Britain and survives in early Arthurian literature as Mabon son of Madron ("the divine mother").

Caesar says that the war-loving Gauls would often dedicate the spoils of an upcoming battle to Mars—and, indeed, there is archeological evidence for this practice. If successful in war, Caesar says, they would sacrifice all living things captured in the battle to the god and gather together the material spoils into a sacred place in his honor. He says many tribes throughout Gaul had such sanctuaries that were rarely violated. Those who did so, if caught, faced unimaginable torture and punishment. The Celtic Mars overlaps in his duties with Apollo by also serving as a healing god, but his main functions were war and territorial protection. He bears many Celtic names, such as the guardian deity Mars Albiorix in southern Gaul, Mars Caturix ("king of fighting") near Geneva, and the popular healing god Mars Lenus in Gaul and Britain. He is often pictured on stone carvings with a goose, a sentry animal known for its aggressiveness. The god is also called Mars Teutates, which matches the name of a ferocious Gaulish deity described by the first-century A.D. Roman poet Lucan as "cruel Teutates satisfied only by human sacrifice." Eight hundred years later a commentator on Lucan says that this Teutates was in fact the god Mars and that he was appeased by the drowning of his victims. It's difficult to know if this is an accurate description of earlier Gaulish religion, but the god of the medieval commentary bears a striking resemblance to an image carved on an ancient cauldron found in a bog at Gundestrup in Denmark, in which a superhuman figure plunges a man upside down into a giant vat.

Caesar's Jupiter often appears in Gaulish sculpture as a toga-clad ruler of the sky with a scepter in hand. In a few inscriptions he is expressly identified by the name Taranis, a Celtic word meaning "thunderer." The previous passage of Lucan says that Taranis was as vicious as the Scythian goddess Diana, while Lucan's medieval commentator claims that victims dedicated to Taranis were burned alive in wooden cages, a practice mentioned by Caesar himself. But Gaulish Jupiter bears many other names as well, such as Jupiter Brixianus in northern Italy, Jupiter Ladicus in Spain, and Jupiter Poeninus in the Alps. Whatever his name, the sky-god was worshiped widely across the Celtic world and is the subject of a remarkable set of a hundred columns found mostly along the Rhine River. These tall pillars are carved to resemble oak trees, confirming a passage in the writings of the second-century A.D. Greek writer Maximus of Tyre, in which he says the Celtic image of Zeus (the Greek name for Jupiter) was a lofty oak tree. Jupiter rides a horse at the top of these columns, sometimes with a wheel of the sun and lightning in his hands, as he tramples a giant, serpent-legged monster beneath him. Zeus also fights giants and monsters in Greek mythology, but never from atop a horse, suggesting a distinctly Celtic story behind these carvings. We can only guess about the myth the columns represent, but it's possible there was an ancient and widespread Celtic tale about the god of the sky defeating the dark powers of the underworld with the blinding power of the sun and his mighty thunderbolts.

Caesar lists only one goddess among the Gauls—Minerva, who was the mistress of all arts, a description that closely matches her role in Greek and Roman mythology. But just as Roman Minerva (Greek Athena) was much more than a goddess of craft, it's likely that the Celtic goddess also had other areas of concern, such as victory in war and healing. A Roman writer of Gaulish origin named Pompeius Trogus who wrote during the time of the emperor Augustus tells the story of an attack on the city of Massalia (modern Marseilles, France) during which a goddess appeared to the besieging Celtic war leader in a dream and warned him to cease his assault. He entered the city peacefully and saw in a temple there a statue of Minerva, the very goddess who had appeared to him in his dream. The third-century geographer Solinus says that in Britain, Celtic Minerva was worshiped as Belisama ("brightest") and had in her sanctuary a perpetual fire burning in her honor. She was also honored in Britain as the goddess Sulis at the famous thermal springs at Bath, known as Aquae Sulis ("the waters of Sulis") throughout Roman times. Indeed, Celtic Minerva seems to have been one of the longest surviving of the Celtic gods. The Christian church fathers Salvianus of Marseilles and Gregory of Tours mention her active worship in Gaul during the fifth and sixth centuries. As late as the seventh century, Bishop Eligius of Noyon in northern France was warning women of his diocese not to pray to Minerva when weaving and dyeing cloth.

Caesar includes one final god of the ancient Gauls after all the others. This is Dis, a Roman name for the Greek Hades, god of death and the dark underworld. He records that the Gauls all believed they were descended from Dis, as the druids taught. Because of this, they marked the beginning of each day with sunset, not sunrise. In early Celtic art Dis appears holding a scroll, sometimes accompanied by a maternal goddess named Aericula. It may seem strange that the Celts believed they were descended from the god of the dead, but the same belief is found in ancient India and other mythologies around the world. In later Irish stories, the god Donn ("the dark one") appears as a kindly, paternal figure who lives on a rocky island in the western sea where the souls of the Irish journeyed after death.

There were many other ancient Celtic gods apart from those listed by Caesar, but again we know very little about them. One is Esus, who appears in the poem of Lucan as "dreadful Esus," who demands human blood shed on savage altars. The medieval commentator says that victims of this god were suspended from trees—as were those of the Norse god Odin—after they had been fatally wounded. The only certain image we have of Esus is a pillar discovered in 1711 underneath the cathedral of Notre Dame in Paris. In this carving, dedicated by local sailors and dated to the first century A.D., the god is named in an inscription and appears as a muscular woodsman chopping at a tree. On the panel next to him is a bull with three cranes and the name Tarvos Trigaranus. The pillar is similar to an ancient relief from Trier dedicated to Mercury, which shows another woodsman about to chop down a tree with an axe while three birds and the head of a bull watch from the foliage above. These enigmatic carvings may well depict a lost myth about the god.

Among the many other gods of the ancient Gauls is Sucellus ("the good striker") who appears in stone relief as a man with a curly beard and hair with a long-shafted hammer in his hand. Beside him on one carving is a goddess named Nantosvelta, who is often pictured with a raven. Another widespread god is Cernunnos ("the horned god"), a divine lord of the animals who appears in a Celtic rock carving from northern Italy as early as the fourth century B.C. The pillar found under Notre Dame bears the only surviving inscription with his name, but his figure appears in many locations. In these he is often seated in a cross-legged posture like the Buddha surrounded by stags and other wild animals, notably a snake with ram horns, and has large antlers springing from his own head on which hang torques, the neck rings found throughout the Celtic world. This divine power over animals survives in many later Irish and Welsh stories, while a medieval Christian tale tells of a suspiciously similar Breton saint named Korneli who was a protector of horned animals.

There is one final Gaulish god about whom we know very little, yet there survives a story about him that is one of the closest things we have to an actual Celtic myth from antiquity. His name is Ogmios and he bears in name and function similarities to a later Irish god named Ogma. The Irish Ogma was a god of poetry who was called *trénfer* ("strong man") and who was credited with inventing Ogam letters, an early Irish writing system based on lines carved in stone.

The Greek writer Lucian, who lived during the time of the Roman emperor Marcus Aurelius, tells a story of his travels in Gaul during which he came across an image of the god Hercules—but it was unlike any representation he had seen in Greek or Roman art. Instead of a muscled youth, this Hercules was a bald old man dark and wrinkled as if from a lifetime at sea. But he carried a lion skin on his shoulder, arrows in a quiver, and a club in his hand—unmistakable signs of the god Hercules. Most striking to Lucian, this Hercules was dragging behind him a group of men fastened by the ears to his own tongue with a delicate chain of gold and amber, from which they could have easily escaped if they had so desired. The god in the image was turning to face the men as he smiled.

At first Lucian thought the Celts were making fun of Hercules, but he was soon approached by a Greek-speaking Gaul who offered to explain the image to him. He revealed to Lucian that the Gauls did not think the god Hermes represented verbal eloquence, but that the power of the spoken word was best shown by Hercules, whom they called Ogmios, since he was much stronger. He also told the visiting Greek that he shouldn't be surprised that they portrayed Hercules as an old man, since eloquence is a quality that shows itself best with age. He also said that their god Hercules achieved his greatest deeds not by physical strength but by the power of the spoken word, represented by fast and sharp arrows that he carried in his quiver.

We should be careful about accepting this story at face value, since Lucian was known for his imaginative comic writings, but we know that he was an itinerant lecturer in Gaul and so it is quite possible this story was based on an actual encounter. An uncommon appreciation of language among the ancient Celts is a quality attested by several classical writers, while the similarities between Gaulish Ogmios and the Irish Ogma are hard to ignore. It seems reasonable to suppose we have in this story by Lucian a taste of the rich Gaulish mythology about Ogmios, a god who led men by the strength of the spoken word.

Goddesses in ancient Celtic religion were more than just consorts of powerful gods. As with Gaulish Minerva described by Caesar, these female deities have their own powers, worshipers, and mythology, though once again there are only tantalizing hints at what these stories were.

One of the earliest comes from a Greek visitor to western Europe named Artemidorus. He records that worshipers on an island near Britain performed sacrifices like those offered to Demeter and her daughter on the Aegean island of Samothrace. We don't know which of the islands around Britain he means, but it may be one of the islands to the north or west of Britain, perhaps even Ireland. He doesn't name the Celtic goddesses worshiped there, though the similarity to sacrifices on Samothrace is an important clue to her powers. The Aegean island was a center for the worship of the great mother goddess, sometimes identified with Demeter, whose control over fertility brought about the fruits of the earth and the seasons of life. We don't know all the details of the Greek worship, since it was a secret religion for initiates only, but we know there were prayers and sacrifices of domesticated animals on hearth stones along with offerings to underworld gods in ritual pits. This suggests that the Celts on the island near Britain also worshiped a mother goddess or goddesses. Like the Greeks and many other cultures, they may have also had a myth about a goddess of fertility withdrawing from the world bringing winter on the earth, only to be enticed back by sacrifice and worship to usher in the new growth of spring.

Images of such mother goddesses are found throughout Gaul and Britain, sometimes as single divinities but most often as a group of three. These carvings show seated women, sometimes with one breast bared, wearing long garments and often carrying symbols of harvest and fertility, such as baskets of fruit, bread, or babies. One particular maternal goddess was known as Matrona, who gave her name to the Marne River of eastern France.

A goddess sometimes pictured with the divine mothers is Epona, whose name means "the horse goddess." Images of her appear throughout Celtic Europe and even in Rome itself. She was the only Celtic divinity to be officially adopted into the Roman pantheon, with her feast day on December 18. Her popularity among the Romans springs from her adoption by cavalrymen of the legions stationed in Gaul who took her worship home. In her depictions she always is accompanied by a horse. Sometimes she rides side-saddle on a mare carrying fruit and bread, while at other times she feeds a foal from a shallow dish. Her symbolism is complex and her role as a goddess was clearly much more than simply as the patroness of horses and riders. There are also elements of fertility, motherhood, healing, and rebirth in her worship. Her ancient roots in Celtic religion and her popularity are shown in echoes of her cult in later Irish and Welsh stories. In Ireland, a supernatural and very pregnant woman named Macha races faster than a horse and curses the men of the Ulster kingdom to endure the pains of childbirth. In Wales, another mysterious figure named Rhiannon rides a magical horse, is falsely accused of murdering her own son, and is forced to carry visitors to the royal court on her back like a horse as punishment. Rhiannon's birds were also known to sing so sweetly they could raise the dead to life.

One of the many goddesses of ancient Britain was Brigantia, whose name means "the exalted one." She was particularly popular among a confederation of tribes in northern Britain during Roman times who called themselves the Brigantes, in her honor. She was also honored in early Ireland, especially in the province of Leinster in the southeast of the island, as the triple-goddess Brigid who presided over fertility, iron-working, and poetry. The Irish goddess had her feast at the beginning of February on a day known as Imbolc, a time when the new lambs were born. Elements of her cult were borrowed by the Christian Saint Brigid, whose feast day is February 1.

As in classical mythology, some goddesses had darker natures. A Gaulish lead tablet from the late first century of our era from Larzac in southern France records a magical text written by a gathering of women who use "secret underworld names" to invoke the otherwise unknown goddess Adsagsona to render two other women "enchanted and bound." Another goddess, Andraste, was supposedly worshiped in groves in Britain by the torture and sacrifice of captured Roman women by the rebel queen Boudicca in the first century A.D. Boudicca also invoked Andraste before beginning her campaign against the Romans by releasing a hare.

There are dozens of other ancient Celtic gods and goddesses whose names we know—Alisanos, Dunatis, Sequana, and Nehalennia, among them—but we can say little about their powers and nothing of their mythology. In the end, most of the gods of the Gauls and the other early Celts remain a mystery that we will probably never solve. Their worship disappeared over time with the victory of Christianity and their stories vanished with them. We don't even know which god or goddess in Celtic mythology brought the world into being—for unlike almost every other early culture, we have no creation myth from the ancient Celts. But we do know how they believed the world would end. The Greek traveler Posidonius says that while he journeyed in Gaul, he heard from the druids themselves that the human soul and the universe itself were eternal, but that at some time in the future both fire and water would destroy our world.

2

THE BOOK OF INVASIONS

THERE WAS PRESERVED IN EARLY Ireland a remarkable story of how the Irish came to their island. It is a tale that stretches over centuries, with waves of invasions by outsiders and brutal wars to possess its hills and fertile plains. It is a story of magic and monsters, of death and devastation, and of gods, like the Tuatha Dé Danann, who seem almost human, and of heroes who fight like gods. Like almost all Irish stories, it was recorded by Christian monks. These scribes blended biblical tales and early Christian writings with the ancient pre-Christian mythology of their island. The result is a sweeping saga that begins with Adam and Eve in the Garden of Eden and weaves its way through Irish mythical history until the gods at last are banished to the world of the underground *síd* mounds and the ancestors of the Irish rule over the land.

The name of this work is *The Book of Invasions* (Irish, *Lebor Gabála Érenn*), a pseudo-historical epic written down in its final form in the twelfth-century *Book of Leinster*, but with tales woven into it composed by writers and storytellers of earlier centuries. The first hero in the saga is a young woman named Cesair, a granddaughter of Noah, who leads a band of a few dozen men and women to Ireland in a vain attempt to escape the coming flood. Years later the

Partholonians arrive, but they in turn die in a plague save for a single man named Tuán, who survives for centuries to come by shape-shifting into various animals before being born again as a human in the days just before Saint Patrick. The Partholonians are followed by the Nemedians, who battle the monstrous Formorians before being driven from the island. The Fir Bolg rule next, then the magical Tuatha Dé Danann, who defeat the Fir Bolg in battle. But the Formorians, more human in form by this point, return and fight the Tuatha Dé in a separate tale called the *Second Battle of Mag Tuired* that is arguably one of the oldest and most mythologically rich stories from early Ireland. In this battle, the Tuatha Dé are thinly disguised gods engaged in a primal war with the forces of chaos reminiscent of the Olympian gods fighting the Titans of Greek mythology. The sons of Míl from Spain are the final invaders of the island and victors over the Tuatha Dé, who in time become identified with the fairy folk of Ireland.

On the first day of creation, God made unformed matter and the light of the angels. Then came the earth and seas, the sun and stars, and the birds and beasts. On the sixth day of that week he made Adam to hold stewardship over the earth, while the beautiful angel Lucifer was granted rule over heaven. But Lucifer grew jealous of God and was cast down from heaven with the angels who followed him. In revenge, he tempted Eve to sin by eating the forbidden fruit, so that she and Adam were exiled from Eden. The sons of Adam multiplied upon the earth until they grew wicked with greed and envy. God sent a flood to destroy humanity and drown everyone except Noah and his family on the ark. After they safely reached land, they and their descendants repopulated the earth.

But Noah had tried to save his granddaughter before the great flood by sending her to Ireland. Cesair, daughter of Bith, son of Noah, led three ships west to Ireland after her grandfather had warned her of the coming flood, and cautioned that perhaps it would not reach such a distant land. On the voyage she took her father Bith along with many settlers, but two of the ships sank so that only fifty maidens and three men survived. The men divided the fifty women among themselves as wives and settled the empty land forty days before the flood. But Noah was wrong. As Bith stood atop a mountain later named for him, he saw the great wall of water coming and knew that he, his daughter, and their people would not survive. The flood overtook Cesair in her valley in Connacht in the most distant part of Ireland, so that she was the last to die in the mighty deluge that swept the earth.

Ireland was uninhabited for three hundred years after the flood, until Partholón came from the east with his followers to settle the land. Ten years after he reached Ireland, he fought and won the first battle ever waged on the island, against the evil Formorians, hideous creatures then, each with a single arm and leg. Partholón and his followers reshaped the landscape of Ireland, building lakes and clearing plains for farming and grazing. But then a plague struck Ireland and killed every human in the land within seven days—except for Tuán, the grandson of Partholón's brother. Tuán was nearly driven mad from loneliness and fear. For thirty years he lived a solitary life in cliffs and caves to protect himself from wolves. He grew into an old man, shriveled, naked, and miserable. One night at last as he lay down to die he saw himself transformed into a mighty young stag. In this form he roamed the hills of Ireland, leader of a great herd, until he saw the coming of a new people to Ireland.

Nemed son of Agnoman sailed from the Greek lands of distant Scythia for Ireland with over thirty ships, but only the vessel with his own kin survived the voyage. He and his four sons settled across the island and many children were born to their wives over the years. They cleared plains throughout the land until they were attacked by Formorians who came by sea. Nemed and his army fought many battles against this monstrous race, but in the end Nemed died and the Formorians prevailed. They imposed a harsh tribute on the descendants of Nemed, demanding two-thirds of their children along with their grain and milk every autumn. The children of Nemed at last rose up against the Formorians and attacked them by land and sea. Few of either race were left alive by the end of the war. Most of those of Nemed's tribe who survived succumbed in time to a deadly plague, though a few fled Ireland for distant lands. Only Tuán remained on the island, living as a stag until he grew old and returned to his favorite cave. There he passed into the shape of a wild boar and became the leader of a herd of pigs that traveled all around the provinces of Ireland.

Some of the survivors of Nemed's people went to Britain, but Sémión journeyed all the way to Greece. There he prospered and had many children, but the Greeks enslaved them and made them haul soil up into the rugged mountains to build fields for growing crops. At last, five thousand of Sémión's descendants escaped and made ships from the bags they had used to haul soil. They then sailed away from Greece all the way back to Ireland.

From Sémión come the Irish people known as the Fir Bolg and the Fir Domnann. Five kings of the Fir Bolg ruled Ireland, but they fought each other constantly and many of their people died. Of those who survived the wars, a great multitude perished from disease. At last, Eochu son of Erc took the throne and ruled for ten peaceful years. During his time there was no rain, but dew watered the prosperous land. Spears and weapons were banished from Ireland and laws were enacted for the first time. But at the end of ten years, Eochu was killed and those who stayed alive in Ireland lived in a world of chaos and brutality. Only Tuán remained apart from the misery of the Irish as he wandered the land as a boar. After many years he returned to his cave and transformed into a hawk, soaring over the land and learning all things.

It was then that the Tuatha Dé Danann came at last to Ireland from the far north. Some say they were angels cast out of heaven with Lucifer, while others say they were children of men who had traveled to the northern islands of the world and learned their magical arts. But no one knew their true origins.

They came wrapped in dark clouds and landed on the shore of Connacht, in the far west. They cast darkness upon the whole island for three days and three nights. With them they brought four instruments of power. The first was the great stone of knowledge, called the Lia Fáil, that still stands on the royal hill of Tara. When a true king of Ireland would step on the stone, it would shriek beneath him. The second was the spear of Lug, which made its bearer invincible. The third was the sword of their king Nuadu, from which no one could escape once it was drawn. And finally there was the cauldron of the Dagda that could satisfy the hunger of all.

The Tuatha Dé demanded that the Fir Bolg either grant them the kingship of the land or meet them in battle. When the Fir Bolg refused to yield, the Tuatha Dé fought them and slew tens of thousands on the plain known as Mag Tuired. Eochaid mac Eirc, king of the Fir Bolg, was slain, while the survivors of his people who escaped the battle fled to the Formorians and settled on islands near Ireland.

Nuadu, king of the Tuatha Dé, lost his hand in the battle when the Fir Bolg warrior Sreng mac Sengainn cut it from his arm. His people loved Nuadu, but no man could rule over them who bore such an injury. They held an assembly and decided to give the kingship to Bres, whose mother was of the Tuatha Dé but whose father was Elatha, king of the Formorians. The mother of Bres was Ériu, who as a young woman in years past had stood on the shore of the ocean and seen a remarkable sight.

As she looked out at the calm sea, a ship of silver appeared in the distance. The current brought it to the shore, and a man stepped out of it. He was the most handsome man she had ever seen. He had golden yellow hair down to his shoulders, a cloak and shirt embroidered with golden thread, and a jeweled brooch on his chest. He carried two shining silver spears with shafts of bronze and a gold-hilted sword with inlaid studs of silver and gold.

The splendid man looked at Ériu and said, "Shall we make love together for an hour?"

"But I don't know you," she replied.

"Lie with me anyway," he answered.

And so they lay on the beach and made love for an hour. When they were done, the man got up and Ériu began to weep.

"Why are you crying?" he asked.

"Because all the young men of the Tuatha Dé have been wooing me in vain, but I gave myself to you—and I don't even know your name."

"I am Elatha mac Delbaith, king of the Formorians," he replied. "You will bear me a son. Name him Bres the

Beautiful, for every beautiful creature in Ireland—be they man, woman, or horse—will be compared to him."

Then he drew a golden ring from his finger and gave it to her, saying she should not part with it until she found the man whose finger it would fit perfectly. After that, he went back into his boat and sailed away.

And so nine months later, Ériu gave birth to a son and named him Bres, as his father had said. The boy grew twice as fast as a normal child until he reached manhood. At last he was chosen as the new king of the Tuatha Dé and given sovereignty over Ireland. It was then that his mother came to him with the ring that had been left with her by her lover Elatha. When she placed it on her son's finger, it fit perfectly.

But Bres was an evil king who cared nothing for his people. The knives of the Tuatha Dé were not greased by him at feasts nor did their breath smell of ale. There was no music or poetry. The crops withered and the people starved because Bres neglected his royal duties. In time, Formorian kings imposed tribute on the land so that there was no smoke from a house on the island that was not under their dominion. Even the great warriors of the Tuatha Dé became servants, so that Ogma carried firewood and the Dagda was made to build a fortress for Bres.

At last, the Tuatha Dé came to Bres and complained that he was not a just king. He asked that he might have seven more years to rule and change his ways. The people at last consented—but Bres had no intention of reforming. He planned to use the time to gather an army from the Formorians so that he might destroy the Tuatha Dé.

Bres went to the land of his father Elatha and asked for soldiers to fight the Tuatha Dé. When the Tuatha Dé discovered this, they expelled Bres from the throne and made

Nuadu king again. Since no one who was not perfect in body could be king among the Irish, the physician Dian Cécht made for him a new hand out of silver that moved as if he were born with it. Nuadu then gathered together all his warriors on the royal hill of Tara for a great feast.

The doorkeeper Camall mac Riagail stood guard at Tara during the feast with orders to keep out anyone who was not useful to the kingdom. As he was on duty, he saw a young and handsome warrior coming toward him.

"Who are you?" asked Camall.

"I am Lug," said the young man.

"What is your skill?" asked Camall. "For no one without a skill may enter Tara."

"I am a builder," said Lug.

"We don't need you," replied Camall. "We already have a builder."

"I am a smith."

"We already have a smith."

"I am a champion of warriors."

"We already have a champion."

"I am a poet."

"We already have a poet."

"I am a physician."

"We already have a physician."

"I am a sorcerer."

"We already have a sorcerer."

"Then ask the king," said Lug, "if he has anyone who possesses all these skills together."

Camall went to Nuadu and told him of the young man at the gate.

"Let him enter Tara," said the king. "For no man like that has ever come here before."

Lug came into the fortress and took the seat next to the king reserved for the greatest sage of the land. Ogma was so angry at this that he picked up a giant stone that could only be moved by fourscore oxen and threw it at the brash young man. Lug caught it and tossed it back at Ogma. Lug then picked up a harp and began to play, so that his sorrowful music caused the whole assembly of warriors to weep and his joyful tunes filled them with happiness.

When Nuadu had seen what Lug could do, he held an assembly of his men and decided to give him power over the Tuatha Dé to fight against Bres and the Formorians. Lug accepted and held a council with the Dagda and Ogma at his side. They summoned all the Tuatha Dé to them—druids and sorcerers, charioteers and smiths, physicians and warriors—and asked what they could contribute to the coming battle. They all promised their loyalty and skills to the defeat of Bres. The sorcerers even pledged to shake the roots of the mountains so that the Formorians would think the land of Ireland itself was against them. The Mórrígan, the fearsome goddess of battle and prophesy, also pledged herself to Lug and urged him to fight against those who oppressed their island.

A week before Samain—the day known as All Hallows' Eve—Lug sent the Dagda to spy on the Formorians. He went to their camp under a flag of truce and waited to be fed according to the rules of hospitality. The Formorians knew the Dagda loved porridge, so they boiled a huge vat for him with eighty gallons of milk, vast quantities of lard, and countless sheep and swine as well. They poured it into a hole in the ground and told him he would be killed unless he ate it all—which he did, scraping the pieces from the bottom of the hole with his hand. He then fell asleep with his belly as big as an enormous cauldron.

When he woke, he left the Formorian camp and went on his way, carrying his swollen belly before him. He met a beautiful young woman on the way whom he desired, as she did him, but because of his belly he was impotent. The woman began to mock him and finally threw him to the ground. Then all that he had eaten came out of him so that he was himself again and made love to the beautiful woman.

The Formorians and Tuatha Dé advanced to the great plain of Mag Tuired where they would meet in battle. When Lug had assembled all his men around him, he asked what they would do to defeat their enemy.

"I will provide new weapons for every one that breaks," said Goibniu the smith, "even if the battle lasts seven years."

"I will heal every man who is injured," said Dian Cécht the physician, "unless his head is cut off."

"I will kill a third of the Formorians all by myself," said Ogma the warrior.

"I will shame and satirize them all," said Coirpre the poet, "so that they won't be able to stand against us."

"We will enchant the very trees and rocks against them," said Bé Chuille and Dianann, women who were weavers of magic.

"And you, Dagda," asked Lug, "what will you do?"

"Not hard to say," he replied. "I will fight for the men of Ireland with power and destruction. I will crush their bones with my club like hail beneath the feet of horses on the plain of Mag Tuired."

When the time came for the great battle, the Formorians marched out of their camp against the warriors of the Tuatha Dé. Bres was there leading the Formorian army, while Lug was at the front of his own battalions, urging his men to throw off the bondage they had suffered. Every man on both sides was armored, with a helmet on his head, a spear in his hand, a sword at his side, and a shield on his shoulder. When they met, it was as if the raging sea were striking against a cliff.

The battle fought between the races of Ireland was keen and cruel. Many men from both the Formorians and Tuatha Dé fell there in death. Streams of blood flowed over the white skin of young warriors. Harsh was the noise of a multitude of swords and shields, sharp weapons piercing the warm flesh of men with screams of pain. Harsh, too, was the shouting of warriors and the clashing of ivory-hilted blades and the sound of spears flying through the air. As they hacked at each other, their fingertips and feet almost met, and because of the slippery ground soaked in blood, the warriors fell to the earth to be slain by their foes in the red mud.

The battle lasted for days, but no matter how many Tuatha Dé fell to the Formorians, they were back to fight again at the next sunrise, for Dian Cécht and his children cast each mortally wounded man into a well and chanted incantations over him until he rose again whole. But the Formorian warriors did not rise once they fell.

Lug met the monstrous champion Balor of the deadly eye on the battlefield. His eyelid was so big it was only lifted in war, and then only by four men. Whoever looked at it would lose all will to fight and would soon be slain. But just as the men began to lift Balor's eyelid, Lug cast a sling stone at him that carried his eye all the way through his head and killed Balor, along with a score of his men he crushed when he fell.

As the battle drew at last to a close, Bres pleaded for his life.

"It is better to spare me than kill me," he said.

"What good will come from that?" asked Lug.

"Spare me, and the cows of Ireland will always produce milk," cried Bres.

"That will not save you," answered Lug.

"Then I will teach you the secret of abundant sowing and reaping forevermore," said Bres.

And so he did. For that, Lug spared him.

The battlefield of Mag Tuired was silent then, save for the crows who came to feast on the dead. The Formorians had been utterly vanquished and the Tuatha Dé once again ruled over Ireland, while Tuán still soared over the island in the form of a hawk.

Now among the many descendants of Noah after the flood were a people known as the Gaels, who were always searching the world for their true home. They helped to build the tower of Nimrod, after which God separated the proud races of the earth by giving them different languages. The Gaels wandered to Egypt, then at last to Spain, where they conquered the native people and built a great watchtower on the northern coast known as Breogon's Tower. It was there on the clearest of winter evenings that Íth son of Breogon climbed his father's tower and saw in the far distance the land of Ireland.

Íth sailed to Ireland with a hundred and fifty warriors, but the rulers of the island slew him on the plain that now bears his name. It was for revenge of Íth that the Gaels came from Spain to Ireland.

Thirty-six lords of the Gaels came with their wives and slaves and households. Among the Gaels were the sons of Míl, including Amairgen, the greatest of their bards. The sons of Míl had a rowing competition as they approached Ireland. The mighty warrior Ír drew ahead of the other ships. Éber Donn, his brother, cursed him so that Ír's oar broke, causing him to fall over backwards and die.

As Amairgen set his right foot upon the shore of Ireland, he recited this poem:

I am a wind upon the ocean.
I am a wave upon the land.
I am the roaring of the sea.
I am a stag that battles seven times.
I am a tear-drop of the sun.
I am a boar for valor.
I am a salmon in a pool of still water.
I am a spear that wages war.

The Gaels met a force of the Tuatha Dé in battle at the mountain of Sliab Mis and defeated them there. Then Banba, a woman of the Tuatha Dé, appeared to them and said: "May your journey not be prosperous if you have come to conquer Ireland."

"Indeed," said Amairgen, "that is why we have come."

"Then at least grant me this request," she said. "Let my name be upon this island."

"It will be so," said Amairgen.

They continued their journey across Ireland and met another woman of the Tuatha Dé named Fótla. She asked if her name could also be upon the island. And so Amairgen agreed.

Then at Uisnech, at the center of Ireland, they met a third woman of the Tuatha Dé, Ériu the mother of Bres, and she spoke to them: "Warriors, you are welcome. It was foretold long ago that you would come and that the island would be yours forever. I only ask that my name be upon this island."

"Your name will be first among the names of Ireland," said Amairgen.

The Gaels then came to the royal hill of Tara, where they met the kings of the Tuatha Dé. These kings asked the Gaels to return to their boats and withdraw from Ireland for three days so that they might prepare for a fair fight. But they had no intention of fighting an honorable battle. They planned to have their druids use magic against the Gaels to destroy them at sea. But the kings said they would submit the issue to the judgment of Amairgen.

Amairgen decreed that the Gaels would withdraw in their ships from Ireland—beyond the ninth wave—and then return to fight for possession of the land. They went south from Tara and embarked in their ships to the sea. But the druids of the Tuatha Dé recited magical incantations against them as they waited on the water. A furious wind tossed the Gaels upon the sea and threatened to drown them all until Amairgen mounted the bow of his ship with his harp in hand and sang with all his strength:

I invoke the land of Ireland,
surging are its mighty seas,
mighty are its upland meadows,
filled with meadows are its rainy woods,
rainy are its rivers full of waterfalls,
filled with waterfalls are its spreading lakes,
spreading widely are its many springs,
springing with people are its assemblies,
the chief assembly is at Tara,
Tara is a tower of tribes,
the tribes of the warriors of the sons of Míl,
warriors of ships to conquer the land.

At once the waves grew still. The Gaels returned to Ireland and conquered the land, driving the Tuatha Dé to the world beneath the *síd* mounds, where they remain to this day. Then the sons of Míl divided the land among themselves and ruled it.

All these things Tuán saw as he soared above the island in the form of a hawk. When he grew old and could fly no longer, he fasted nine days and became a swift salmon. One day he was caught in a net by the wife of a king named Cairell. She cooked and ate him, after which he grew in her womb until he was born as a baby boy and called Tuán the son of Cairell, who became a great druid prophet. After that Patrick came to the island and preached the word of God, converting many to the new way, including Tuán, who became a monk and lived alone in his hermitage for many years, telling anyone who would ask the ancient story of Ireland.

THE WOOING OF ÉTAÍN

THE *WOOING OF ÉTAÍN* (IRISH, *Tochmarc Étaíne*) is an ancient tale in three parts about the enduring power of love. In the first part of the story, Midir, a chief of the Tuatha Dé Danann, wins and falls in love with his bride Étaín, the daughter of an Ulster king. But when he brings Étaín home, his first wife magically turns her into a pool of water, which transforms into a butterfly, then drives her away from Midir for a thousand years until she is reborn as a girl, also named Étaín. This reborn Étaín marries a king named Eochaid, whom Midir ultimately defeats in a battle of wits to win back his former wife.

There was once a king of the Tuatha Dé Danann ruling over Ireland named Eochaid Ollathair, the Father of All, who was also known as the Dagda. He was a powerful lord who could control the storms of the heavens and bring a bountiful harvest to the land.

One of his subjects was Elcmar, whose home was the *síd* mound of the Bruig na Bóinne. Elcmar's wife was Eithne. The Dagda very much wanted to sleep with Eithne and she with him, but they were afraid to do so because of her husband's magical power. The Dagda therefore used his own magic and sent Elcmar away on an errand using spells that made time seem to pass not at all for Elcmar while he was away. Night was banished for him and he did not grow hungry or thirsty. Nine months passed for him as if a single day.

The Dagda meanwhile went to Eithne and lay with her so that she bore a son named Óengus. When Elcmar returned from his journey, he had no idea that his wife had shared a bed with the Dagda or that a son had been born to her.

The Dagda took the child to the house of Midir in Brí Léith to be fostered. Óengus was raised there for nine years among three times fifty boys and the same number of girls. Óengus was the greatest among the youth and the favorite of Midir because of his beauty and nobility. He was also known among them as the Mac Óg, the young son, for his mother had said: "Young is my son who was conceived at the beginning of the day and born the same evening."

One day Óengus had a quarrel with one of the boys in the house of Midir named Triath of the Fir Bolg, a tribe conquered by the Tuatha Dé when they came to Ireland.

"I shouldn't even be speaking to the son of a slave," said Óengus to Triath contemptuously. For Óengus thought he was a son of Midir and would one day be king at Brí Léith. He did not know he was in fact the son of the Dagda.

"I lower myself," replied Triath, "to speak to a boy who has no mother or father."

Óengus went to Midir in tears and told him what Triath had said.

"That is not true," said Midir. "Your father is Eochaid Ollathair, the Dagda, and your mother is Eithne the wife of Elcmar of the Bruig na Bóinne. I have raised you so that Elcmar might not know that his wife was unfaithful to him."

"Come with me," Óengus said to Midir, "so that my real father may acknowledge me and so that I will not be mocked by the Fir Bolg."

The two traveled to Uisnech, in the middle of Ireland, where the Dagda had his house. From Uisnech it was equally far in every direction: north, south, east, and west. The Dagda was holding an assembly of his tribe, so that Midir called him aside to speak with him and the boy privately.

"What does this child want?" asked the Dagda.

"He wishes to be acknowledged by his father and given land, for it is not fitting that a son of a king be without territory of his own."

"You are most welcome," the Dagda said to the boy. "You are indeed my son. But the land I would gladly give you is not yet empty."

"What land is that?" asked Midir.

"The Bruig na Bóinne on the north side of the Boyne River," said the Dagda. "Elcmar lives there. I have done him wrong by sleeping with his wife and fathering this child, so I do not wish to shame him further by removing him from his land by force."

"What should the boy do?" asked Midir.

"Let him go to the Bruig na Bóinne at Samain," the Dagda said, "and bring weapons with him. It is a day of peace across the land, so Elcmar will have no arms with him. He will be standing on his *síd* with a forked stick of hazel and a golden brooch on his cloak. Let the boy go and threaten to kill him. It is best not to slay him, but instead make him promise to grant Óengus rule over the Bruig na Bóinne for a day and a night. But when Elcmar returns, let him not give back the Bruig. Let Óengus tell Elcmar that the *síd* is his now forever, for all of time is day and night."

Midir then took Óengus back home and on the next Samain gave him weapons and sent him to Elcmar at the Bruig na Bóinne. Óengus did as the Dagda had said and threatened Elcmar so that he was granted possession of the Bruig for a day and a night. On the next day when Elcmar returned and demanded his home back, Óengus refused and spoke as the Dagda had said. But Elcmar said he would not yield the Bruig to Óengus until the matter had been submitted to the judgment of the Dagda in the presence of the men of Ireland.

The Dagda held an assembly and ruled that the Bruig was now the land of Óengus, since Elcmar had yielded to fear and granted the boy possession for a day and a night. But the Dagda granted Elcmar other lands across the river in recompense, so that Óengus became ruler of the Bruig na Bóinne and all the people who lived near it.

Midir came back to the Bruig a year later on Samain to visit Óengus. He found the young man standing on the *síd* mound watching two bands of boys playing their games on the plain below. On the far side of the river to the south, Elcmar was watching also. A quarrel arose among the boys, so that Óengus was about to intervene, but Midir stopped him.

"Stay here," said Midir. "If you go, Elcmar will come also and there will be a trouble. I will go myself and separate them."

So Midir went down to the plain and with difficulty stopped the fighting among the boys, but he was wounded while doing so with a holly javelin that gouged out one of his eyes. He returned then to Óengus.

"This was a cursed visit," Midir said to the young man, "for now I am disfigured and cannot see from where I have come or where I am going."

"I will make things right," said Óengus. "I will fetch the physician Dian Cécht to heal you."

Óengus brought Dian Cécht to the Bruig na Bóinne and the physician healed Midir.

"Now that you are whole," said Óengus to Midir, "stay with me a year as my guest."

"I will not," replied Midir, "unless I have a gift."

"Name what you want," said Óengus, "and it will be yours."

"I desire," he said, "a chariot worth seven slave women, a cloak befitting my rank, and the most beautiful woman in all of Ireland as my own."

"I will gladly give you the chariot and the cloak," said Óengus, "but the fairest woman in the land is not mine to give. She is Étaín, the daughter of Ailill, a king in Ulster."

And so Óengus went to Ailill to ask for his daughter. He declared that he was a prince of the Tuatha Dé Danann and it was for Étaín that he had come.

"I cannot give her to you," said Ailill. "Your race and standing are far above my own. If you do any harm to my daughter, I would not be able to exact a payment of wrong-doing from you due to your lofty status."

"Then I will buy her from you outright," said Óengus.

"Agreed," replied Ailill, "but you must know first the price I ask."

"Name the price," said Óengus.

"In exchange for Étaín," said Ailill, "you must clear twelve plains that are now wilderness and woodland so that I may graze my cattle there and build dwelling places for my people."

"It will be done," answered Óengus,

Óengus knew there was no way he could accomplish such an immense task himself. He went therefore to his father the Dagda, who listened to his son's plight and cleared the plains for him in a single night.

Óengus then returned to Ailill to receive Étaín.

"Not yet," said Ailill. "You must first change the course of twelve rivers from this land to the sea. These streams are now bogs and marshes, but I want them to be rivers flowing to the sea that I may add riches from the ocean to my territory."

"It will be done," said Óengus.

Óengus went to the Dagda and complained about the impossible task he had been given, so his father changed the course of the twelve rivers in a single night.

When this was done, Óengus came to Ailill and asked for Étaín.

"Not yet," said the king. "First you must give me the girl's weight in gold and silver, for I will get no good out of her once she is gone."

"It will be done," said Óengus.

Étaín was set in the middle of Ailill's hall and weighed. Then Óengus give her father her weight in gold and silver, after which Óengus took Étaín with him from her father's house.

When Óengus returned to the Bruig na Bóinne, he gave Midir a fine chariot and cloak, along with Étaín. Midir slept with Étaín that night and was grateful to Óengus his foster son. He stayed with him at the Bruig for a full year.

At the end of the year, Midir bade farewell to Óengus and took Étaín with him. But before he left, Óengus said to him: "Be careful, Midir, for there is a fearsome and powerful woman angry at you, your wife Fuamnach, the foster daughter of the druid Bresal. She is shrewd and full of magic. She will not welcome another woman into her house."

At first Fuamnach seemed to welcome Étaín to her home. She took her around their holdings and led her at last to the sleeping hut. But when they were alone, Fuamnach struck her with a branch of purple rowan so that Étaín turned into a pool of water on the floor. Fuamnach then went home to her foster father Bresal.

The heat of the hearth fire, the power of the earth, and the warmth of the air turned the pool of water that had been Étaín into a purple butterfly. The butterfly was the size of a man's head and the most beautiful creature in all the land. The sound of her humming wings was sweeter than the music of pipes and harps. Her eyes shone in the darkness like precious stones and her fragrance would drive hunger and thirst from anyone wherever she went. The drops of dew that fell from her wings would cure all illness and disease.

The butterfly followed Midir wherever he went throughout the land. Armies of men would gather to gaze on her beauty and listen to the sound of her wings. Midir knew it was Étaín and was happy without a woman as long as she was by his side. He would fall asleep each night to her humming by his bed, and she would wake him if any danger came near.

Fuamnach, the estranged wife of Midir, came to him one day accompanied by three of the Tuatha Dé as guarantors of her safety—Lug, Ogma, and the Dagda. Midir was very angry at Fuamnach, but she said she did not regret what she had done to Étaín. Moreover, she declared she would make Étaín miserable in the future, no matter what form she took.

Fuamnach brought great spells and magic from Bresal the druid to banish Étaín from Midir. She stirred up a hostile wind that drove Étaín away from Midir so that she could not light on a tree or anywhere else for seven years. During all that time she was blown about on the wind until finally she landed in the lap of Óengus at the Bruig na Bóinne.

Óengus recognized her immediately and sang:

Welcome, Étaín,
worn down by travel and sorrow,
driven by the winds of Fuamnach.
You have not found rest
by Midir's side.
Fruitless is your suffering,
but you are most welcome
in my home.

Óengus took Étaín and folded her up in the fleece of his cloak. He brought her into his house and sat her in the bright sun by his windows. He clothed her in purple garments and slept beside her every night.

Fuamnach heard of how Étaín was honored and made welcome by Óengus. She sent a message to Midir asking him to invite his foster son Óengus to visit him so that she might make peace between them. But as soon as Óengus had left the Bruig, Fuamnach journeyed there and found Étaín the purple butterfly alone. She struck her with a fierce wind and drove her from the house of Óengus across the hills and valleys of Ireland for many years.

When Óengus had come to speak with Midir, he was told that Fuamnach had deceived them both. Óengus rushed back to the Briug na Bóinne to save Étaín from Fuamnach, but she was gone. Óengus found the tracks of Fuamnach and followed them to the house of Bresal the druid. He cut off her head there and took it back to the Bruig, where he stuck it on a pole.

After many years, Étaín landed on a ceiling pole in the house of Étar, a warrior from Ulster. She fell from the ceiling into a gold cup held by the wife of Étar, so that the woman swallowed the butterfly unaware. The wife of Étar then conceived a child in her womb and bore a girl nine months later. Étar gave the name Étaín to the child and welcomed her into his home.

Étar raised Étaín in his home along with fifty daughters of kings who waited on her. One day the girls were washing themselves in a river near the sea when they saw a horseman on the plain, coming toward them. He was riding a brown horse and was dressed in green with red embroidery. He wore a golden brooch and carried a silver shield and a five-pointed spear. His fair yellow hair was braided and a band of gold held it from his face.

He paused and looked at the girls bathing, then recited a poem:

Étaín is here, swallowed
in the cup of Étar's wife.
There will be wars, Étaín,
fought because of you.
You are the White Woman
who seeks the king,
our own Étaín.

Then the horseman went away. They did not know who he was or from where he came.

Eochaid Airem was high king of Ireland at this time. He summoned all the men of the island to the great feast at Tara to celebrate his inauguration and confirm their fealty to him—but they would not come. They said they would not go to the feast at Tara unless Eochaid had a queen.

Eochaid sent messengers to every province of Ireland to search for the most beautiful woman in Ireland to be his bride. Not only must she be beautiful, he instructed them, but she must also be pure and have never slept with a man. The messengers searched the whole land, but no maiden was more beautiful in shape or form than Étaín.

Eochaid had a brother named Ailill Anguba, who fell in love with Étaín at the feast of Tara after Eochaid had slept with her. Ailill was tormented with guilt and shame because of his feelings for Étaín, and he fell ill. He would tell no one of his love for his brother's wife nor would he even speak to Étaín. When he was on the verge of death, Eochaid's physician came to him and told him he suffered from a disease he could not cure—the pain of love.

Eochaid then departed from Tara to go on a royal circuit of Ireland. He left his brother Ailill with Étaín so that she might see to his funeral when he died. She would come every day to sit beside Ailill's bed. When she was near him, his eyes would follow her the whole time and he would feel better. Étaín noticed this and asked him one day what was truly the cause of his illness.

"My sickness," he said, "is because of my love for you."

"I wish you had said so before now," she replied. "For I could have made you well long ago."

After that she came every day to feed him and wash his face and body. In time, he was almost healed.

"There is only one thing lacking to make me whole," Ailill said to Étaín.

"You will have that one thing tomorrow," she said, "but not here in the court of your brother Eochaid. Meet me at dawn near the hidden tree behind the hill and I shall heal you."

Ailill could not sleep that night in anticipation of lying with Étaín, but at sunrise he fell asleep until three hours after dawn. Meanwhile Étaín went to the tree and found a man there who looked like Ailill. He spoke of the illness he had suffered and talked with her as Ailill would. But they did not make love.

Ailill awoke at mid-morning and lamented to Étaín that he had slept through his tryst with her. She was surprised he spoke so, but she arranged for them to meet under the tree again the next morning at dawn.

Ailill was determined to meet with Étaín this time, so he built a roaring fire in his hall and sat in front of it. He also brought a bucket of cold water to pour on his head. But once again he fell asleep.

Étaín went to the tree to meet Ailill and found the man who was like him there. She did the same the next day and spoke to him.

"You are not Ailill, the man I have come to lie with and heal," she said. "Who are you and why have you come to meet me?"

"It would only be right," said the man, "to meet my own wife. Long ago we were married. My name is Midir."

"Why did we part?" asked Étaín.

"Because of the magic of Fuamnach and the spells of Bresal," he answered. "Will you come with me now, Étaín?"

"How can I leave Ailill without healing him?" she asked.

"He is healed," said Midir. "It was I who caused his sickness so that I might meet you thus. I have made him whole now. Will you come with me?"

And then Étaín began to remember.

"Yes," she replied, "but only if Eochaid my husband freely gives me to you."

"I will see that he does so," Midir said.

Étaín returned to Ailill and found him healed in body and soul. The guilt he had felt for planning to lie with his brother's wife was gone. Soon Eochaid returned from his circuit of Ireland and was full of joy that his brother had been healed by Étaín.

One beautiful summer day not long after this when Eochaid arose from sleep, he went to the walls of Tara and gazed out at his kingdom. The fields were covered with flowers of every color and hue.

Suddenly Eochaid saw in front of him on the walls a strange warrior wearing a purple cloak and golden yellow hair to his shoulders. His eyes were a piercing blue and he carried in one hand a five-pointed spear, while in the other he held a white shield inlayed with gems and gold.

Eochaid was struck speechless, for the man had not been inside the walls of Tara the night before when the gates were shut.

"I welcome you, warrior," said Eochaid, "but I do not know you."

"Few men do," said the stranger. "I am Midir of Brí Léith."

"Why have you come?" asked Eochaid.

"To play a board game of *fidchell* with you," answered Midir.

"That would be fine, said Eochaid. "I am quite good at *fidchell*."

"We will see," said Midir.

He then brought from beneath his cloak a silver board with pieces made of gold.

"I will not play without a wager," said Eochaid.

"If you win," said Midir, "I will give you fifty fine horses with red ears and broad chests, fitted with fifty crimson bridles."

"Then let us begin," said Eochaid.

They played the game of *fidchell* together and Eochaid won.

The next day the king went to the walls of Tara again and saw Midir standing there. Below him beneath the walls were the fifty horses he had promised Eochaid.

"Would you like to play *fidchell* again?" asked Midir.

"Indeed I would," answered Eochaid, "but only for a greater wager."

"If you win," said Midir, "I will give you fifty young pigs, fifty golden swords, fifty red-eared cows each with a calf, and fifty sheep with red heads."

"Then let us begin," said Midir.

They played the game of *fidchell* together and Eochaid won.

The next day Eochaid went to the top of the walls and saw Midir there with all the gifts he had promised.

"Let us play *fidchell* together again," said Midir.

"Gladly," said Eochaid, "but I demand a much greater stake this time."

"What is it you wish?" asked Midir.

"If you lose," said the king, "you must clear all the stones from the fields of my kingdom and build a causeway for me across the great bog of Lámraige."

"You ask too much," said Midir.

"Then I will not play," said Eochaid.

"Then I accept your wager," said Midir.

They played the game of *fidchell* together, and Eochaid won.

"Have all your people remain inside their homes tonight," said Midir, "and I will give you what we have wagered."

That night the people of Tara heard a thunder of sounds outside their walls and throughout the countryside. When Eochaid arose the next morning, he rode out and saw that all the stones had been cleared from the fields of his kingdom and that a sturdy causeway had been built across the impassible bog of Lámraige. When he returned to Tara, he found Midir waiting for him.

"Let us play *fidchell* together again," said Midir.

"What will be the stake?" asked the king.

"Whatever the winner wishes," answered Midir.

They played the game of *fidchell* together and Eochaid lost.

"You have beaten me," said Eochaid. "What do you wish from me?"

"I wish," said Midir, "to put my arms around Étaín and receive a kiss from her."

"Return in a month," said the king, "and you shall have what you have won."

When a month had passed, Eochaid put a guard around Tara and the best of all the outlaws of Ireland with them to prevent anyone from entering the walls. Then he locked the gates and the doors of his feasting hall. He and Étaín were inside surrounded by his greatest warriors. The king was sure that Midir could not enter.

But suddenly Eochaid saw him standing before him in the hall.

"Give to me what you owe me," said Midir to the king.

"You may hold Étaín in your arms and receive her kiss," said Eochaid, "but only here inside the hall."

"That will do," said Midir.

Étaín rose from her chair and went gladly to stand before Midir. He wrapped his arms around her and she kissed him.

As they embraced, Midir and Étaín flew up through the skylight in the roof. The king and his warriors rushed out the door, but all they saw were two swans flying swiftly away from Tara.

The wise men of Eochaid advised the king to dig up all the *síd* mounds of Ireland to find Étaín, for they knew then that Midir was a ruler among the people of the Otherworld. Eochaid and his laborers spent a year and three months destroying the *síd* mounds—but each one they destroyed was found whole again the next morning.

When the king went to the mound at Ban Find, a man came forth from the *síd* and rebuked him.

"What wrong have we done to you that you destroy our homes?" he asked. "We haven't taken your wife."

"I will not cease," said Eochaid, "from digging up the *síd* mounds of Ireland until you tell me how to find Étaín."

"That is not difficult," the man said. "Take blind puppies and cats to the *síd* of Brí Léith and leave them there. That will call forth Midir."

And so the king did as he was told. Then as soon as he began to dig up the mound of Brí Léith, Midir appeared before him.

"Give me my wife," demanded Eochaid.

"You sold her to me," replied Midir.

"You cannot keep her," said the king.

"Go home," said Midir. "I will send Étaín to you tomorrow. You may keep her—if you can recognize her."

The next morning there appeared before the walls of Tara fifty women all with the same appearance and clothing as Étaín. There was an old gray hag in front of them.

"Choose your wife, Eochaid," said the hag.

The king divided the women into two groups and asked them to approach a vessel of wine in the middle of his hall, for he knew Étaín was the best at pouring drink in Ireland and was certain he could recognize her if the women took turns pouring the wine.

When all but two had come forth and poured from the vessel, Eochaid was still certain he had not seen Étaín. But when the last woman poured, the king was sure he had found Étaín and chose her to stay. The hag and all the other women then disappeared.

One beautiful day not long after, Eochaid and his queen were conversing in the middle of the fort at Tara when they saw Midir approaching them.

"Are you content?" Midir asked of Eochaid.

"I am," the king said. "I have my wife back and I have defeated you."

"Are you sure?" asked Midir. "Étaín was pregnant with your child when I took her from you and she bore a daughter in my home. The girl grew remarkably fast and learned everything from her mother—even how to pour drink—and she looks just like her."

"No!" said Eochaid.

"Yes," said Midir. "Étaín is safe with me. Your chose your own daughter, Étaín the young, as your wife and have slept with her. And now she is with child from you."

"By the gods, that was an evil trick!" exclaimed Eochaid.

When the king's daughter was born, he sent her away without looking at her to a farm in the middle of the wilderness to be fed to the dogs. The men of Eochaid threw the child to the ravenous hounds and left, but the cowherd who lived there and his wife returned home before she could come to any harm. They then raised the child as their own.

Eochaid never regained his spirits after losing Étaín and was killed one day by his enemies, who placed his head on a pole for all to see.

But Midir and Étaín lived together in love from that day forward.

4

CÚ CHULAINN AND THE TÁIN BÓ CUAILNGE

THE *TÁIN BÓ CUAILNGE*, USUALLY known as "The Cattle Raid of Cuailnge," is the heart of a series of interrelated Irish stories known as the Ulster Cycle, which tell of the exploits and adventures of the Ulster or Ulaid people of northern Ireland. The surviving manuscripts that preserve the *Táin—The Book of the Dun Cow, The Book of Leinster, The Yellow Book of Lecan*—were written from the twelfth to fourteenth centuries, but the language of the stories is from several centuries earlier. As with many other Irish tales, there is much controversy among scholars concerning how much, if any, of the story preserves elements of an era before the introduction of Christianity to Ireland. I have included in this chapter several of the *remscéla*, or pre-tales, which are not strictly part of the *Táin* but are important to its plot.

The central character of the *Táin* is the great Irish hero Cú Chulainn. He was born from divine and human parents; there begins the hero's journey found in many mythologies, consisting of remarkable boyhood deeds, astonishing feats of bravery and combat, and finally a hero's death.

THE DISCOVERY OF THE TÁIN

One day Senchán Torpéist, the chief bard of Ireland, went to visit Gúaire, a king in the province of Connacht. Senchán took with him a retinue of three hundred master and apprentice poets, along with their wives and servants. They soon began to eat Gúaire out of house and home. Gúaire's brother Marbán the hermit heard about this injustice and pronounced a curse on Senchán and his band, saying they would lose their gift of poetry unless they could recite the whole of the *Táin Bó Cuailnge*. Among them they knew only pieces of the *Táin*, so they searched all of Ireland for a year and a day looking for a bard or storyteller who knew the whole tale, but they could find no one who did.

At last one night a young poet named Emine and his friend Muirgen came upon the grave of a famous warrior of old, Fergus mac Roich. Emine left to search for shelter, but Muirgen stayed by the tomb. In despair, Muirgen chanted a poem above the grave of Fergus:

Oh Fergus, if only this rock
were your true self, mac Roich,
then poets looking for a roof
to cover them here
would recover the Táin,
plain and perfect Fergus.

A heavy mist descended suddenly on Muirgen—and out of it walked the ghost of Fergus mac Roich in great majesty wearing a green cloak, a dazzling red tunic, and a golden sword. For three days and three nights Fergus recited to him the whole *Táin* from start to finish. After that, the spirit disappeared and Muirgen returned to Senchán to narrate the story and lift the curse that had been placed on them. And so the *Táin* was recovered for all to hear.

THE CONCEPTION OF CONCHOBAR

The story begins with a young woman named Nes, the daughter of Eochaid Sálbuide. One day she was sitting outside of the great Ulster fort of Emain Macha when the druid seer Cathbad passed by.

"Cathbad, what is this day good for?" asked Nes.

"It's a perfect day for conceiving a king," said Cathbad.

"Are you speaking the truth?" she demanded.

"Indeed, I am," he said. "I swear by all the gods."

Since Cathbad was the only man present that day, Nes took him to her bedroom and lay with him so that she would become pregnant. And just as she had hoped, that very day she conceived a child within her womb. A long three years and three months later, she gave birth to a boy and named him Conchobar.

Nes raised Conchobar for seven years, teaching him the ways of his people and the love of power. Nes was beautiful and was sought after by none other than the king of Ulster, Fergus mac Roich.

"Marry me," pleaded Fergus.

"Only if you give me something in return," replied Nes.

"Anything you desire," the king promised.

"Just a small thing," she said. "I want you to name my son Conchobar as king for a year, so that some day his own sons may be called the heirs of a king. You'll still rule over Ulster, my dear Fergus, in all but name."

And so Fergus agreed. After Nes married Fergus and went to bed with him, she set out to obtain the kingship for her son permanently. She gave generous gifts of gold and silver to the warriors of Ulster to win their favor and advised her son to take everything he could from half the people of the land and give it to the other half. By these means she won over the nobility of Ulster.

When the year of Conchobar's kingship was at an end, Fergus went to his warriors to take back the crown from Conchobar. But the nobles were none too pleased that Fergus had used the kingship as a dowry, and they were grateful that they had received so many fine gifts from Conchobar and Nes.

"Let what Fergus sold stay sold," they declared, "and let what Conchobar purchased continue to belong to him."

And so Conchobar became king of the Ulstermen.

Conchobar was loved by all the people of his province. His judgment was always considered and fair, so that the land was fruitful and prosperous. He was the bravest of all the Ulster warriors, even as his fellow fighters risked their own lives to keep him safe in battle. All the province regarded him so highly that every man who took a wife gave her on the wedding night first to Conchobar. When he traveled, at any house he stayed the husband would send his own wife to warm Conchobar's bed. His home was full of captured treasures and the heads of enemy warriors he had slain decorated his walls. His generosity was legendary and his feasting hall was always full of guests dining from the bounty of his table.

He seemed in every way the perfect king.

THE CURSE OF MACHA

One of the noblemen of Conchobar was Cruinniuc mac Agnomain, a wealthy but lonely widower who lived with his sons in the mountains of Ulster. One day when he was alone at his farm he saw a beautiful woman walking toward him. She went into his home and began to do the household chores as if she had lived there for years. When night came, she climbed into Cruinniuc's bed and made love with him.

The woman stayed with Cruinniuc after that and took care of him and his sons. While she was there, the farm was prosperous and there was never a lack of food, clothing, or anything else they needed.

One day Conchobar called all the people of Ulster to a great festival. Men, women, boys, and girls all gathered with great excitement wearing their finest clothes, including Cruinniuc and his sons, but his wife stayed on the farm since she was nine months pregnant.

"Don't boast or say anything foolish at the festival," she warned Cruinniuc.

"That's not likely," he said.

At the end of the celebrations there was a great horse race on a nearby field. Conchobar and all the warriors brought their horses and chariots to compete, but the king's team always won. Everyone in the crowd said that no one could best Conchobar.

"My wife can run even faster than the king's horses," boasted Cruinniuc.

When the king's men heard him say this, they hauled him before Conchobar, who was stung by the claim and demanded Cruinniuc make good on his boasting. He sent a messenger to the farm to fetch the woman.

"I can't race now," she pleaded with the messenger. "I am pregnant with twins and will give birth any day."

"If you don't come," said the messenger, "your husband will die."

And so the woman went, her labor pains beginning even as she arrived. She begged the king not to make her run, but he refused to listen. She turned to the crowd gathered there and pleaded with them: "Please, help me. A mother bore each of you. At least wait until my children are born before you force me to race."

But the crowd stood silent.

"Very well," said the woman. "But I warn you that a great evil will come upon Ulster because of this."

Then the king asked her name.

"I am Macha, daughter of Sainrith mac Imbaith, the wondrous son of the ocean. From this day forward my name shall be on this place."

And then the race began. Macha flew around the field like the fastest of horses alongside the chariot of the king until she crossed the finish line just ahead of the team.

When she reached the end of the course she gave birth to twins, a son and a daughter. It was from them that the Ulster capital, Emain Macha or the Twins of Macha, was named.

In her labor pains Macha screamed at the king and his warriors that thenceforth in the hour of their greatest peril they would fall into the pangs of birth for five days and four nights. From that day her curse held for nine generations. Whenever danger came upon the province, all the men of Ulster would collapse in labor pains, unable to move in their agony. Only the women, young boys, and the great warrior Cú Chulainn were spared from the terrible curse of Macha.

THE EXILE OF THE SONS OF UISLIU

One day Conchobar and the warriors of Ulster were gathered together for a feast at the home of the king's chief storyteller, Fedlimid mac Daill. Fedlimid's pregnant wife was serving them even though she was great with child and about to give birth. Meat was set before the warriors on overflowing platters and drinking horns full of ale were passed around the hall until drunken shouting and laughter filled the night. At the end of the evening when the men had all fallen asleep, Fedlimid's wife at last crossed the hall to her own bedchamber. Suddenly the child in her womb cried out in a scream that woke everyone in the house.

All the warriors jumped to their feet as if under attack, but Sencha mac Ailella, the chief judge of Conchobar, ordered everyone to be still and for the woman to be brought before them. Her husband Fedlimid then asked her what was the fearful cry that had burst from her full womb. The woman shook her head in bewilderment:

Even though the cry came from the cradle of my own body,
no woman knows
what her own womb bears.

She turned to the druid Cathbad hoping that he might explain the cry. And Cathbad said:

From the hollow of your womb there cried
a woman with twisted yellow hair
and beautiful grey-green eyes.
Her cheeks are flushed like foxglove

and her teeth the color of new-fallen snow.
Her lips are lustrous like Parthian red.
Queens will envy her,
heroes will fight for her,
kings will seek her for their bed.
Because of her, great will the slaughter be
among the chariot-warriors of Ulster.

Cathbad placed his hand on the woman's belly and the child moved at his touch.

"Yes, this child is a girl. Deirdre will be her name—and she will bring evil on us all."

After the girl was born, everyone proclaimed that she was the most beautiful child they had ever seen.

"Kill her!" shouted the Ulstermen.

"No!" said Conchobar. "I will take this child for myself and have her reared in secret away from all jealous eyes. When she is of age, I will bring her to my bed."

And so Conchobar sent her away to a hidden place so that no one could see her. Only her foster father and foster mother saw her, along with a woman poet named Leborcham who was a satirist and couldn't be kept away.

One day when Deirdre had grown into a beautiful young woman, her foster father was outside in the snow skinning a calf to cook for her. A raven settled on the snow next to the pool of blood and drank from it.

Deirdre saw it and said: "I could love a man with those three colors—hair black like a raven, cheeks red like blood, and a body white as snow."

Leborcham, who was standing nearby, said: "Luck and fortune are with you, my dear, for such a man is not far away—Noíse son of Uisliu."

"I will be ill," Deirdre said, "until I see him."

It happened that one night soon after, Noíse was standing alone on the walls of Emain Macha, the stronghold of the Ulstermen, and was singing. The songs of the sons of Uisliu were so sweet that every cow who heard them gave two-thirds more milk, and every person who heard them was filled with peace. The sons of Uisliu were also great warriors. If they stood back to back, they could hold off the whole province of Ulster. They were moreover as swift as hunting hounds and could outrun wild beasts.

While Noíse was on the walls alone, Deirdre slipped away from her hidden farm and came near as if she were merely walking past him. He didn't recognize her at first.

"That's a fine heifer going by," he said.

"The heifers are bound to be fine when there are no bulls around," she replied.

But then he realized who she was.

"You have the greatest bull of this province to yourself," he said, "the king of Ulster."

"Between him and you," she said, "I would choose a fine young bull for myself."

"Don't say such things!" cried Noíse. "Remember the prophecy of Cathbad."

"Are you rejecting me?" she asked.

"Yes, I must," he answered.

Then Deirdre seized him by both ears.

"Two ears of shame and mockery these will be," she said, "if you don't take me with you."

"No! Get away from me, woman."

"Too late. You will do it," she said, binding him with her curse.

A shrill cry began to rise from the throat of Noíse. As it grew, the men of Ulster heard it and began to take up arms. But the brothers of Noíse knew what it was and ran to quiet him.

"What are you doing?" they asked. "The Ulstermen will come to blows because of you."

Then Noíse told them what had happened.

"Evil will come from this," they said. "But you will not be disgraced while we are alive. Come, we'll leave here and go to some other place. No king in Ireland will deny us welcome."

And so Noíse and his brothers left that night with Deirdre among them, as well as three times fifty warriors along with three times fifty women and the same number of hounds and servants.

The band of warriors and their followers traveled across Ireland searching for a safe place to settle, but everywhere they went Conchobar laid a trap for them. At last they crossed the sea to Britain, where they lived in the mountains and hunted wild animals to survive. Finally when the game was gone, they hired themselves as mercenary soldiers to the king of Britain. But they built their houses to hide Deirdre so that no one might see her and seek to take her by force.

One day a servant of the king happened to enter the home of Deirdre and Noíse early in the morning and saw them sleeping. He went at once and woke the king, saying that he had found the most beautiful woman in the world for him. All he had to do was to kill Noíse and she would be his to sleep with. The king was reluctant to openly kill Noíse and lose his Irish mercenaries, so he sent the servant each day to try and win her favor in secret. Each night, however, Deirdre told Noíse what the king's servant had said to her.

Soon the king began to send Noíse and his brothers into the most dangerous battles so that they might be killed, but they were so fierce in fighting that no one could touch them. At last the king sent his own soldiers to kill Noíse, but Deirdre heard of the plan and urged her husband and his followers to flee back to Ireland immediately. They did so that very night.

When the warriors of Conchobar heard that Noíse was back on their island, they told the king that it was time to forgive him and allow the couple to settle in their own land in peace. Conchobar sent them a message guaranteeing their safety. Noíse and his brothers agreed if the previous king Fergus, along with the great warrior Dubthach and Conchobar's own son Cormac, would pledge themselves as guarantors of Conchobar's good will. Fergus and the others then went down to the sea to meet Noíse.

But Conchobar had other plans. He knew that Fergus was bound by a *geis* or prohibition put upon him that he could never pass by a feast without joining it, so the king held banquets along the way to delay him from joining Noíse. Since Noíse and his brothers had sworn an oath that they would not eat in Ireland until they dined at Conchobar's table, they were compelled by hunger not to wait for Fergus. When the sons of Uisliu came to Conchobar's fortress at Emain Macha along with Fergus's son Fiacha who had gone to meet him, the whole of Ulster was waiting for them on the walls. Éogan mac Durthacht was the first to greet Noíse—but with the thrust of a spear through his chest that came out the back and broke his spine in two. Fiacha threw himself across Noíse to protect him, though it was in vain. The Ulster warriors slaughtered Fiacha and the brothers of Noíse and all of his followers until the grass ran red with blood.

Deirdre alone was left alive and was brought to Conchobar with her hands bound behind her back.

When Fergus was told of this, he and Dubthach and Cormac the son of Conchobar attacked Conchobar at Emain Macha and killed many of the warriors of Ulster. Then they and three thousand others fled west to the kingdom of Ailill and Medb in Connacht, where they were welcomed by the king and queen as exiles. For sixteen years they remained there, lamenting their betrayal and the loss of honor that Conchobar had inflicted on them.

As for Deirdre, once she was taken captive by Conchobar she never again smiled or raised her head in the presence of the king. She mourned without ceasing the loss of Noíse, until Conchobar in anger determined to give her to Éogan mac Durthacht, the very man who had murdered her husband.

The morning that Éogan took her from Emain Macha, she stood between him and Conchobar in his chariot as they left the gates.

"Deirdre," laughed Conchobar, "don't look so downcast. Between me and Éogan you are powerless, just a sheep between two rams."

But as they passed a large boulder on the road, Deirdre threw herself out of the chariot and smashed her own head against the stone. There she lay dead on the road, depriving both men of their prize forever.

THE BIRTH OF CÚ CHULAINN

And so it was that Fergus and the exiles of Ulster went to live in Connacht with the enemies of their tribe. But there were still many great warriors among the men who served Conchobar, though none was greater than Sétanta, who later took the name Cú Chulainn.

The story of Cú Chulainn's birth is strange and wondrous. There was a day when the crops of Ulster were attacked and eaten by nine scores of male and female birds, each pair bound by a silver cord between them. Conchobar and his men were furious to see their harvest destroyed, and so mounted their chariots to drive the birds away. Along with them came Deichtine, Conchobar's sister, the warrior Conall, and the troublemaker Briccriu.

They chased the birds south across the mountains and plains of Ireland until darkness fell, and they reached the ancient *síd* mound of the Bruig on the Bóinne River. Conchobar sent Conall and Briccriu to seek shelter for the night, but the only place they could find was a small hut in which a poor couple lived. Briccriu told the king that they needn't bother going there unless they brought their own food, but Conchobar took his men to the hut nonetheless and crowded inside. They broke down the door of the store-room and helped themselves to all the couple had. Soon they were drunk and in a festive mood.

The woman who lived in the hut then began to go into labor, at the same time as a mare in the yard was giving birth to two foals. Deichtine went in to help the woman deliver her child and not long after brought out a baby boy. The Ulstermen took charge of the child and decided to give him the two foals as a present, while Deichtine nursed him at her own breast. Then the whole company fell asleep.

When the sun rose the next morning, the Ulstermen awoke to find there was nothing to be seen of the hut or the couple. Only the baby and the foals remained. They took the boy back to Emain Macha and Deichtine raised him as her own son.

But soon the baby was struck with a fever and died. Deichtine was heartbroken and all the women of Ulster sang a song of lamentation for the child. She came home after lamenting and asked her servant for a drink. A cup was brought and Deichtine drank it—but she didn't notice that a tiny creature was in the cup, and so she swallowed it.

When Deichtine fell asleep that night, she dreamed that a man came to her and told her she would bear a child by him. He said that his name was Lug and that he had led her and her company to the Bruig on the Bóinne River. The boy who had been born there was his son. Even though the child had seemed to die, he was in fact now in her womb. She was to name the boy Sétanta and the two foals were to be raised with him.

Deichtine grew great with child, though no one knew who the father was. Some said it was Conchobar himself who had slept with his own sister in his drunkenness. The king said nothing, but gave his pregnant sister to Sualdam mac Roich to marry. Deichtine was so ashamed to go to her husband's bed pregnant that she miscarried on her wedding night. Then she slept with Sualdam, became pregnant, and gave birth to a son she named Sétanta—a boy who had been born three times.

When Sétanta was born, the greatest men and women of Ulster contended to some day take him as a foster son, as was the custom. They went to Conchobar the king to decide between them.

"My sister Finnchaem should take the boy," he said.

"I do love him," she replied, "as if he were my own son Conall."

Briccriu the troublemaker spoke up: "Of course you love him so. There's little difference between a son and a nephew."

"Wait," said Sencha, chief judge and wisest man of Ulster. "I would be a better foster parent than Finnchaem. I am a fine warrior as well as the best judge and advisor in all matters to the king. I settle all disputes in Ulster and everyone acknowledges my wisdom."

"No," said Blaí Briuga, the warrior most renowned among the Ulstermen for his hospitality. "The boy should come to live with me. I can feast all the men of Ireland in my house for a week without want. I can support him better than anyone else."

"Not true," said Fergus. "I am second to no man in courage, skill in battle, and honor."

"Sit down, Fergus," said Amairgen the poet, "and listen, all of you. I am most worthy to raise this boy. For in eloquence and brave deeds I have no equal."

"There is nothing to be gained by all this fighting," said Conchobar at last. "Let Morann the druid decide."

And so Morann gave his judgment: "Let him be given to Conchobar as his foster son, for he is the brother of Finnchaem, and to Finnchaem as a mother and Conall as his foster brother. But let him also be given to Sencha to teach him eloquence of speech and to Blaí Briuga for sustenance and to Fergus to sit on his knee and to Amairgen as his teacher. In this way he will be raised by everyone, as warrior, prince, and sage. This boy will be cherished by all and will save us someday from our enemies."

THE BOYHOOD DEEDS OF CÚ CHULAINN

While Sétanta was very young, he lived with his mother and father to the south of Emain Macha on the plain of Muirthemne, near the sea. While there he heard stories of the boys of Ulster and how three times fifty were always playing hurley ball with their sticks.

"Mother, let me go and join the boys at Emain Macha," he said.

"No," she replied. "You are much too young and you have no warrior to escort you from here to there. The journey is too difficult for you."

"I'm going to go anyway," he answered.

Sétanta gathered his wooden shield and toy javelin along with his hurley stick and ball and set off to the Ulster capital alone. Along the way he kept throwing the javelin into the sky in front of him and running to catch it by its end before it hit the ground.

At last he came to the playing fields of Emain Macha and rushed to join the game.

"This boy insults us," said Follomon the son of Conchobar. For Sétanta did not know that it was forbidden for anyone to join the game unless he had first sought permission and protection.

The other boys threw three times fifty javelins at him all at once, but he repelled each one with his toy shield. Then they threw all their balls at him, but he caught them against his chest. Then they threw their hurley sticks, but they could not touch him.

At last Sétanta became furious at the ill treatment he was receiving from the boys and began to change in form and appearance. In his battle fury each hair on his head stood straight up as if it were hammered into his skull. One of his eyes narrowed until it was like the eye of a needle while the other opened as wide as a mead goblet. He bared his teeth from ear to ear and glowed with a warrior's fire. The boys began to run.

Then he attacked them and knocked down fifty of them before they reached the gates of Emain Macha. He pursued the rest past the king as he sat playing chess at the gate and leapt over the chess board.

Conchobar seized him by the arm.

"You aren't treating these boys very well," said the king.

"I treated them just as they deserved," Sétanta said. "I came all the way from my home to play with them, but they were not kind to me."

"What is your name?" asked Conchobar.

"I am Sétanta the son of Sualtaim and your sister. I did not expect to be treated badly here among my own people."

"Why didn't you ask them for protection?" said the king.

"I didn't know that was required," replied Sétanta. "And so I now ask you for your protection."

"Agreed," said the king.

The boy then turned and started attacking the boys throughout the fort.

"Why are you still fighting with them?" asked the king.

"Because now," said Sétanta, "I want them to ask for *my* protection."

"They will do so," said Conchobar. "I give you my word."

"Then I agree that I shall do them no more harm," said Sétanta.

After this, the people of Emain Macha went into the hurley fields and helped the boys to their feet, each going to the aid of their own foster son.

When he first came to Emain Macha, Sétanta did not sleep inside the fort.

"Why don't you sleep here?" asked Conchobar.

"Because I can't sleep unless my head and feet are equally high," said the boy.

And so Conchobar ordered a pillar-stone placed at Sétanta's head and another at his feet. In between he made a special bed for him.

One day when a certain man went to wake him, Sétanta jumped up with a start and struck the man on the forehead, driving his broken skull into his brain and killing him. He also knocked down one of the pillar-stones.

From that time forward no one dared to wake him, but allowed him to sleep until he woke of his own accord.

At another time, Sétanta was playing hurley ball on the field east of Emain Macha by himself against three times fifty boys. In every game he beat them until they couldn't stand it anymore and attacked him. He struck back and killed fifty of them, then ran away to hide under Conchobar's bed. The people of Ulster rose up to kill the boy while Conchobar rushed to defend him, but Sétanta lifted up the bed with thirty warriors on top of it and threw it into the middle of the house. At last, Conchobar and Fergus calmed the angry crowd and made peace between them and the boy.

Once when Sétanta was still a child, war broke out between Ulster and Éogan mac Durthacht, who had been Conchobar's ally and slain Noíse for him when he returned to Ireland with Deirdre.

When the battle began, Sétanta was left behind asleep at Emain Macha. The fighting went poorly for the Ulstermen so that Conchobar and many of his men were left for dead on the battlefield. Their groans woke up Sétanta and he went to help his countrymen.

Along the way he met a man with half a head carrying half of another man on his back.

"Help me, boy," the man with half a head said. "I am wounded. Take my brother from my back and take a turn carrying him."

"I will not," said Sétanta in fear.

The man threw his brother on the boy, but Sétanta cast him off and wrestled the man until the man beat him and threw him on the ground. Then he heard the war goddess crying from among the corpses: "A poor warrior you are to be beaten by a phantom."

Sétanta then took his hurley stick and struck off the half head of the man who had beaten him. He then began to drive the head before him across the plain like a ball.

"Conchobar, are you there?" Sétanta shouted.

The king called out to him until the boy found him.

"Why are you here, boy?" Conchobar asked. "A grown man could die of terror amid such a scene."

Sétanta picked up the king from the ditch and put him on his shoulders. Six grown men could not have done the same.

"Go to that house there and make a fire for me," said the king after a time.

The boy carried him into the house and made a fire.

"If I had a roasted pig to eat," said the king, "I might just live."

"I'll find you one," said Sétanta.

He went off into the woods and found at last a man roasting a pig over a fire. The ferocious-looking man had one hand on the pig and another on his weapons. But Sétanta attacked him and cut off his head, carrying it and the pig back to Conchobar, who then ate the pig.

"Let us go home," said the king.

And so Sétanta helped him back to Emain Macha. Along the way they found Conchobar's son Cúscraid, whom Sétanta put on his back and carried all the way home.

Once when Sétanta was only five years old, Ulster was attacked by twenty-seven fierce and dark warriors from the isles of Faiche. The Ulstermen immediately collapsed into labor pains because of the curse laid on them by Macha. But the curse did not fall on young boys. When the invaders poured over the walls of Emain Macha, the women screamed and the boys who saw the men of Faiche ran away—all except for Sétanta. He attacked them with stones and killed nine of them with his hurley stick, driving the rest out of Ulster and saving his people.

When Sétanta was seven years old, the smith Culann prepared a great feast for Conchobar and his best warriors. As the king was leaving Emain Macha, the king drove his chariot past the playing fields and saw Sétanta defeating all the boys there.

"Come with me to the feast, little Sétanta," said the king. "You will be my guest."

"I'll come later, uncle. I'm not done playing here yet."

And so Conchobar went to the home of Culann and forgot that Sétanta would be following him.

"Is there anyone else coming?" asked Culann.

"No," said the king.

Culann then locked the gate of his fort and released his fierce hound outside the walls to guard his home. This animal was so ferocious that it took three men with three chains to control him. When that was done, they began the feast.

Meanwhile, young Sétanta was approaching the fort of Culann. As he walked he threw his hurley ball into the air and tossed his stick after it to strike it, then caught both before they hit the ground.

It was at this moment that Conchobar remembered that Sétanta was coming. He cried out to Culann and ran to the top of the rampart above the gate, but it was too late.

The hound had seen Sétanta coming near and rushed him with his teeth bared ready to tear the boy apart. But when Sétanta saw the animal, he took his hurley ball and threw it so hard at the hound that it went into his throat and drove its entrails out the back end of his body. A great shout of joy went up among the Ulstermen.

"I welcome you, lad, and am glad you are safe," said Culann, "but for my sake I wish I had never prepared this feast. That hound was the greatest in Ireland and guarded my farm and cattle from all harm. Without him I am ruined."

"Don't worry," said Sétanta. "I will raise a pup just as good for you. Until he is grown, I myself will guard your farm and animals."

Then Cathbad the druid spoke: "From now on, boy, your name shall be Cú Chulainn. For you will be the *cú*, the hound of Culann."

"A fine name," said the boy. And from then on he was known as Cú Chulainn.

One day Cathbad the druid was instructing his students when one of them asked what that day would be good for.

"Today is a good day," said Cathbad, "for a warrior to first take up arms. For whoever receives weapons for the first time today will have fame forever throughout Ireland."

Cú Chulainn overheard these words and went quickly to Conchobar the king and asked for arms.

"Who sent you to do this?" asked Conchobar.

"Cathbad the druid," said the boy.

And so the king gave him a spear and a sword. Cú Chulainn brandished these about the royal hall and broke them, then went through fifteen more sets of weapons that also broke in his hands. Finally, Conchobar gave him his own arms, which were strong enough for the boy.

Cathbad came and saw what was happening.

"Who gave this child weapons today of all days?" the druid asked.

"I did," said the king. "Didn't you send him?"

"No," said Cathbad, "for whoever takes up weapons today will be a warrior of great fame, but his mother will weep, for his life will be short."

"Why did you deceive me?" Conchobar asked Cú Chulainn.

"Because a short life means nothing to me," said the boy. "Let me live on this earth only a single day if my fame as a warrior may be everlasting."

On another day someone asked Cathbad what that day would be good for.

"The name of the man who goes forth in battle in a chariot today will live throughout Ireland forever," said the druid.

Cú Chulainn heard this and went to Conchobar to ask for a chariot, which the king gave him. The boy broke the chariot and the next twelve, until Conchobar gave him his own chariot.

He climbed into this chariot with Ibor, Conchobar's charioteer, at the reins and they rode around the yard inside the gates. After a short time Ibor said that was enough.

"Not yet," said Cú Chulainn. "Let's circle around Emain Macha. I'll give you a fine reward if you drive me."

So Ibor took the boy outside and around the fortress so the other boys could see him. Then he turned back to the gates.

"Not yet," said Cú Chulainn. "Put the whip to the horses."

"Where do you wish to go?" asked the charioteer.

"As far as the road will lead," said Cú Chulainn.

They went along the road to a mountain called Sliab Fúait, where Cú Chulainn's foster brother Conall Cernach was standing guard. It fell to a different warrior of Ulster each day to stand at Sliab Fúait and protect the province from invaders.

"Greetings, Conall," said Cú Chulainn. "Return to Emain Macha. I'm here to relieve you as guard."

"You are too young," said the warrior.

Then Cú Chulainn took a stone and threw it at the shaft of Conall Cernach's chariot, breaking it.

"Why did you do that?" asked Conall in anger.

"Because no warrior of Ulster can stand guard with a broken chariot," said the boy. "Go back to the fort and leave me here to protect Ulster."

Conall reluctantly agreed. Cú Chulainn then asked his charioteer about the enemies of Ulster who lived nearby. Ibor said the nearest were the three sons of Nechta Scéne named Fóill, Fannall, and Túachell. They were fierce men and had killed many brave warriors of Ulster.

"Take me to them," said Cú Chulainn.

Ibor drove him to a small river on the border of Ulster where the sons of Nechta Scéne had their fortress. In the middle of the stream was a pillar-stone with a wooden branch set on top as a warning to trespassers. Cú Chulainn took the branch and cast it into the water, letting it float away downstream. He then lay down on the far bank for a nap.

"Wake me if any warriors show up," said Cú Chulainn.

The sons of Nechta Scéne saw what the boy had done and rushed down to the stream while Cú Chulainn slept peacefully.

"Who dares to enter our lands?" asked the men.

"Just a lad here on his first outing," said the charioteer Ibor. "There's no need for trouble. My hands are on the reins already to take him home. The boy is merely sleeping."

"There's no boy here," said Cú Chulainn as he awoke, "but a man ready to do battle."

"Don't be a fool," said his charioteer. "This first man is Fóill the Sly. If you don't kill him with your first spear thrust you'll never touch him."

"Then I swear by the god by whom my people swear," said Cú Chulainn, "the spear my lord Conchobar gave me will not miss."

Cú Chulainn cast the spear at Fóill and broke his back in two. The boy then cut off the warrior's head as a trophy and took his spoils.

"Watch out for this next man," said his charioteer. "He is Fannall the Swallow who moves as swiftly as a bird."

But Cú Chulainn was even faster. He killed the warrior, cut off his head, and took his spoils.

"Beware this last man," said Ibor. "He is Túachell the Cunning. No weapon has ever touched him."

"Then I will use my finest spear on him and riddle him full of holes," said Cú Chulainn.

The boy knocked him down with his spear and cut off his head. He then gave it and the spoils to Ibor to place in the chariot.

Cú Chulainn told the charioteer to then turn toward the plain and drive as fast as he could. With Ibor at the reins the horses flew like the wind. When they reached the middle of the plain, Cú Chulainn saw a herd of deer grazing there.

"What would be more impressive to the Ulstermen," he asked the charioteer, "to bring the deer back dead or alive?"

"No one can capture a live deer," said Ibor.

"I can," said Cú Chulainn. "Drive them into that bog."

Ibor used the horses to drive the deer into the bog, where Cú Chulainn then leapt from the chariot and captured the largest stag in the herd. He tied it to the back of the chariot and told Ibor to drive on.

Soon they saw a flock of swans.

"What would be more impressive to the Ulstermen," Cú Chulainn asked the charioteer, "to bring back the swans dead or alive?"

"No one can capture swans alive," said the charioteer.

Cú Chulainn then threw stones at the birds and stunned twenty of them with two stones so they fell to the ground. He gathered the birds and tied them with cords to the chariot. He then told Ibor to turn back to Emain Macha with the twenty birds flying above, the deer trailing behind, and three severed heads hanging from the chariot.

When they approached Emain Macha, Cú Chulainn ordered Ibor to turn the left side of the chariot toward the fort, which was forbidden. Cú Chulainn then cried out for all to hear: "I swear by the god by whom the men of Ulster swear that unless some man is found to fight with me I will slaughter everyone in the fort."

The watchman on the walls cried out to the king.

"A warrior in a chariot is here and a great battle fury is upon him. He will shed the blood of everyone in Emain Macha unless naked women go out to meet him."

"Send forth the naked women!" shouted Conchobar.

The women of Emain Macha came out of the gate led by Mugain the wife of the king himself. They marched up to Cú Chulainn and bared their breasts to him.

"These are the warriors you will face today," Mugain told him.

Cú Chulainn grew red and his face blushed crimson in embarrassment. The warriors of Ulster then seized him and threw him into a tub of cold water. That tub burst from the heat of the boy. They threw him into a second tub of cold water that began to boil. Then they threw him into a third tub, which warmed just enough for a bath.

When he came out of the tub, the queen placed on him a blue mantle with a silver brooch and a hooded tunic. Cú Chulainn then went and sat beside Conchobar in the place of honor, which was his ever after.

THE WOOING OF EMER

One day when the men of Ulster were in Emain Macha feasting, they decided that Cú Chulainn needed a wife, since all of their own wives and daughters were falling in love with him. They also thought that such a great warrior should father a son.

Cú Chulainn agreed and so went to a place called the Gardens of Lug to woo a beautiful girl he knew there named Emer, the daughter of a cunning man named Forgall Monach. Cú Chulainn found Emer seated on the grass with her foster sisters sewing. She was wearing a low-cut dress, so that her breasts rose over the top.

"I see a sweet country where I could rest my weapon," he said to her.

"No man will travel in this country until he has killed a hundred men," Emer answered.

"Still, in that country I'll rest my weapon," he said.

"No man will travel this country until he has done a salmon leap with twice his weight in gold and struck down three groups of nine men each with one blow, leaving the middle man of each untouched," she answered.

"It will be done—and in that country I'll rest my weapon," said Cú Chulainn. Then he went home.

That evening Emer told her father what the young man had said.

"I'll put an end to this," he said to himself. "He'll never have what he wants."

Forgall disguised himself as a royal messenger from Gaul and came to the court of Conchobar at Emain Macha pretending to pay tribute. At the king's command, Cú Chulainn and the other warriors put on a demonstration for him of their martial skills.

"Not bad," said Forgall, "but of course if you really want to be a fine fighter you must study with Scáthach the great warrior-woman in Britain. Then you could beat any man in Europe."

Cú Chulainn was then determined to leave Ireland and swore to study with Scáthach—which was exactly what

Forgall had intended. But before the young man left, he went to Emer to say goodbye, swearing he would be faithful to her until they met again.

Cú Chulainn made the long journey across the sea to find Scáthach in the wild lands of Britain, taking his foster brother Ferdia with him. He came at last to Scáthach's fortress, but the only way to reach it was to cross a deep gorge by a way known as the Pupil's Bridge. This bridge would throw off anyone who tried to cross it unless he was a skilled warrior. Three times Cú Chulainn tried to cross and was tossed on his back. But then he went into his battle fury and leapt across the bridge.

Scáthach was told of his arrival and sent her daughter Uathach to greet him. When she saw Cú Chulainn, she was amazed by his beauty and fell in love with him.

"I see you've fallen for this young man," said Scáthach. "Go to his bed tonight if you want."

"That would be no hardship," said Uathach.

And so that night she dressed as a maidservant and went to his chamber. Cú Chulainn reached out to draw the beautiful maiden into his bed, but in his eagerness he hurt her so that she cried out. Cochar Cruibne, one of Scáthach's finest warriors, rushed to the chamber to defend Uathach and was killed by Cú Chulainn, who cut off his head. Cú Chulainn regretted what he had done and promised to train with Scáthach and take the place of Cochar as her champion in battle.

Cú Chulainn was the best student Scáthach had ever seen and learned every skill she could teach him, including the use of the fearsome *gae bolga*, a spear no man could avoid.

One day when Scáthach's greatest enemy, the warrior queen Aife, marched on her land, Cú Chulainn challenged the invader to single combat. The two met and clashed as champions, but at last Cú Chulainn seized her by her breasts and tossed her to the ground with a sword held over her.

"A life for a life, Cú Chulainn," she said.

"I will spare you if you grant me three things I desire," he said.

"If you can ask them in one breath, you shall have them," she answered.

"Give me hostages for Scáthach, promise you'll never attack her again, and sleep with me tonight so that you bear me a son."

"I grant you all you ask," said Aife. And she went to bed with him that very night.

A few weeks later, Aife came to Cú Chulainn and told him she was pregnant with his son.

"Give him the name Conla," said Cú Chulainn. "I'll send for him to come to Ireland in seven years."

Then he presented Aife with a ring to give to the boy when he came of age, with the command that the boy reveal his name to no man, make way for no man, and never refuse combat.

When his training was complete, Cú Chulainn returned to Ireland and went to Emer's home. Her father had heard of his coming and had posted men as guards around his fort, including Emer's three brothers, each with eight powerful warriors at their sides. Cú Chulainn killed eight men from each group with one stroke and left the center man untouched. When he entered the fortress, he put Emer and her sister on his back, each with a bag of gold in their arms, and leapt back across the walls of the fort. Emer's father Forgall tried to flee, but fell from his own rampart and died.

As he escaped back to Emain Macha, Cú Chulainn killed a hundred men along the way.

The young man and his bride were welcomed to Emain Macha by Conchobar, but Briccriu the troublemaker said that the young man's plans to have the girl for himself would have to wait. By tradition the king must sleep with every bride before the groom.

Cú Chulainn flew into a rage and would have killed every man at Emain Macha, but the warrior Fergus and Cathbad the druid told him they would sleep in the bed between the king and Emer to protect his honor. Cú Chulainn agreed and Emer remained untouched that night. The next day Conchobar paid Cú Chulainn his full honor-price and provided the dowry of Emer himself. After that, Cú Chulainn took her to bed.

THE DEATH OF AIFE'S ONLY SON

Seven years passed until one day some men of Ulster who were at the beach saw a small bronze boat with golden oars coming toward them across the sea. There was a boy inside who was slinging rocks at birds so skillfully that he only stunned them, then he let them go again. The men sent word of the boy to the king, who ordered his warrior Condere to find out who he was.

When he reached the shore, Condere asked the boy his name.

"I give my name to no man," he replied, "and yield to no man."

Condere returned to the king and reported what the boy said.

"No one challenges the honor of the Ulstermen in such a way," said the warrior Conall Cernach. And so he went to the shore to challenge the boy. In no time at all, Conall was lying in the sand knocked out from a sling stone. The boy then tied Conall's arms together and sent him back to the king.

"This is shameful," said Conchobar. "Who will stand against this boy for the honor of Ulster?"

No one stepped forward.

"I will go," said Cú Chulainn at last.

Emer implored her husband not to meet the boy, fearing this was the son Cú Chulainn had told her of. He said that he feared the same, but he could not refuse the king. Then he went to the shore to meet the boy.

"Name yourself or die," Cú Chulainn said.

"Then I will die," the boy replied.

The two clashed fiercely at arms for hours, but Cú Chulainn could not defeat him. At last he forced the boy into the water and drew forth the *gae bolga* from his pack of weapons. He sent the fearsome spear speeding across the waves until it pierced the bowels of the boy and mortally wounded him. Cú Chulainn carried him to the shore and laid him on the sand.

"Men of Ulster," said Cú Chulainn, "this is my son, Conla."

All the warriors gathered there wept when they heard this. Conla asked to greet each of the great warriors he had heard so much about from his mother, then he breathed his last as his father held him in his arms. He was buried in a grave beneath a stone, and for three days no calf in Ulster was allowed to go to its mother on account of the death of Cú Chulainn's only son.

THE TÁIN BEGINS

One night far away in Connacht, when the royal bed was prepared for Ailill and Medb in their fort at Cruachan, the couple engaged in pillow talk.

"It's true what they say, my love, that the wife of a wealthy man does well for herself," said Ailill to his wife.

"I suppose," replied Medb. "What makes you say that?"

"I was just thinking how much better off you are today than when I first met you," he said.

"Oh, really?" she said. "I think I was doing quite well before you came along."

"If you were, I never heard about it," Ailill replied. "All you had were a few woman's things that your enemies kept stealing from you."

"Are you serious?" asked Medb. "My father was Eochu Feidlech, high king of Ireland, descended from generations of kings. He had six daughters in all and I was the most celebrated of them—and the most generous in bestowing favors. I had fifteen hundred royal mercenaries at my command and an equal number of freeborn native men, and those were just my household guard. My father gave me this province of Ireland to rule from Cruachan. Men came from the whole island to woo me, but I turned them down, for I asked a harder wedding gift than any bride before me—a husband with no meanness, fear, or jealousy.

"If I married an ungenerous man, our union would be wrong, since I am always giving gifts and favors. If I married a coward our marriage would be equally wrong, because I thrive on conflict and battle. And if I married a jealous man he could never stay my husband, for I never had one man without another waiting for me in the shadows.

"You're the man I wanted, Ailill of Leinster. You aren't greedy or fearful or jealous. When we married I brought you the best bride price a man could hope for—clothing for a dozen men, a chariot worth seven female slaves, the width of your face in red gold, and the weight of your left arm in white bronze. All that you have I gave you. You're a kept man, Ailill."

"I am not!" he replied. "I only let my brothers rule in Leinster because they are older than me, not because they are more generous. I had never heard of a province in Ireland run by a woman, so I came here to rule with the daughter of the high king of Ireland."

"Even so," said Medb, "it remains that I am wealthier than you."

"You astonish me," he said. "No one has more property or jewels or precious things than I do."

And so they both jumped out of bed and ordered all that each of them owned brought before them—buckets, tubs, iron pots, thumb rings, golden treasures, purple cloth, bracelets, and sheep. These were all counted and found to be equal in number. From the pastures horses and pigs were brought in. For every stallion or fine boar of Medb, Ailill owned one to match it. Finally, they brought in the herds of cattle from the fields. These were measured and counted. All were equal, but for one bull held by Ailill—Finnbennach the White Bull was his name. He had been born to one of Medb's cows but had refused to be owned by a woman and so had gone over to Ailill's herd. Medb had no equal to this bull and her spirits fell as if she owned nothing at all.

She was determined to find a bull of her own to match Ailill's, so she called her messenger Mac Roth and asked him where she might find the greatest bull in Ireland.

"I know the very animal," Mac Roth said. "He lives in the province of Ulster, in the territory of Cuailnge, in the house of Dáire mac Fiachna. The bull is called Donn Cuailnge, the Brown Bull of Cuailnge."

"Go there," commanded Medb, "and ask Dáire to lend me his bull for a year. At the end of that time I'll give it back to him along with fifty yearling heifers in payment for his loan. I'll also give him a portion of the beautiful Plain of Ai as his own, and a chariot worth seven slave women—and my own friendly thighs on top of all that."

Mac Roth and his men journeyed east across Ireland to the house of Dáire and asked him for the loan of the bull. Dáire was delighted to agree to Medb's terms and settled his guests into his home for the night. But when darkness fell one of Dáire's men heard one of Mac Roth's men say that it was a good thing they had been granted the loan of the bull, for they would have taken it by force if he had refused. When Dáire heard this he sent Mac Roth back to Medb empty-handed.

"What did Dáire say to my offer?" asked Medb.

When Mac Roth explained what had happened, Medb spoke: "He was afraid his bull would be taken by force, was he? Then taken it shall be."

Ailill and Medb began to gather their army for the invasion of Ulster and the taking of the Brown Bull of Cuailnge. Ailill sent word to his brothers to come to Cruachan along with their men. They also gathered many other war leaders with thousands of men. Soldiers from all four provinces of Ireland came together to invade the rich lands of King Conchobar of Ulster.

Medb went in her chariot to see her chief druid before she departed for war.

"I have called this army together," she said to him. "They have left lovers, friends, and family to follow me. I lead them, druid, but will I return with them alive?"

"Whoever comes back or not," he said, "you will return."

Satisfied, she turned the chariot back—but suddenly there in front of her she saw a young woman with golden hair. Her eyebrows were dark, her teeth were white, and her lips were the color of bright blood.

"Who are you?" asked Medb.

"My name is Fedelm," said the woman. "I am a poet of Connacht."

"Where have you come from?" asked the queen.

"From Britain where I was studying poetry."

"Do you have the *imbas forasnai*—the second sight?" Medb asked.

"I do," said Fedelm.

"Then look into the future," said Medb, "and tell me what lies ahead for my army."

Fedelm replied: "I see it crimson, I see it red."

"But that can't be," said Medb. "I have heard that Conchobar and all the warriors of Ulster are laid low by the curse of Macha. They are defenseless. My spies have told me this. Now look again and tell me what lies ahead."

Fedelm closed her eyes and looked into the future once more.

"I see it crimson, I see it red."

"No!" cried Medb. "Conchobar cannot fight and the best of his warriors are in exile here with me. Look again and tell me what you see."

"I see it crimson, I see it red."

"You must be seeing something else," said Medb. "Whenever a great army gathers there is always fighting and strife. Warriors fall wounded and some die, but not the whole army. Look again, Fedelm, and tell me what you see now."

"I see it crimson, I see it red—for I see a young warrior standing in your path. I see your men dead, corpses torn, women wailing. I see the blood of your army dripping from his sword."

As they marched from Connacht into Ulster, Medb went to inspect her armies. She came back to camp that night and complained to Ailill about the three thousand Galeóin troops from Leinster.

"What's wrong with them?" asked Ailill.

"Nothing," said Medb. "That's the problem. While the other warriors were still pitching their tents, the Galeóin had made theirs and were cooking dinner. When the other troops were cooking dinner, the Galeóin had finished and were playing their harps by the fire. They make the rest of the army look bad by comparison."

"Well, do you want to send them away?" asked Ailill.

"No," the queen replied. "They would seize our lands while we're gone."

"What do you want me to do then?"

"Kill them," said Medb.

"That's a wicked, womanly thing to do," said Ailill. "These men are our friends. I will not have them killed."

Fergus, the exile from Ulster, had heard all this and said: "There's no need to leave them behind or kill them. Divide them in small bands among the rest of the army so that they don't stand out."

And this seemed good to Medb.

Fergus meanwhile sent a secret message to Cú Chulainn to warn him of the approach of the Connacht army. He also led them in a winding path to give the Ulstermen time to recover from Macha's curse. Medb noticed this and accused him of betraying her.

"Not at all," said Fergus. "I'm simply taking a roundabout path to avoid Cú Chulainn. He isn't affected by the curse and will destroy this army if he gets a chance."

"Bah!" cried Medb. "No one man can stop such a great army."

"Cú Chulainn can," said Fergus.

The next day they came to a ford in a river and saw the heads of four men on a forked branch by the water. Their horses were there unharmed but covered in blood. Warnings written in Ogam script were carved onto the branch.

"Are these our men?" asked Medb.

"Yes," said Ailill. "Four of our best warriors."

"But who could do such a thing?" she asked.

"Only Cú Chulainn could do this," said Fergus.

"Then Cú Chulainn must die," said the queen.

SINGLE COMBAT

Medb waited until morning, then called the great warrior Fróech mac Fidaig to her tent.

"Fróech, we need your help to rid us of this nuisance. Go find Cú Chulainn and challenge him to single combat."

And so the next day Fróech took nine men with him and found Cú Chulainn washing in the river.

"Wait here," Fróech said to his men. "He isn't good at fighting in water. I'll meet him there."

So Fróech stripped off his clothes and came to Cú Chulainn.

"If you come any closer," Cú Chulainn said, "I'll have to kill you."

"You can try," said Fróech.

And so the two warriors began to grapple in the water. Finally, Cú Chulainn bested Fróech and held him underwater for a long time before raising him up.

"Now," he said to Fróech, "will you let me spare your life?"

"Never could I live with such shame," replied Fróech.

Cú Chulainn thrust him under the water once more and held him there until he was dead.

Every morning after that Medb sent a new warrior to face Cú Chulainn and each was killed by the Ulster hero. She promised the warriors gold and land and her daughter in marriage and the friendship of her own thighs, if only they would kill Cú Chulainn. Every day and night Cú Chulainn would slay dozens more in ambush and combat until hundreds of Connacht soldiers were dead. But the fighting was taking its toll on Cú Chulainn. He was exhausted and injured, with no time for his wounds to heal.

Still the army of Medb went forward. Soon they had crossed all of Ireland and came to the land of Ulster where they found the Brown Bull of Cuailnge. Then Medb took it for herself and ordered her army back to Connacht.

One morning as Cú Chulainn was following the Connacht army, he knelt by the stream bathing his wounds and saw a man approaching him.

"Who are you?" asked Cú Chulainn.

"Someone who will help you," said the stranger. "I am Lug, your father from the *síd*. Your wounds are grievous. They need time to heal. Sleep, Cú Chulainn. Rest and be well."

Lug put his son into a deep sleep for three days and labored to heal him. He worked herbs and medicine into his wounds so that Cú Chulainn began to recover in his sleep without knowing it.

While Cú Chulainn was sleeping, the boys of Ulster rose up to fight, for they were too young to be laid low by Macha's curse. They wanted to help Cú Chulainn in his battle against the forces of Queen Medb, and so they went out to attack the armies of Connacht with Follamain son of Conchobar leading them. One hundred and fifty of the best young men of Ulster came to the plain before the army of Connacht.

"Kill them all," said Ailill.

The warriors of Ailill and Medb met the boys there on the plain by a stone known as the Lia Toll and slaughtered every one of them save for Follamain, Conchobar's son. He survived the battle, but swore he would not return to Ulster until he took Ailill's head and crown with him. The Connacht men only laughed and sent out two brothers against him. They attacked him and slew him there.

Cú Chulainn meanwhile was still asleep healing from his wounds. When he awoke after three days, he felt ready for feasting or love-making or battle, whichever came first.

He found his father Lug sitting beside him.

"How long have I been asleep?"

"Three days and three nights," the man replied.

"This is disgraceful," said Cú Chulainn. "For that time the armies of Connacht have been free from attack."

"Not so," said Lug. "The boy troop came from Ulster led by Follamain and fought the armies of Ailill and Medb on the plain. They all perished in battle aside from Follamain, who was killed afterward by the Connacht warriors."

"This is to my everlasting shame," said Cú Chulainn. "Because of my weakness all these boys have died."

"Then go and fight," said Lug. "Your wounds have healed and the men of Connacht have no power over your life."

"Ready my chariot," Cú Chulainn said to his driver, "and put all the weapons of battle inside it."

Cú Chulainn strapped on his armor and belt. He then took with him eight swords with ivory hilts, eight spears and javelins, eight dark-red shields with razor-sharp rims, and a crested battle helmet. Around his shoulders he fastened his magical cloak from Tír Tairngaire, the Land of Promise, a gift from his father.

Then, ready for battle, a battle fury seized him. He became monstrous in appearance with a bright red face and twisted mouth. One eye sunk into his head while the other bulged out. His heart pounded like a lion among bears and flames of fire rose from his head.

He stepped into his war chariot and drove out to meet his enemies in battle. In his fury he killed a hundred, then two hundred more, then three hundred, then five hundred. In six great circuits around the camp of the Connachtmen he drove, killing as he went, so that afterward the place was known as Seisrech Bresligi, the Place of the Sixfold Slaughter. No man of Medb's army escaped without some kind of wound, but Cú Chulainn remained untouched.

The next morning Cú Chulainn rose from his camp and put on his best clothing to display himself to the women of Connacht among the army. The day before he had seemed a monster in his spasm, but now he was the handsomest man in Ireland, with loose-flowing golden hair spreading over his shoulders.

The women climbed on top of their own husbands to catch a glimpse of Cú Chulainn as he rode past their camp in his chariot.

"This is a nuisance," said Medb. "The women are crowding so close that I can't even see this man."

Then she climbed onto the backs of her own men to see Cú Chulainn and was awed by his beauty.

CÚ CHULAINN AND FERDIA

"Send someone out to fight me!" shouted Cú Chulainn.

"Not me," cried each of the Connacht warriors. "My family owes no sacrifice to the gods—and even if they did, why should I be the one to die?"

The next day Medb sent twenty-nine men against Cú Chulainn in a swamp known as Blood Iron. These were Gaile Dána and his twenty-seven sons along with his nephew. On the weapons of each was deadly poison. Any man who was even scratched by their swords and spears would die. But Cú Chulainn killed them all without being touched.

Day after day Medb sent more warriors against the Ulster hero, but Cú Chulainn slaughtered them all. At last she sent for one of the Ulster exiles, Ferdia, the beloved foster brother of Cú Chulainn.

"Well now, Ferdia," Medb said. "Do you know why you're here?"

"I can guess," he replied. "But I won't fight Cú Chulainn. He is my friend and brother."

"But I will give you a chariot worth three times seven female slaves, weapons for a dozen men, a rich portion of the fertile Plain of Ai, wine flowing for as long as you live, freedom from all taxes and tribute, gold and jewels beyond your dreams, and my own daughter Finnabair as your wife—plus my own friendly thighs on top of all that."

"Those are fine gifts," said Ferdia, "but you can keep them. I will not fight Cú Chulainn."

"Oh, really?" Medb said. "Then I suppose what Cú Chulainn said was true."

"What did he say?" asked Ferdia.

"He said that slaying you in battle would be no great accomplishment," Medb lied.

"He shouldn't have said that," answered Ferdia. "I am as good a warrior as he is. I swear by the gods I will meet him at the ford of battle in the morning."

"You have my blessing," said Medb with a smile, "and all that I promised will be yours. Now go and prepare for battle."

Ferdia went to the ford where Cú Chulainn was waiting for him.

"I have no wish to harm you, my brother," said Cú Chulainn. "It would be better if you returned to Medb and the Connachtmen without facing me in a fight."

"I cannot return to them without fighting you, my brother" Ferdia said. "Either you will die or I must fall."

"So be it," said Cú Chulainn. "The choice of weapons is yours."

"Do you remember when we learned from Scáthach in Britain to throw short spears in battle?" asked Ferdia. "Let us do that."

And so the two of them fought all day with spears and shields, but neither drew blood from the other. Then they took long spears and battled, but neither Ferdia nor Cú Chulainn was harmed, try as they might to kill each other.

"It is growing dark, Cú Chulainn," said Ferdia. "Let us stop for the night and begin again at sunrise."

They gave their spears and shields to their charioteers and embraced each other. They ate together that night and slept by the same fire in peace. The next morning they arose ready to do battle once again.

"Your choice of weapons today," said Ferdia.

"Then let us try our large stabbing spears this morning," said Cú Chulainn.

And so they passed the day in fierce combat with their enormous spears. Soon both were landing wounds on the other, but neither would yield. As the sun was setting, Cú Chulainn spoke: "Let us cease fighting for the evening and begin again tomorrow."

"Agreed," said Ferdia.

They passed that night together again and tended each other's wounds before falling asleep exhausted. The next day they rose early and Cú Chulainn offered Ferdia his choice of weapons.

"Our large swords today," said Ferdia.

They took up their swords and shields facing each other until the night, each wounding the other terribly. When darkness fell they ceased from fighting, but each withdrew to his own fire for the night.

The next morning both warriors were grim as they put on their best armor and went to the ford to battle for the last time. Ferdia used marvelous feats of war craft as he leapt and danced, striking at Cú Chulainn. At last Cú Chulainn went into his battle fury and grew in size until he was like a giant. He called on his charioteer for the *gae bolga*, the magical spear that none could resist. With a single throw

Cú Chulainn sent the spear flying at Ferdia so that it went straight through his body with its terrible barbs.

"That is enough, my brother," Ferdia gasped. "You have slain me."

Cú Chulainn ran to him and held him in his arms. When Ferdia breathed no more, Cú Chulainn laid him gently on the ground.

"Get up, Cú Chulainn," said his charioteer Laeg. "The men of Connacht will be here soon and will slay you in your weakness."

"What difference does that make?" asked the warrior. "For I have slain my brother whom I loved."

Cú Chulainn then began to sing a lament over Ferdia's body. In the morning, he arose at last and went back to his camp.

THE FINAL BATTLE

After the death of Ferdia, Cú Chulainn continued to fight the warriors of Medb and Ailill as they took the stolen bull back to Connacht, hoping to delay them in their retreat until the men of Ulster had recovered from the curse of Macha. But his wounds grew worse every day and he was exhausted beyond measure. Even Cú Chulainn could not fight alone forever.

At last the day came when the curse was lifted from the Ulstermen. Conchobar the king gathered his warriors together and marched west as fast as they could to overtake the soldiers of Connacht and help Cú Chulainn. Hundreds of the fiercest soldiers in Ireland advanced through the hills and valleys to face their enemies. But Ailill and Medb were not afraid.

"Let them come," said Ailill. "We have warriors of our own to meet them."

When both armies met at last, they filled the plain with hundreds of fires like the stars of the sky while they waited for battle in the morning. The Mórrígan, the goddess of war, came too and sang over the sleeping warriors:

Ravens tearing at the necks of men,
blood spurting, flesh hacked to pieces,
blades in bodies, the deeds of war.
Hail, men of Ulster, woe to Connacht.
Hail, men of Connacht, woe to Ulster.

Cú Chulainn lay by his fire as he heard the armies arrive for battle. He tried to rise and help the Ulstermen, but he had no strength left that night. All he could do was wait for the battle to begin.

It was noon the next day before Cú Chulainn could join his countrymen. By then the battle was raging with unspeakable slaughter on both sides. Cú Chulainn found Medb relieving herself away from her army, but he spared her, not being a killer of women.

The battle began to turn at last against the Connachtmen, but Medb and Ailill had already sent the stolen bull back to Connacht. Fergus the exile of Ulster was bitter in blaming the queen for the death and destruction of so many men, all for the sake of her pride.

"We have followed the rump of a misguided woman," he said as the survivors marched home. "It serves us right. This is what happens when a herd is led by a mare."

Cú Chulainn and the Ulstermen made a treaty with Connacht and returned home in victory to Emain Macha, but both sides had lost many men. For seven years thereafter the kingdoms of Ulster and Connacht were at peace.

All that remained was the judging of the two bulls in Connacht to see if Ailill or Medb now owned the finest animal. The bulls were brought together on the Plain of Ai at a place known afterward as Tarbga, the Field of Bull Strife, to be judged. The animals fought there all day, with neither the Brown Bull of Medb nor the White Bull of Ailill able to gain the advantage over the other.

At last at nightfall the Brown Bull pinned the horn of the White Bull to the ground with his hoof and would not let him rise. But then the Brown Bull was thrown back and broke his leg while the White Bull had his horn torn away. Both animals fought through the night in the darkness so that none of the men could see what was happening.

Then, in the morning light, the men of Connacht saw the Brown Bull heading west with the remains of the White Bull hanging from his horns. Pieces of the slain bull fell from the victor's horn as he roamed throughout Connacht, so that many places in the province were named for parts of its body.

Ailill and Medb returned to their fort at Cruachan. They had lost the war with Ulster, but Medb had won the contest with her husband.

5

TALES FROM THE ULSTER CYCLE

THERE ARE MANY EARLY IRISH stories apart from the *Táin Bó Cuailnge* that feature Ulster warriors such as Conchobar, Fergus mac Roich, and Cú Chulainn. Ailill and Medb are also regular actors in the conflicts between the provinces of Ulster and Connacht. Some, such as the *Story of Mac Dá Thó's Pig*, are clearly meant to be humorous, while others, such as the *Death of Cú Chulainn*, are poignant and solemn. Together with the *Táin*, all these stories came to be known as the Ulster Cycle.

THE STORY OF MAC DÁ THÓ'S PIG

There was once a famous landowner in the province of Leinster named Mac Dá Thó, the Son of the Two Mutes. All of Ireland knew of his magnificent hound, so that every ruler wanted the animal for himself. Messengers came to Mac Dá Thó from Ailill and Medb in Connacht asking for the dog, but at the same time messengers arrived at his home from Conchobar of Ulster seeking the hound. Each promised magnificent gifts in exchange for the dog Ailbe—threescore hundred milk cows, along with chariots, horses, and the friendship of a powerful kingdom.

The messengers were taken to guest house of Mac Dá Thó and made welcome while their host pondered what to do. There were seven doors to the guest house and seven cauldrons and seven fireplaces inside, each with a pig and an ox cooking in them. The custom was that a man entering the guest house would thrust a flesh fork into the cauldron and whatever he brought out the first time was his to eat. But if he brought out nothing, he received no second chance.

Mac Dá Thó went to his room and fell into a great silence for three days and nights, eating and drinking nothing. At last his wife came to him and asked why he was so quiet.

"I will never open my heart to a woman," he said, "any more than I would trust my wealth to a slave."

"Oh, really?" she replied. "It seems to me, my husband, that you're having no luck solving a problem. Perhaps a woman can find an answer you cannot."

Mac Dá Thó shrugged and began: "What should I do, wife? If I don't give the hound to Conchobar, his army will come and ravage my land. But if I refuse Ailill and Medb, they will do the same. I am doomed no matter what I decide."

"Not so," said his wife. "Give the dog to both Ulster and Connacht. Let them come here to take it home and their armies can destroy each other rather than you."

This seemed a good idea to Mac Dá Thó, so he called the messengers secretly in turn and told them he had decided to give the hound to their masters. But they should come to him personally with all their warriors to take it home.

And so the messengers returned to Ulster and Connacht to report the happy news.

On the appointed day, the rulers and greatest warriors of the two most powerful kingdoms of Ireland came to the home of Mac Dá Thó. He welcomed them and showed them to his magnificent guest house.

Mac Dá Thó ordered his best pig killed for the feast. This pig was so big that threescore milk cows had been feeding it for seven years.

The roasted pig was brought to the great wooden table in the guest house where Conchobar and his warriors, as well as Ailill and Medb with their men, were all seated.

"How shall the pig be divided?" Ailill asked Conchobar.

While Conchobar considered this, Briccriu the troublemaker of Ulster spoke up: "The greatest warriors of Ireland are at this feast, but it is only right that the best man of all should plunge his knife first into the pig and take away the choicest cut. Let those who think they are best tell of their exploits to win this prize."

The kings both agreed and so began the contest.

All the warriors of Ulster and Connacht stood and told the assembled crowd of the men they had slain and the cattle they had taken from their enemies. At last Cet mac Mágach, a great warrior of Connacht, was the only one left standing.

"Let a man come forward better than me," he said, "or I will divide the pig."

"Wait," said Lóegaire of Ulster. "I am a better man than you, Cet."

"Is that so?" asked Cet. "Isn't it a custom among your tribe that on the day a youth takes up arms he meets the enemy at your border? I was there that day and put a lance through you, keeping your horse and chariot for myself. Sit down, Lóegaire."

And so he sat down.

"Wait," said Óengus of Ulster as he stood. "Do not carve the pig yet, Cet. I am a better warrior than you."

"Óengus," said Cet, "isn't your father called Lám Gabuid, the Wailing Hand? Do you remember how he got that name? Once when I invaded your western lands, many of your warriors came out to meet me, including your father. He threw his lance at me, but I caught it and threw it back at him, cutting off his hand. What makes you think his son can stand up to me? I am going to carve the pig. Sit down, Óengus."

"You shall not plunge your knife into that pig," said Éogan Mór of Ulster. "I am a greater warrior than you."

"Don't make me laugh," said Cet. "Don't you remember when I came to your farm and took your cattle from you? You chased after me and threw your spear into my shield, but I pulled it out and cast it back at you so that it passed through your head and came out your eye. You've seen the world with a single eye ever since. Sit down, Éogan."

"The pig is not yours yet," said another Ulster warrior. "I am a better man than you."

"Munremar, is that you?" asked Cet. "Well, wasn't it just three days ago that I raided your lands and took away the heads of three of your men along with the head of your own son? Sit down, Munremar. It's time to carve the pig."

"Not yet," said a gray and terrible warrior of Ulster named Celtchair son of Uithechar.

"Celtchair," said Cet, "do wait a moment before you try to pound me to pieces. Wasn't it not long ago that I came to your house? The alarm was raised and you attacked me, but I cast my spear into your loins and cut away the upper part of your testicles, so that now you can't get your wife pregnant or even piss straight any more. Sit down, Celtchair."

"Don't carve the pig yet, Cet," said an Ulster warrior named Mend. "I am a better man than you."

"Mend son of Sword Heel, isn't it?" asked Cet. "I remember how your father got that name, since I was the one who cut off his heel with my weapon and sent him limping away. And he was a better man than his son. Sit down, Mend."

"W-w-wait!" said Cumscraid the Stammerer, a warrior of Ulster. "Do not carve the p-p-pig yet, Cet. I am a b-b-better fighter than you."

"Oh, my dear Cumscraid," laughed Cet. "Don't you remember how you got your name? You tried to raid the borderlands of Connacht, but I met you there and sent a spear through your throat. Ever since no word comes rightly from your lips. Sit down, Cumscraid."

And so Cet made ready to carve the pig, since no more Ulstermen rose up to challenge him. But then through the door walked Conall Cernach—and a great shout arose from the men of Ulster.

"Get away from the pig, Cet!" shouted Conall. "I swear by the god my tribe swears by that I am a better man than you. Since I first took up weapons, I have not passed a day without killing a Connacht warrior or a night without plundering your lands. Nor have I slept a single night without the head of a slain Connacht fighter under my knee."

"It is true," said Cet as he put down his knife. "You are a better man than I am, Conall. But if my brother Anluán were here, he would challenge you, for he is a better warrior than you."

"Oh, but he is here," said Conall.

Then the Ulsterman reached into the satchel on his belt and pulled out the severed head of Anluán. He threw it at Cet and covered the man's chest with his own brother's blood.

Then Conall went and sat before the pig and began to carve it for himself. But the men of Connacht pelted him with stones while the Ulster warriors protected him with their shields. To the Connacht men he gave only a token amount of the meat.

The warriors of Ailill and Medb rose in anger at their meager share and attacked the men of Conchobar. Spears were thrown and swords flashed throughout the hall until there were bodies of men from both sides piled on the floor as high as the roof beams and rivers of blood flowed through the seven doors. Then the slaughter burst out of the hall and spread to the yard.

At this point Mac Dá Thó came out with the hound Ailbe and let him loose to see which side he would choose. The animal chose Ulster and so began to attack the men of Connacht.

Ailill and Medb jumped into their chariot and rushed away from the fight in terror, but Ailbe chased after them. Their charioteer struck the head from the hound with his sword as they drove through what was thereafter known as Mag nAilbe, the Plain of Ailbe.

Conchobar also fled the slaughter in his own chariot, but another charioteer of Ailill named Fer Loga lay in wait for him behind the heather. As the Ulster king passed by, Fer Loga jumped into the chariot and seized him from behind with his sword to his throat.

"You're not going to escape so easily, Conchobar," said Fer Loga.

"Spare me," said the king, "and I will grant you whatever you wish."

"I don't want too much in exchange for your life," said Fer Loga. "Only that you take me as a guest to your fort at Emain Macha and have your maidens sing 'Fer Loga is my darling' to me every night for a year."

And Conchobar agreed.

Thus every night for a year the maidens of Ulster gathered before Fer Loga and sang love songs to him. At the end of the year, Conchobar sent Fer Loga back to Connacht in safety with gifts of horses and gold.

THE CATTLE RAID OF FRÓECH

There was once a young man named Fróech who was the most handsome warrior in all of Ireland. His father was Idath of Connacht, but his mother was Bé Find, a magical woman of the Otherworld *síd* and sister of Bóand, a goddess of the swift Boyne River. Fróech's mother had given him twelve white cows with red ears from the *síd*. Fróech was rich and prosperous, but he had no wife.

Finnabair, the daughter of Ailill and Medb, heard stories of Fróech and fell in love with him without ever seeing the lad. When Fróech heard of this, he decided to go and speak to the girl. His family told him to go first to his mother's sister and ask for gifts so that he might present them to Ailill as a bride price for his daughter.

Fróech went to Bóand and brought back fifty blue cloaks and tunics with embroidery of gold, fifty silver shields with golden rims, fifty candles with golden decorations, fifty spear blades with precious stones that shone in the darkness like the sun, fifty gray horses with golden bridles, seven hounds on silver chains, shoes of bronze, seven horn blowers with golden yellow hair, three fools with silver shields, and three harpers in royal clothing.

Fróech and his company arrived at Cruachan, the fort of Ailill and Medb, and were welcomed by the king and queen. There was such a crowd to see the arrivals that sixteen men died of suffocation in the turmoil. Fróech and his people were then shown to the guest house and feasted by their hosts. Fróech brought forth his three harpers to play and twelve men died of weeping and sorrow at their songs. Fróech then stayed for a week at Cruachan and hunted with Ailill and Medb every day.

But Fróech was anxious because during his time at Cruachan he had not yet seen or talked with Finnabair. So one morning he rose early and went down to the river to bathe, hoping to see the girl there. Soon Finnabair and her maidservant came to the water. Fróech took her hand and greeted her: "Stay and talk with me, for it is for you I have come to Cruachan."

"You are most welcome here, Fróech," said the princess.

"Will you come away with me?" he asked.

"Indeed, I will not," she replied, "for I am the daughter of a king and cannot elope with a man. But take this thumb ring which my father gave me as a token of my love for you. I will tell him I have lost it."

And the two of them parted.

Later that day Ailill was talking with Medb.

"I fear that our daughter will run away with Fróech," said Ailill.

"It wouldn't be a bad idea to give her to him," said Medb, "for he would bring many cattle to us as a bride price and go with us on our raid against Ulster."

Fróech entered the room and asked if he might speak with them.

"Will you give me your daughter as my bride?" he asked.

"Indeed, I will," said Ailill, "if you will pay the bride price."

"Gladly," said Fróech.

"Then the price is threescore dark gray horses with golden bridles, twelve milk cows along with a white calf with red ears with each cow, and yourself and your whole company to come with us to raid Ulster."

"I swear by my shield and sword," Fróech said, "that I would not pay such a high price for Medb herself!"

And he stormed out of the room.

"Just as I had hoped," said Ailill to Medb. "For if we had given him the girl every king in Ireland would attack us out of jealousy. I think it would be best to kill him now before he tries something foolish."

"That would be dishonorable," said Medb.

"Then I will arrange it so that we don't get the blame," said her husband.

Ailill, Medb, and Finnabair went out to hunt the next day and invited Fróech to join them. At noon they were hot and tired, so they went to bathe in the river. After Fróech took off his clothes and went into the water, Ailill looked through his bag and found the thumb ring he had given his daughter."

"Look at this, wife," he said to Medb. "Do you recognize this ring?"

"I do," she replied.

In his anger Ailill threw the ring into the river. But Fróech was watching him and saw a salmon leap into the air and swallow the ring. Fróech quickly caught the salmon and buried the fish in a hidden place on the riverbank.

After that Fróech was about to leave the water when Ailill asked him to first bring him a branch with red berries from a rowan tree on the opposite bank, which Fróech did. As Finnabair watched him she thought she had never seen anyone so beautiful. His body was white, his hair was fair, his eyes were blue, and his naked body was without blemish.

"Excellent berries," said Ailill. "Bring us some more from that other bank."

And just as Ailill had intended, Fróech walked into a deep pool in the center of the river where lived a monster. There the creature seized him.

"Someone bring me a sword!" cried Fróech. But no man dared to bring him a weapon for fear of Ailill and Medb. Then Finnabair threw off her outer clothes and jumped into the water with a sword. Her father threw a five-pointed spear at her so that it tore her inner garments. Fróech caught the spear and threw it back at Ailill so that it ripped through his shirt. Finnabair gave Fróech the sword and after a great battle he cut off the monster's head. After that the place was known as the Black Pool of Fróech.

Ailill and Medb returned to their fortress.

"We did a great evil against that man," said Medb.

"Yes, but tomorrow the girl will die," said her father.

When Fróech returned to Cruachan he was injured badly from his fight with the monster and was near death. Supper was made ready for him and he was bathed by a company of women. When he was carried to bed, the people of Cruachan heard three fifties of women in scarlet mantles, bright green head scarves, and silver bracelets weeping outside the walls of the fortress. When they were asked why they were weeping, one of them replied: "Fróech son of Idath is the favorite youth of all the *síde* of Ireland."

Fróech then heard the sound of their lamenting and asked to be carried outside. The weeping women gathered about him and carried him into the *síd* of Cruachan, into the land of the Otherworld.

On the evening of the following day, the women carried him from the *síd* and back to the fort of Cruachan. They left him at the gate of the courtyard, healed of all his wounds.

Ailill and Medb welcomed Fróech and were in awe that he had returned from the Otherworld safely. They held a great feast for him that night. While he was seated at the table, he called one of his men and gave him instructions: "Go to the pool where I fought the monster yesterday and find the spot where I entered the water. There is a salmon hidden there. Take it to Finnabair and tell her to cook it. The thumb ring is inside the fish. I expect she may need it later tonight."

As the evening went on and everyone became drunk, Ailill called for all his treasures to be brought to him that he might show his great wealth to his guests.

"Finnabair," said the king to his daughter, "bring me the thumb ring I gave you so that I may show it to everyone."

"I'm sorry, father," she said, "but I'm afraid I lost it."

"If you do not find it," he replied, "then I swear by the god my people swear by that you will die."

The guests all cried out that the ring was not worth her life and that he should spare the girl, but Ailill would not change his mind.

"Father, if the ring is found and I give it to you," she said, "may I be released from my obligations to you as a daughter? May I choose another man to watch over me?"

"If you give me that ring," he answered, "you can go with the stable boy for all I care." For Ailill was sure the ring was lost forever.

She called then for one of her maidservants to bring in the salmon on a platter to the king. On top of the fish was the thumb ring.

Ailill and Medb looked at the ring in wonder, then their daughter rose and said to her father: "My lord, you have promised me the freedom to choose my own husband and so I give myself to Fróech. There is no other man in the world I would prefer to him."

"Let it be done," said Ailill. "Fróech, when you return with your cattle as a bride price for my daughter, then you may sleep with her."

"I will do that," said Fróech.

The next morning Fróech and his company left Cruachan and went east to retrieve his cattle. But while he was on the journey, a messenger arrived and said that his cattle had been stolen. That night his mother came to him from the *síd* and told him what had happened.

"The news is terrible," she said. "Outlaws have seized your cattle and family and have taken them far away beyond the Alps. They are lost forever."

"No," said Fróech. "I have sworn that I would bring those cattle to Ailill and I will."

So Fróech set out to cross the sea with three times nine men along with a falcon and a hound on a leash. As he was passing through the province of Ulster, he met the great warrior Conall Cernach and told him what had happened.

"A difficult task lies ahead of you," said Conall.

"Help me then," said Fróech.

"Gladly," replied the Ulster warrior.

The company crossed the sea to Britain, then sailed to France and journeyed many weeks until they reached the Alps. There one day they saw a small woman herding sheep.

"Who are you?" asked the woman.

"We are men of Ireland," said Fróech. "We come in search of my stolen cattle."

"My mother was from Ireland," she replied. "I will help you. But you must know that the men of this country are grim and frightful warriors. They travel far and steal whatever they want. I have heard that they have your cattle. The woman who tends them is from Ulster. Go and speak with her. Perhaps she can help you. But beware, for a terrible serpent guards those cattle now."

Fróech and Conall went secretly to the cowherd and spoke to her. Conall revealed that he too was from Ulster. The woman was thrilled and threw her arms around him, for it had been foretold that Conall of Ulster would destroy the fortress of thieves.

"Let me go now," said the woman. "It is time for me to milk the cows. But I will leave the door to the fortress open. When everyone is asleep, go inside the door and slay the serpent if you can. But beware that many have died trying."

When all was dark and everyone was asleep, Fróech and Conall crept inside the fortress. They found the serpent and were ready to do battle with it, but instead it leapt into the bag Conall had on his belt. They then killed the thieves, rescued Fróech's cattle, freed his family, and burned the fortress to the ground. After that, Conall released the serpent from his bag and it went away from him, neither doing harm to the other.

The Irish warriors drove the cattle back across Europe to Ireland, where Fróech bade farewell to Conall and went to Cruachan at last to join Ailill and Medb on their raid against Ulster.

THE DESTRUCTION OF DÁ DERGA'S HOSTEL

There was once a famous king over all of Ireland named Eochaid Feidleach. Once when he was crossing the assembly ground at Brí Léith he saw a young woman standing at the edge of a well. Her hair was like burnished red gold and she wore a cloak of green silk embroidered with gold, with clasps of silver and gold above her breasts. Eochaid watched her as she loosened her hair to wash it. Her hands were long and white as snow, her teeth like pearls, her eyes like hyacinth, her lips as red as rowan berries, and her two thighs sleek and warm. She bore herself with the dignity of a queen, and indeed to Eochaid it seemed she was the loveliest woman in the world.

A desire for the woman seized him and he asked her if she would sleep with him.

"That is why I have come here," she said. "I am Étaín, daughter of Etar, king of the horsemen from the Otherworld. I was born in the *síd* twenty years ago. Kings and nobles there have wooed me, but since I have been able to speak I have loved you, Eochaid Feidleach."

"I will never look upon another woman," said Eochaid, "and with you alone will I live the rest of my life."

"I will have my proper bride price," she said, "and then my desire."

"You shall have it," Eochaid said.

The king paid her father the worth of seven slave women and married her.

Étaín bore a daughter, also named Étaín, to her husband. But Eochaid died and in time the younger Étaín was married to Cormac, king of Ulster. She bore him only a single daughter, though he desired a son. The younger Étaín went to her mother for a magical porridge to help her bear a son, but she had no other child.

"Your porridge has failed, mother," she said. "I have only a daughter."

"No matter," said her mother. "She will be pursued by kings."

Cormac divorced his wife because she was barren, save for the single girl she had borne. In time, however, he changed his mind and took her back again, but he desired to kill their daughter. He gave the child to two slaves and told them to throw her in a pit. But as they were about to toss her in, she smiled and laughed at them. They were kind of heart and could not kill her, so they took her to a king named Eterscél, who raised her as his own daughter.

Eterscél built a fence of wickerwork around a hut with no door and kept the girl there so that no one might see her. Only a skylight in the roof gave her light. But one day years later a young cowherd looked through the skylight and saw the girl, who had grown into a beautiful young maiden. He told King Cormac about the girl and her father sent a band of warriors to bring her to him, for it had been prophesied to him by the druids that an unknown woman would bear him a son.

While young Étaín was in her hut the next morning, a bird flew in the skylight. He shed his bird skin on the floor and stood before her as a shining young man.

"The king's men are coming for you," he told her. "They will destroy this house and bring you before the king. But you will first become pregnant by me. In time you will bear a son and name him Conaire."

And so the bird man lay with her and she conceived a child. After he left, the king's men burst into the hut and destroyed it, taking the girl back with them to Cormac. He was struck so by her beauty that he immediately married her, for he did not know she was his own daughter. Nine months later, she bore a son and named him Conaire.

Conaire was fostered with three other boys named Fer Le, Fer Gar, and Fer Rogain. Conaire had special gifts of hearing, eyesight, and judgment, one of which he taught to each of his foster brothers. The four shared everything, dressed alike, and even had the same color horses.

One day King Eterscél died and a Bull Feast was held to decide the next king. In this feast a bull would be slain and cooked, then one chosen man would drink the broth. A spell of truth was said over him in his bed and whoever he saw in his dream would be the new king. If the sleeper lied, he would perish.

That night the sleeper dreamed of a naked man passing along the road of Tara with a stone in his sling.

At this time Conaire was on the plain of the River Liffey hunting with his three foster brothers when he left them and turned his chariot to Dublin. There he saw a flock of white-speckled birds of great size and beauty. He pursued them all the way to the sea, where the birds settled on the waves. He rushed at them with his sling, but suddenly they shed their bird skins and attacked him with spears and swords. One of them, however, protected him and spoke to him.

"I am Némglan, king of your father's birds. Go now to Tara, for there has been a Bull Feast there tonight. A naked man passing there with a stone and sling shall be the new king. You are that man."

The bird king then taught Conaire what he must not do as king.

"Your reign will be noble," Némglan said, "but there are nine *gessa*—prohibitions—on you.

"You must never harm a bird. You are forbidden to cast your stones at birds, for we should be dear to you as family.

"You must never pass righthandwise like the sun around the Hill of Tara or lefthandwise around the Plain of Brega between the River Liffey and the River Boyne.

"You must not hunt the crooked beasts of Cerna.

"You must not be absent more than nine nights from Tara.

"You must not spend the night in a house from which the light of a fire is visible from outside.

"You must not allow three red men to go before you into a red man's house.

"You must not allow raiding in your lands during your reign.

"You must not allow a lone man or woman to visit you after sunset.

"And finally, you must not try to settle a quarrel between two of your slaves."

When he had said this, the bird king and his company disappeared.

After this young Conaire shed his clothes and came near to Tara. He saw noblemen on the road waiting for their new king with fine clothing, for they had been told that a naked man would rule over them. They put royal raiment on him and sent him in a chariot to Tara.

But the people of Tara were not pleased.

"We were waiting for a king and we get a mere boy?" they exclaimed. "This will not do!"

"My age is not important," Conaire said. "I am young, but generous, and I am of royal birth."

And so the people of Tara welcomed him as king.

During the beginning of the reign of Conaire, all of Ireland prospered. Ships brought goods from faraway lands, pigs feasted on acorns up to a man's knees every autumn, the rivers were full of fish, the weather was fair and fine, and no man slew another.

But Conaire's three foster brothers were not pleased. They were thieves and raiders by trade, as their father and grandfather had been before them. Each year during Conaire's reign they stole a pig, an ox, and a cow from the same farmer and beat him to within an inch of his life, just to see if the king would punish them. Each year the poor farmer would come to Conaire to seek justice, but the king would send him away without hearing his complaint.

And so the foster brothers of Conaire grew bold and took to marauding like wolves around Ireland with three times fifty men. But they were captured by the men of Connacht and taken before the king at Tara for judgment.

"Let the father of each outlaw slay his own son," proclaimed Conaire, "but my foster brothers shall be spared. I banish them from Ireland, but they may raid in Britain if they wish."

There was great anger at the king for this, but his three foster brothers were released and traveled to Britain, where they were joined by other outlaws from both Ireland and Britain, including one-eyed Ingcél Cáech, the son of the British king, and the exiled sons of Queen Medb, all named Maine.

One day after this when Conaire was traveling along with his friend Conall Cernach back to Tara through Uisnech, the center of Ireland, the king and his men saw war bands of naked men going to battle and burning all the farms around him.

"What is this?" asked Conaire.

"Not hard to answer," the people said. "The king's law has broken down and the land begins to burn."

Conaire fled from there righthandwise around Tara and lefthandwise around the Plain of Brega. He hunted beasts along the way, but did not know that they were the beasts of Cerna until the hunt had ended.

The night known as Samain had then arrived when the boundary between the world of humans and the Otherworld was easily broken.

"Where shall we go now?" Conaire asked his companion Mac Cécht.

"Let us seek out a hostel to spend the night," Mac Cécht answered.

"I know a man of this land," the king said. "Dá Derga the Red of Leinster is his name. I have given him many gifts."

"I know his house," said Mac Cécht. "There are seven doorways there and seven bedrooms between every two doorways."

Conaire turned to the hostel of Dá Derga along the Road of Cuala, but as he rode he saw three horsemen going before him. They each wore a red tunic and mantle. All three had blazing red hair, carried red shields and spears, and rode red horses.

"This cannot be," said Conaire. "It is a *geis* of mine that three red men cannot ride before me to the house of a red man."

Conaire sent his son Le Fer Flaith after the red riders to stop them by offering them gifts, but no matter how fast he rode he could not catch them. Again he tried, shouting to them, but they merely rode faster and sang to him:

We ride the steeds of the síd mounds,
from the Otherworld.
Though we were alive, now we are dead.
Death is coming

And then they passed out of sight.

When Conaire heard what the men sang, he was struck with foreboding.

"Every *geis* I have is seizing me tonight."

The king continued toward the hostel with his companions, but along the way he suddenly came upon a man on the road with black hair, one hand, one eye, and one foot. He carried on his back a squealing pig and was followed behind by a hideous, dark woman with an enormous mouth.

"Welcome to you, dear friend Conaire," said the stranger. "Long has your coming been foretold."

"Who welcomes me?" asked Conaire.

"I am Fer Caille, the Man of the Woods. I've brought you a pig so you won't go hungry tonight. My wife Cichuil follows me."

"Forgive me," said Conaire. "Any other night I would stop and feast with you, but I must be on my way."

"Not to worry," said the man. "We will follow you to the place you go."

Now at this time the marauding foster brothers of Conaire had returned to Ireland from beyond the sea along with countless other outlaws to raid and ravage the land of the king. And it so happened that they landed that night on the shore at the Hill of Howth, near the hostel of Dá Derga, just as Conaire was approaching. They saw him coming in the darkness, and so they waited until he entered the hostel.

"Welcome, Conaire," said Dá Derga. "I would welcome you even if you brought all the men of Ireland with you to feast at my table."

Conaire sat at the place of honor, near the three red men who had preceded him and Fer Caille, who was still carrying his pig on his back.

While the guests were seated, a lone woman came to the door of the hostel after the sun had set and asked to be let in. She wore a great gray mantle of wool on her shoulders and her long hair was as black as night.

She leaned on the doorpost of the entryway and cast her dark eye on the king and his men. She stood in the doorway on one foot with one hand raised above her.

"Who are you?" asked Conaire fearfully.

"Some call me Cailb," she answered, "but I have many names."

"Woman or phantom, whatever you are," said Conaire, "if you are a seer, tell us what fortune awaits us."

She stared hard at the king.

"I see," she chanted, "that no one of flesh will escape this place tonight, except what the birds carry away in their talons."

"What do you want from me? "asked Conaire.

"A seat at your feast," she replied.

"It is a *geis* of mine," he said, "that I cannot allow a lone person inside after the sun has set. You cannot enter."

"Indeed," she replied, "if you have no place for me at your table, then the hospitality of the king has departed."

"Wait," said Conaire. "Though it bodes my destruction, enter and join us."

While the king and the other guests began the feast, the foster brothers of Conaire and the other raiders arrived outside Dá Derga's hostel. Ingcél, the one-eyed son of the king of Britain, was their leader. He had seven pupils in the single eye on his forehead and from a far distance could see Conaire seated on the champion's throne in the hostel. Ingcél was filled with a desire to slaughter the whole household. He had killed his father and mother and all his brothers, so he thought nothing of slaying the rightful king of Ireland.

Ingcél ordered his men to surround the hostel and attack. The king heard the host outside and roused his warriors to fight. The first to fall was Conaire's fool, Lomna Drúth, who had predicted his own death. The king and his men did not wait inside for the marauders, but charged through the doors and met them before the hostel.

The fighting was terrible, with hundreds slaughtered on both sides. Three times the hostel was set on fire by the outlaws and three times the fire was put out. The king was at the front of the battle, killing many of the raiders with his own sword as his men fell around him. At last a great thirst came upon Conaire.

"Bring me a drink, Mac Cécht," the king said to his companion, "or I will surely perish."

"There is nothing to be had, my lord," he replied, "neither water nor wine."

Then with his last ounce of strength, the king charged the marauders. He fell to the ground in death, slain not by the outlaws but by his consuming thirst. Two of the outlaws cut off his head as a trophy, but Mac Cécht slew them and retrieved Conaire's head. The rest of the outlaws fled for their lives.

Wounded, broken, and maimed, Mac Cécht lay on the battlefield. But with the little strength he had left, he took Conaire's head, opened the mouth, and poured into it a cup of water.

And the head of the king spoke:

A good man, Mac Cécht!
an excellent man, Mac Cécht!

He gives a drink to a king,
a worthy deed he does.

For three days Mac Cécht lay in the blood and gore outside the hostel. At the end of the third day a woman passed by and he called out to her. She was afraid to come near at first, but he pledged that he would not harm her.

"Woman," he said, "I don't know if it is a fly, a gnat, or an ant that gnaws at my wounds. I am too tired to move and see. Tell me what it is."

"It is a wolf," she said. Then she grabbed the animal by the tail and pulled it away from him.

"I swear by what my tribe swears," Mac Cécht said, "it seemed no bigger than an ant to me."

He then seized the wolf by the throat and killed it with a single blow to the head. Mac Cécht afterward carried the body and head of Conaire back to Tara for a royal burial.

Now Conall Cernach had escaped from Dá Derga's hostel with three times fifty wounds through his shield arm. He made his way wearily back to the home of his father.

"Have you any news of the king?" the old man asked.

"He is dead," said Conall.

"I swear by the gods by whom the great tribe of Ulster swears," declared his father, "that it is cowardly for a man to abandon his lord."

"Look at my shield arm, father!" said Conall. "The sinews barely hold it together. I fought for Conaire with all my strength."

"Aye, that arm did fight tonight," said the old man.

"That it did," said Conall. "And I lived. But there are many men to whom this arm gave drinks of death this night before Dá Derga's hostel."

ATHAIRNE AND AMAIRGEN

There was once a famous blacksmith among the Ulstermen named Eccet Salach. A son was born to him named Amairgen. For fourteen years Amairgen did not speak a word. The young man's belly grew until it was the size of a small house and snot ran from his nose without ceasing. His skin was black and his feet had crooked toes. His eyes were red and sunken, while his hair was rough and prickly. His back was bony and his skin covered with scabs. He had neglected to move for so long that his own excrement piled up around him. His favorite foods were boiled curds, sea salt, unripe berries, burnt ears of grain, bunches of garlic, and nuts, which he played with on the floor.

Athairne, the chief poet of Ulster, one day sent his servant Greth to Eccet Salach the smith to order an axe. Greth saw the monstrous figure of Amairgen sitting on the floor in the house and was terrified. Eccet's daughter was there alone with the boy, looking after him.

Suddenly Amairgen spoke: "*In n-ith Greth gruth?*—Does Greth eat curds?"

The boy repeated the words twice more and added: "A fair bush, a foul bush, bunches of garlic, hollow of pine—*In n-ith Greth gruth?*"

Greth ran away from the house as fast as he could and returned to his master Athairne. He told the poet what the boy had said.

Soon Eccet returned home and his daughter told him the words her brother had spoken. Eccet knew immediately that Athairne would come to kill Amairgen, for a boy who spoke such perfect words of poetry after saying nothing for fourteen years would certainly become the greatest poet in Ireland.

Eccet made a likeness of his son out of clay and put it into the boy's bed. Then Athairne and Greth came that night and saw what they thought was the boy sleeping. Athairne took his axe and brought it down on the head of the figure in the bed. Then they fled from the house. There was an outcry raised behind them.

Eccet and his men chased Athairne back to his fort and captured the poet inside. The judges of the Ulstermen decided that Athairne would have to pay Eccet the value of seven slave women as restitution, along with the blacksmith's own honor-price. In addition, Athairne would have to take Amairgen as his apprentice and teach him the art of poetry. Thus in time Amairgen became the chief poet of Ulster.

BRICCRIU'S FEAST

Briccriu Poison Tongue of the Ulstermen decided once to host a great feast for his tribe. He ordered a magnificent feasting hall to be built that surpassed any dwelling in Ireland for beauty and expense. Gold and silver decorations covered the walls and a royal dining couch was set up in the front of the house for Conchobar, the king of Ulster. Briccriu built a chamber for himself looking down on the hall since he knew the Ulstermen would never let him join them.

When Briccriu had finished the building, he furnished it with beds and blankets, food and drink, and set out for Emain Macha, the royal capital of Ulster, to invite Conchobar and his nobles to his feast.

It happened that Briccriu arrived at Conchobar's hall on a day when all his warriors were gathered there. He was made welcome and addressed the assembly: “Men and women of Ulster, come to my feasting hall to share a banquet with me.”

“Gladly,” said Conchobar, “if my people agree.”

“We do not!” shouted Fergus mac Roich. “If we accept his invitation Briccriu will cause strife among us so that the dead will outnumber the living.”

“If you don’t come,” said Briccriu, “I will stir up worse trouble for you here. Warrior shall fight warrior, father shall fight son, mother will quarrel with daughter, and the breasts of women will strike against each other until they are destroyed.”

“Let us take counsel together,” said Sencha, the wisest of the Ulstermen.

The Ulstermen then decided to take hostages from Briccriu to guarantee his good behavior while they feasted at his hall. In addition, they would assign eight swordsmen to remove him from his hall as soon as the feast was ready.

“To that,” said Briccriu, “I gladly agree.”

The king and men of Ulster set out at once for the feast with Briccriu among them, with their ladies soon to follow. The trickster couldn’t help but stir up strife on the way. He approached Lóegaire Buadach the Victorious as they rode along the path.

“Hail now, Lóegaire,” cried Briccriu. “It is an honor to accompany such a fine man as yourself to my feast. I’ve always thought you should claim the honor of being the greatest of Ulster warriors. I wonder if you might take some advice?”

“I will if it is good,” said Lóegaire.

“Then tonight at my feast,” said Briccriu, “claim the champion’s portion of the meal for yourself. It is certain you deserve it.”

"I will do that," said Lóegaire, "and men will die if they stand in my way."

Briccriu next went to Conall Cernach and said the same. When Conall had agreed to seek the champion's portion, Briccriu went to Cú Chulainn to urge him to claim the choicest portion of the meal.

"By the god of my tribe," declared Cú Chulainn, "I will do it. If any man stands in my way he will lose his head."

The king and his company arrived at last at the house of Briccriu and took their seats. Half of the hall was set aside for Conchobar and his warriors, while the other half was reserved for the wives of Ulster.

Briccriu spread a fabulous feast before them all, then was ordered to leave. As he was passing out the door he turned and said to the crowd: "Enjoy yourselves—and give the champion's portion of the roasting pig to the hero you honor most."

The charioteer of Lóegaire rose to claim the finest cut of meat for his lord, but the charioteers of Conall Cernach and Cú Chulainn did the same. A fight arose among the three heroes with swords and shields that threatened to destroy the feasting hall.

"Enough!" shouted Conchobar. "Sencha, you are wisest of us all. What should we do?"

"Let us," said Sencha, "divide the champion's portion among every warrior here in equal shares. When the feast is done, let the three heroes travel to King Ailill in Connacht to judge among them who is the greatest."

This suggestion was acclaimed by all. Soon the meat was apportioned to the banqueters and everyone was in high spirits once again.

From outside the hall Briccriu saw what had happened and was furious that his plan had been ruined. But when he saw the ladies of Ulster approaching the feast, he had an idea and ran to greet them before they reached the door.

"Fedelm," said Briccriu, "daughter of King Conocha, wife of the glorious hero Lóegaire Buadach, welcome to my hall. It is only right that you among the ladies of Ulster should enter my hall first."

After that Lendabair, wife of Conall Cernach, drew near.

"Greetings to you, radiant Lendabair," said Briccriu, "fairest of the women of Ulster and wife of our greatest hero. You must enter the hall first."

Then came forward Emer, the wife of Cú Chulainn.

"Hail to you, Emer of the Fair Hair," said Briccriu. "As the sun surpasses the stars of heaven, so do you outshine the women of Ulster in beauty and wisdom. Of course, it is you who must enter the hall first."

As the three women drew near the door of Briccriu's house, they began to walk faster—and then they ran. They lifted their dresses up above their thighs as they raced to reach the entrance first. There was so much shouting and commotion that the men inside the hall thought they were being attacked by enemies. They sprang to arms and began to swing their swords as they ran to the door.

"Stop!" shouted Sencha. "You fools are going to kill us all. It is your wives at the door, stirred up, I would guess, by the poison tongue of Briccriu. Shut the door, now."

And so the guards closed and barred the doors against the women outside.

Conchobar then declared that there would be a war of words, not weapons, by the wives to see who might enter first. The women took turns declaring why they were most worthy to enter first. When they had finished, Lóegaire and

Conall each rose up and declared his own wife the winner. They knocked away two posts of the hall and let their wives in through the holes. But Cú Chulainn simply lifted up the side of the house to let Emer inside. The ground shook and Briccriu along with his wife fell into the mud with their dogs.

But it was still not decided who among the three heroes was the greatest in Ulster. They went first to Connacht to be judged by Ailill, but after many trials to test the heroes, Lógaire and Conall Cernach would not accept Ailill's judgment that Cú Chulainn was the best of the three. After this they went south to the wise and magical Cú Roí in Munster, but he also decided for Cú Chulainn. The other two rejected his decision as well, so that all three warriors started home to Emain Macha with no one satisfied.

While Lóegaire, Conall Cernach, and Cú Chulainn were journeying back to the Ulster capital at Emain Macha, the rest of the warriors of Conchobar were gathering in the hall of the king for a great feast. As they were eating and the wine was flowing like water, suddenly a man entered the hall. He was enormous in size and his appearance was ugly and horrible to gaze at. About his shoulders he wore an old ox hide and in his left arm was a club the size of a small tree. His eyes were yellow and his fingers were as thick as another man's wrist. In his right hand was an axe larger than any man had ever seen and so sharp that it would cut in half a hair the wind blew against its blade.

Then the giant spoke: "Neither in Ireland nor in Britain nor across the whole world have I found a man on my quest who would play my contest fairly."

"State your quest," said Fergus mac Roich. "The men of Ulster are known to be honorable above all others."

"Then," spoke the giant, "let one of you come forward so that I may cut off his head tonight, then he may cut off mine tomorrow."

The warriors all shouted that this was absurd.

"Let me cut off *your* head," laughed one called Fat Neck, "then you can cut off mine tomorrow."

"That is not my bargain," said the giant. "But if there is no man brave enough to meet my terms, then I will do as you say. But whoever cuts off my head must swear to let me cut off his tomorrow."

"Fine," said Fat Neck. "I swear that if you survive, you may cut off my head tomorrow."

All the warriors mocked the giant as a fool and cheered as Fat Neck took his axe from him. The giant then lay his head on the chopping block. Fat Neck brought down the axe so hard that the giant's head was completely severed from his body and blood spilled across the hall.

The warriors all shouted in triumph—but then the giant rose up, lifted his bloody head, and walked silently out of the hut. Conchobar and his men stared in disbelief, but none more so than Fat Neck.

The next evening, the giant, with his head back on his body, returned to the king's hall and demanded that Fat Neck fulfill his bargain.

"No!" he shouted in fear. "It was a trick. I cannot keep my word."

"This is shameful!" shouted Lóegaire, who had returned to the feasting hall that night with Conall Cernach and Cú Chulainn. "I will let you cut off my head tomorrow if I may cut off yours tonight."

And so Lóegaire decapitated the giant. But when the man returned the next evening, Lóegaire ran away. Conall

Cernach rose and likewise pledged to let the giant cut off his head tomorrow if he would let him sever his that night. But when the giant agreed and the deed was done, Conall hid in his own home the next night.

On the fourth night the giant returned and was furious.

"You cowards!" he declared. "You think you are so brave and you fight to claim the hero's portion of a feast, but you break your word and run away like children. Even you, Cú Chulainn, are afraid to die."

With that Cú Chulainn sprang toward him and grabbed the axe from his hand. The young warrior cut off the giant's head with a single stroke. The giant arose, took up his head, and walked away.

The next night Cú Chulainn returned to the hall to face the giant. The men and women of Ulster sang a lamentation for him. Some of the warriors urged him to run away.

"I would rather die," said Cú Chulainn, "than live in dishonor."

It was then that the giant entered the hall.

"Where is Cú Chulainn?" he asked.

"I am here," said the warrior.

"Your voice is quaking tonight," said the giant, smiling. "Are you afraid to die?"

Cú Chulainn went in silence to the chopping block and laid his neck across it.

"Stretch out your neck, boy," said the giant. "I want to get a clean cut."

"Why do you torment me?" asked Cú Chulainn. "I have kept my word. Do what you will do quickly."

The giant raised his axe until it reached the roof beams of the feasting hall, then waited. At last, he brought it down to Cú Chulainn's neck—but the axe was turned to the blunt side.

The giant laughed and threw back his cloak, revealing himself as Cú Roí, the man to whom the three heroes had gone to be judged.

"Cú Chulainn," he declared, "of all the warriors of Ulster and Ireland, none has been found who can compare with you in courage and honor. You are the greatest hero of Ireland."

And from that day forward, all the Ulstermen agreed that Cú Chulainn should receive the champion's portion at every feast.

THE INTOXICATION OF THE ULSTERMEN

When the sons of Míl came from Spain to Ireland, they defeated the magical tribe of the Tuatha Dé Danann. The bard Amairgen then divided Ireland in two, so that the sons of Míl received the portion above ground and the Tuatha Dé ruled beneath the earth. The Tuatha Dé went into the *síd* mounds of Ireland, but they left behind five of their tribe in each province to stir up trouble. In the days of Conchobar, the Tuatha Dé in the land of Ulster divided the province into three parts. One part they gave to Conchobar to rule, one part to the prince Fintan mac Néill, and the third to Cú Chulainn.

For a year the province of Ulster was divided this way, then on Samain, Conchobar held a great feast at Emain Macha. He set out one hundred vats of ale and invited everyone to join him at his hall, including Fintan and Cú Chulainn.

Sencha the Wise welcomed both men to Conchobar's home and asked a favor of them in exchange for his lord's hospitality. His request was that they give Conchobar the rule of their thirds of Ulster for a year. Both men agreed and joined the feast.

At the end of the year, there was such prosperity throughout Ulster that Fintan and Cú Chulainn agreed to let Conchobar henceforth rule the whole province as king. Both warriors decided to hold a feast for Conchobar and his men at their homes to celebrate the new reign, but by chance they chose the same nights for their feasts. The two arrived at Emain Macha at the same time to invite the king to their halls and neither, because of their pride, would change his plans. They were about to come to blows when Conchobar's counselor Sencha intervened:

"Let us spend the first half of the night with Fintan and the latter half with Cú Chulainn."

This plan seemed good to everyone, and so the feasts were prepared. All the warriors, wives, and servants of Ulster went that night first to the feasting hall of Fintan. Abundant food and drink was laid out on the tables, music filled the air, and songs of praise resounded through the hall. Soon the whole crowd was roaring drunk.

Midway through the night, Cú Chulainn rose and bade all present to follow him to his feasting hall. Stumbling and groggy with ale, the nobility made their way to their chariots and set off with Cú Chulainn leading the way.

Over hills and through valleys the drunken procession traveled through the darkness. Soon, however, they realized that they were lost. To make matters worse, a heavy snow began to fall that covered all the familiar landmarks.

"Lóeg," Cú Chulainn said to his charioteer at last, "Where on earth are we?"

"I have no idea, my lord," he said, "but I don't think we're in Ulster anymore."

"This looks," said Cú Chulainn, "like the province of Munster and the land of Cú Roí. The fort of Temair Luachra is nearby. Let's make our camp there."

Now it happened that on that very night King Ailill and Queen Medb of Connacht had traveled to Munster to the lands of Cú Roí so that he might be foster father to their new son. They had all gathered by chance at Temair Luachra for a feast, along with Cú Roí and many nobles from the province of Munster. Two druids stood guard on the walls of the fort and saw the host of Ulster nearing.

"Are those birds approaching?" asked one of the druids.

"No, you fool, those are deer—or maybe cattle," said the other.

"I'm not sure," said the first. "I think they might be men."

They argued for a long time until at last they went into the feasting hall and told the lords and ladies gathered there what they had seen.

"You idiots," said Queen Medb, "those are the Ulstermen. Come, let us welcome them. This is an opportunity to destroy them that we cannot let pass."

The company rose and welcomed Cú Chulainn, Conchobar, and the nobles of Ulster to Temair Luachra. They were led to the largest and finest building in the settlement—a house made of iron. Servants lit a fire for them and brought in the finest food and drink. As the night drew on, the servants of Medb stole away one by one and finally shut the door behind them.

The Ulstermen were drunk or asleep when chains were put on the door. Seven chains of new iron were made fast on the entrance to the hall and seven stone pillars were placed against the door. Then three times fifty smiths came forth and built a fire surrounding the house. With bellows they stoked the fire until it was blazing hot. A shout from the host outside stirred the Ulstermen—and then they realized they were trapped.

"Cú Chulainn," shouted Briccriu over the roar of the flames, "you have led us into a cage to be destroyed by our enemies!"

The Ulstermen threw themselves against the door, but it would not budge. At last Cú Chulainn kicked a hole in the door with all his might. But before the Ulstermen could escape, the warriors of Munster charged through the entrance and attacked them. Trapped and outnumbered, the men of Ulster picked up the edge of the iron house and overturned it on their enemies, killing three hundred of them. The battle that followed lasted through the next day, until Cú Chulainn broke through the lines with the surviving Ulster warriors and left Temair Luachra far behind. At last they went to the fort of Cú Chulainn and stayed there forty days, feasting and honoring Conchobar as king.

THE WASTING SICKNESS OF CÚ CHULAINN AND THE ONLY JEALOUSY OF EMER

Each year the nobles of Ulster held a festival for seven days on Samain, at the beginning of winter. The celebration would be full of feasting and entertainment for all. There was also a chance for each warrior to rise and boast of his brave deeds against the enemies of Ulster. These men would collect the tongues of their slain foes in a bag to show the crowd, though some were known to include cow tongues to raise their count.

On this Samain, everyone in Ulster had gathered together except the warriors Conall Cernach and Fergus mac Roich. The assembled crowd wanted to begin the festival without them, but Cú Chulainn would not allow it, for Conall was his foster brother and Fergus his foster father.

While they were entertaining themselves and waiting for the two men, a flock of birds settled on the lake near them. No one had ever seen birds so beautiful, so that all the women of Ulster wanted their feathers to decorate their clothing, hoping that this might make Cú Chulainn notice them more. One of the women went and asked Cú Chulainn to kill the birds for them.

"Have I nothing better to do than chase birds for the preening wives of Ulster?" he asked.

"It's your fault," she replied. "They all want to look beautiful for you."

"Yoke the chariot, Lóeg," he said with a sigh. "We're going to hunt birds."

Cú Chulainn set out after the flock and killed them all quickly. He then gave a pair to each woman, but he came to his wife Emer last and had no birds left to give her.

"I'm sorry, my love," he said. "Are you angry?"

"No," said Emer. "After all, it was for love of my husband that the birds were given away. Every woman of Ulster gives you a share of her love, but my love is for you alone."

"Don't worry," said Cú Chulainn. "The next pair of beautiful birds that come near I will give to you."

Not long afterwards, the people of Ulster saw two gorgeous birds bound by a golden chain flying over the lake. The pair sang a beautiful song and sleep fell upon everyone there except Cú Chulainn and Emer.

"I will get those birds for you," said Cú Chulainn.

"No, please," she replied. "Those birds have some kind of magic. There will be other birds."

"I will not be denied," he answered. He then ordered Lóeg to ready for the hunt.

Cú Chulainn chased the birds in his chariot and cast a stone at them from his sling, but he missed. He cast a second stone but missed with that as well. When he threw his spear, it only grazed the wing of one of the birds.

"I am doomed," he said to his charioteer. "For since I took up arms I have never missed my target."

Cú Chulainn walked away from the lake in anger and sat down with his back against a standing stone. Suddenly sleep overcame him and he saw two women approaching. One wore a green cloak and the other a red cloak. They smiled at him and began to beat him with a horsewhip. They struck him so hard and so long that there was scarcely any life left in him. Then they went away.

The Ulstermen came near while he slept and saw that he was in a terrible state. They started to wake him, but Fergus mac Roich said to not disturb him, for it was clear he was having a vision.

When Cú Chulainn awoke at last, he was unable to speak. He was taken to An Téte Brec, the Place of the Twinkling Hoard, and put in a sickbed. For a year he lay there on the edge of death without speaking to anyone.

At the end of the year when the festival of Samain had come again, the Ulstermen were gathered together and came to the bed of Cú Chulainn. Fergus was sitting by the wall, Conall Cernach by the bed, Lugaid Réoderg by his pillow, and Emer at his feet. As they sat there, a man entered the house.

"Who are you and what do you want?" asked Conall.

"I am Óengus son of Áed Abrat. I have come to speak to the man lying there," said the stranger. Then he began to sing:

Cú Chulainn, sick as you are,
they will help you.
Standing beside Labraid Lúathlám,
Lí Ban has spoken.

She says Fand wishes to lie with you
and that were you to come to her land,
he would have gold and silver.
Lí Ban will come to you when you wake.

Suddenly Cú Chulainn sat up in bed.

"It's about time," said the Ulstermen gathered there. "What has happened to you?"

"I had a vision last year at Samain," he said. Then he told them what he had seen.

"You must go back to that stone," they said.

Cú Chulainn left the hut and walked until he reached the standing stone. There he saw the woman in the green cloak from his dream.

"This is good," said the woman.

"It wasn't so good for me last year," he replied.

"We didn't come here last Samain to harm you," she said, "but to seek your friendship. I have come here again from the Otherworld to speak with you about Fand, the daughter of Áed Abrat and wife of Manannán son of Ler. Manannán has left her and now she desires you. My name is Lí Ban and I bear a message from my husband, Labraid Lúathlám. He will send Fand to you if you will come to him in our world and battle for a single day against his three enemies: Senach Síaborthe, Echu Íuil, and Éogan Indber."

"I am in no shape to fight anyone," said Cú Chulainn. "I'll send my charioteer Lóeg to you instead to see what is happening there."

Then Cú Chulainn returned to his bed.

And so Lí Ban took Lóeg into her land to see Fand. They came to the side of a lake facing an island. There they saw a bronze boat coming toward them. They entered the boat and went to the island, where they found a doorway. Lí Ban led Lóeg inside, where they found three fifties of couches with three fifties of women lying on them. He went into a chamber apart from it and was welcomed by Fand, who was the most beautiful woman Lóeg had ever seen.

As they stood in the chamber, they heard the sound of Labraid's chariot coming near. Battle-scarred and silent he was, but Lí Ban welcomed him. She presented Lóeg to him and told how Cú Chulainn would soon come to fight their enemies. Labraid was relieved and sent Lóeg back to his world to fetch Cú Chulainn as soon as he could.

And so Lóeg went back to Ulster and told Cú Chulainn all that he had seen.

Cú Chulainn sent Lóeg to Emer to tell her what had happened, but she rebuked him for not bringing back a cure for his lord from the Otherworld. She then went to Cú Chulainn and rebuked him for lying in bed weakened by the love of women when he had the power to raise himself. Cú

Chulainn sighed and passed his hand over his face. In an instant he was healed and got out of bed.

He went to the standing stone and saw Lí Ban approaching.

"Where does your husband Labraid dwell?" he asked.

"Come and see," she replied, "for Fand is waiting for you and the battle is this very day."

Then Cú Chulainn went with Lóeg and Lí Ban to the Otherworld.

Labraid was waiting there ready for battle and welcomed Cú Chulainn. He showed him the enemy arranged on the plain before them, an innumerable host armed for war.

Cú Chulainn joined in battle with the enemies of Labraid and routed the entire host, killing many of them in his rage. He was so overcome with his battle fury that when he returned to Labraid, Lóeg told them to throw him in three vats of cold water. They did so and the first vat boiled over, the second became too hot to touch, and the third only grew warm.

Cú Chulainn stayed with Fand for a month and slept with her. At the end of that time he bade her farewell. But he arranged to meet her again in his world at a secret place.

Emer welcomed Cú Chulainn back—but there are no secrets from women. She learned of Fand and the secret place of rendezvous Cú Chulainn had arranged. When the day of their meeting came, she went there with fifty of her women armed with very sharp knives.

Cú Chulainn was there resting after making love with Fand.

"Look behind you," said Fand. "There are many clever and able women coming with sharp knives in their hands and gold on their breasts. Your wife Emer is their leader."

"Do not worry," said Cú Chulainn. "I will speak to her so that no harm will come to you."

He went to Emer and pleaded with her. "My dear," he said, "please put down your weapons. I cannot fight with your, the woman I love."

"If you love me so," she replied, "why have you dishonored me before the women of Ireland? If you are planning to leave me for her, you might not succeed."

"Emer, why can't I be with Fand as well as you?" Cú Chulainn asked. "She is pure and modest, beautiful and clever, and a woman truly worthy of a king. She lacks nothing a man could want. And if you leave me, you won't find another man as handsome and brave as I am."

"Perhaps," said Emer, "you will find in time that this woman is no better than me. What's new is bright, while familiar things seem dull. The unknown is honored, the known neglected. We were happy once, you and I. We could be again if I still pleased you."

"Emer, my love," he said, "by my word, you do please me still and will as long as you live."

"Cú Chulainn," said Fand, "you should be with Emer and leave me behind."

"No," said Emer, "Fand is a worthy woman. You should leave me."

"Not so," said Fand, and she began to cry:

Emer, this man is yours.
Good woman, may you enjoy life with him.
But what I cannot hold in my arms,
I can still desire.

Manannán, the husband who had left her, came then and stood before her, but only Fand could see him.

"Well, woman," he said, "what will you do? Will you stay with Cú Chulainn or come with me?"

"In truth," she said, "I would prefer Cú Chulainn, but he loves another. I will go with you."

Manannán then took his cloak and shook it between Cú Chulainn and Fand, so that they might never meet again.

And so Fand left Cú Chulainn behind.

When he realized that Fand was gone, Cú Chulainn ran away to the mountains in his grief. He neither ate nor drank, but slept each night without shelter in the cold.

Emer went to Conchobar and told him of Cú Chulainn's suffering. The king sent warriors to bind him in his sorrow and bring him home. The druids of Conchobar chanted over him and gave him a drink of forgetfulness. When he had tasted it, he forgot about Fand. Then Emer took the cup and drank deeply so that she might also forget her pain forever.

THE DEATH OF CÚ CHULAINN

The warrior Lugaid mac Con Roí had always hated Cú Chulainn because the hero had slept with his mother Bláithíne. Many times he had tried to kill him, but had always failed.

One day Lugaid gathered his men near Emain Macha to lure Cú Chulainn from the fort with magic. His druids caused a great cloud of magical smoke to fall on the Ulster capital so that the weapons of those inside were useless. Cú Chulainn knew then that he would have to go forth and defend his tribe no matter the cost.

Niam, the wife of Conall Cernach, tried to dissuade him from going, along with all the other women of Ulster, but he would not relent.

"Woman," he said, "I know I am doomed, but my honor is at stake. I am not afraid of death."

Cú Chulainn ordered his charioteer Lóeg to make ready for battle. He then leapt into his chariot with his weapons and set forth from Emain Macha. But as he went, one of his chariot horses turned to the left three times, for the Mórrígan, the goddess of war, had broken the chariot the night before to keep Cú Chulainn from going forth, for she knew he would die. But Cú Chulainn did not turn back.

As he drove across the plain, he came upon three witches, each blind in the left eye, beside the road. They were roasting a small dog on a spit of holly. It was a *geis* of Cú Chulainn that he could not pass a cooking fire without eating something from it, but it was also a *geis* to him that he could not eat the flesh of a dog, his own namesake.

"Stop and visit with us," said one of the witches.

"I cannot," said Cú Chulainn.

"We are roasting a little *cú*—a hound—for you, Cú Chulainn," she said. "You must take it."

Cú Chulainn then stopped and the witch gave him the dog's shoulder. He took it in his hand and hid it under his left thigh, but from that point on he lost the strength in that hand and thigh.

Cú Chulainn continued down the road until he came to the army of Lugaid. There was a great battle there and Cú Chulainn slew many men. But Lugaid took one of his three spears and cast it at his chariot, striking his charioteer Lóeg so that he fell dead on the floor. Cú Chulainn drew out the spear and laid his friend on the ground.

"Now I am both warrior and charioteer," he said.

One of Lugaid's men, Erc son of Cairpre, took the second spear and threw it at Cú Chulainn's chariot as he charged, but it struck and wounded Liath Macha, his favorite horse. Cú Chulainn drew it out and released the beloved steed from the yoke. He then put the yoke on himself to pull the chariot and charged forward.

Lugaid took his third spear and cast it with all his might at Cú Chulainn, so that it struck him and the entrails of the Ulster warrior spilled out of him. He came to a stop in the middle of the plain, wounded beyond hope of living.

Lugaid and his men gathered around Cú Chulainn for the kill.

"Let me first," gasped Cú Chulainn, "go to that lake for a drink of water."

"You have my leave," said Lugaid, "if you promise to return to us."

"If I cannot come," said Cú Chulainn, "I will call you to me."

Cú Chulainn made his way slowly to the lake, pressing his hand on his belly to hold his entrails in. He then drank and bathed his wounds as best he could, but he did not have the strength to return to Lugaid and his men. Instead, he crawled to a stone pillar and strapped himself to it with his belt so that he might die standing up. Holding his sword in his hand, he called to his foes to come and face him.

Lugaid and his men came, but they were afraid to come close even as Cú Chulainn was drawing his final breath.

When at last he died, a crow came and sat on his shoulder.

Lugaid approached him, then with sword raised struck off Cú Chulainn's head. But Cú Chulainn's sword fell from his lifeless hand and severed Lugaid's arm.

Conall Cernach and Cú Chulainn had each sworn to avenge the other if he were slain, so the Ulster warrior came looking for Lugaid when he heard of Cú Chulainn's death. Conall found Lugaid on the plain, sitting by his chariot.

"You have slain my friend," said Conall. "It is time for you to die."

"I will fight you," replied Lugaid, "but I have only one arm. Bind yours behind you so that it will be a fair contest."

"Done," said Conall. And the two began to battle with swords.

Neither man could gain the advantage, so Conall signaled to his warhorse Derg Drúchtach. The horse came up behind Lugaid and took a bite out of his side so that his entrails spilled about his feet.

"Unfair!" cried Lugaid.

"Not so," said Conall. "I promised you only a fair fight with me. I said nothing about animals."

With that Conall Cernach struck off the head of Lugaid. He fixed the head upon a pole and it was forgotten there.

When Conall returned to Emain Macha, there was great mourning for Cú Chulainn. Some say the spirit of Cú Chulainn appeared in the air above the fort in a phantom chariot, chanting to them as he rode into the heavens.

Liath Macha, the wounded horse of Cú Chulainn, made his way back to the home of Cú Chulainn and found Emer, the slain hero's wife, crying there. The horse walked three times sun-wise around her and laid his head in her lap, yielding his final breath to her.

STORIES OF THE IRISH OTHERWORLD

THE CELTIC OTHERWORLD IS A strange and supernatural place of gods and spirits. Sometimes it is identified as the bountiful land of the dead, but more often it exists as a parallel world alongside our own that mortals enter at their own peril if not invited by those who dwell there. In Irish tradition, the doorway to the Otherworld is often a *síd* (plural *síde*), one of the many pre-Celtic burial mounds throughout the island that became an integral part of Irish mythology. At other times the entry to the Otherworld can be found in caves or beneath lakes or by sailing to distant islands in the western sea. But however mortals enter this realm, they must beware, as time and space do not function the same as in the human world, sometimes with disastrous consequences for those who try to leave.

THE ADVENTURE OF NERA

One night at the autumn festival of Samain, Ailill and Medb of Connacht were gathered together with all their warriors in their fort at Cruachan. They had hanged two prisoners the day before and were now sitting about a boiling cauldron full of meat waiting for dinner to be ready.

While they were waiting and drinking, Ailill arose and challenged his men:

"Whoever among you ties a supple twig around the foot of one of the dead prisoners on the gallows will have whatever he wishes from me as a reward, even my gold-hilted sword."

Samain was a fearful night for even the bravest of warriors, for horror and spirits roamed throughout the land. Each of the men rose in turn and said he would take the risk—but each returned to the safety of the hall before making it to the gallows.

"I will go out," said the young warrior Nera, "and win that reward."

Then Nera left the hall and made his way through the darkness to where the bodies of the prisoners were hanging. Three times he tied a supple twig around the foot of one of the prisoners, but each time it came off.

"You have to put a special spike into the twig," said the dead prisoner, "otherwise it won't hold."

So Nera put a spike into it.

"Well done, Nera," said the prisoner. "Now by your honor as a warrior, would you do me a favor? I was terribly thirsty when I died. Would you carry me to get a drink?"

"Of course," replied the young warrior.

Nera carried the man on his back to the nearest house. But there was a lake of fire surrounding that place.

"My drink is not here," said the prisoner. "The hearth is always raked in this house. Move on to the next."

Nera carried him to the second house, but there was a lake of water around it.

"Do not go to that house," said the prisoner. "There is never any water left in the tub there after washing and bathing. Move on to the next."

When they reached the third house, the prisoner entered and took a drink from each of the tubs there that had left-over water. Then he spat a mouthful at the faces of the people who lived there so that they died. This is why it is not good to leave water from washing or bathing in a tub after washing or to leave a hearth fire that has not been raked.

Nera then took the dead man back to the gallows. But as he returned to the hall of Ailill and Medb, he saw a strange thing—the fort of Cruachan was on fire and the heads of all inside had been heaped into a pile by enemy warriors.

And so Nera followed the warriors who had killed his people into the cave of Cruachan.

But as the troop entered the *síd*, one of them said, "There is a human with us."

"Yes," said another, "I can feel his heaviness."

They passed the news down the line of marching warriors until they all knew that Nera was among them.

When they reached the hall of the king of the *síd*, the ruler called Nera forward.

"Why are you here?" he asked.

"I came with your army," said Nera.

"Go to that nearby house," said the king. "A woman lives there alone. Tell her I have sent you to stay with her. In payment for my kindness, you are to bring me a bundle of firewood here every day."

Nera went to the house and told the woman what the king had said. She welcomed him there.

For three days as Nera carried his bundle of wood to the king's hall, he saw a blind man with a lame man on his back coming out of the royal house. They would go to the edge of a spring in front of the house and stop.

"Is it still there?" asked the blind man.

"It is indeed," answered the lame man. "Let us go back."

Nera asked the woman he was staying with why the two men went to the spring every day.

"They do so," she said, "to see Brión's crown, which is in the spring. It is a golden diadem that belongs to the king."

"Why do those two go there?" Nera asked.

"The king appointed them to do so," she answered. "He blinded one and made the other lame so they could be trusted to carry out this task."

Nera pondered this, then continued to question her.

"When I came into this *síd*," he said, "I saw the fort of Cruachan burning and all its people slain. How did this happen?"

"What you saw," she said, "was a vision of the future. But it will come to pass unless you warn your people. Go now and tell them. They are still gathered around the hearth fire and it is still Samain evening there. My king will send his men to destroy them, for it has been foretold that Ailill and Medb will ravage our *síd* and carry off Brión's crown."

"But," asked Nera, "how will I convince them that I have gone into the Otherworld?"

"Bring with you the fruit and flowers of summer," she answered. And she gave him wild garlic, primroses, and buttercups.

"Send me warning," she told Nera, "when the Connacht warriors are coming to destroy the *síd*. For I am pregnant and will bear you a son. I will tell my king that you are sick and will take him the firewood myself every day."

Then Nera went back to Cruachan and found his people still sitting around the fire waiting for him, as if no time had passed at all. He told Ailill and Medb all that he had seen and heard, and showed them the fruit and flowers as proof that he had been to the Otherworld.

Nera remained at the court of Ailill and Medb for a whole year, until the next Samain festival. Then Ailill sent him back to the *síd* to fetch his wife, son, and all that belonged to him. When he arrived there, she welcomed him.

"Here is your son," she said. "Now go to the court and take a bundle of firewood. The king is waiting for you."

Nera did as he was told. The king was not pleased that he had slept with the woman without his permission, but he sent Nera away without punishment.

The warriors of Ailill and Medb then attacked the *síd* and ravaged it, taking the crown of Brión and other treasures with them back to Cruachan. But they left Nera in the *síd* along with his family. There he will remain until the end of the world.

THE ADVENTURE OF CORMAC

One day Cormac, king of Ireland, son of Art and grandson of Conn, was at the Hill of Tara when he saw an old warrior by himself approaching him across the grass yard of the fortress. In the hand of the man was a branch of gold with three apples hanging from it. When the man shook it, it made the sweetest sound in the world, so that all would be at peace and without care. Even women in labor and men who were wounded would fall asleep at the sound.

Cormac was overcome with a desire to possess that branch and told the warrior he would give him the three best gifts in Ireland in exchange for it. The man agreed, with a promise from Cormac that he would give him those gifts whenever he might ask for them.

A year later the warrior returned to Cormac. The first gift he asked for was Ailbe, Cormac's daughter. Reluctantly, Cormac gave the man his daughter. Then the women of Ireland wept and wailed until Cormac shook the branch and they all fell asleep.

A year later the warrior returned again and asked Cormac for his second promised gift. This time he demanded Cormac's son Cairpre. The men of Ireland raised an uproar at this, but Cormac shook the branch and they all fell asleep.

At the end of another year, the warrior returned for the third time and asked for Cormac's wife Eithne. With many tears Cormac gave the man his wife, for he had given his word.

But as the warrior was taking Eithne away, Cormac was overcome with jealousy and went after the man to get his wife back. Suddenly a great mist fell between them so that Cormac could not find the man or Eithne.

Cormac wandered through the mist and found himself in the middle of a great plain. Before him was a fortress on the plain with a silver wall around it. The house inside was half of gold and half the roof was made of the wings of birds gathered by troops of horsemen from the Otherworld. The wings were always falling off, so the horsemen were forever putting them back on.

Cormac also saw a warrior there kindling a fire. The man would fetch a whole tree and put it on the fire, then go and bring another. By the time he returned, the first tree was consumed. It was his duty to keep the fire burning, so he could never stop.

Cormac came at last to the central stronghold. A handsome king and beautiful queen were seated there on thrones. The feet of the king were washed, then in came a man with a pig on his back, a staff in one hand and a hatchet in the other. The man with the pig greeted Cormac by name and welcomed him. He slew the pig with the hatchet and cut it up into the cauldron, then chopped up his staff to feed the fire beneath the cauldron.

"This pig," the man said, "will not be cooked until each of the four of us tells a true tale."

"You first," the king said to the man. "Tell us a tale about your pig."

"Indeed, I will," said the man. "When first I came here, your household and property, my king, consisted of six cows, an ox, and myself as your servant. I plowed a single field of wheat with that ox. The farmer next to us owned many cattle that would stray onto your field, so I held them until the farmer gave me the pig, hatchet, and staff. As the farmer instructed me, every night since then I have killed the pig and burned the staff beneath the cauldron to feed many men, but the pig and staff are always whole the next day."

Then a quarter of the pig was cooked.

"On the one day a year when we plow," said the king, "I sow without horse or man to help me. In one hour, the grain is ripe. When I go to harvest it the next day, there are already three stacks in the middle of the field. When I go to bring it home the day after, I find it already inside my fortress where it never spoils."

Then half the pig was cooked.

"Now it is my turn," said the queen. "I have seven cows and seven sheep. The milk of the seven cows is enough for everyone here in the Land of Promise. And the sheep provide enough wool to clothe everyone in the kingdom."

Three-quarters of the pig was then cooked.

Then Cormac told the story of what had happened to him since the mist fell upon him.

"What you have seen," said the king, "is the present world. The horsemen you saw thatching the house are the skilled men of the world who labor continuously, but all of their work vanishes in time. The man kindling the fire is the noblemen and farmers of the world, who consume all they find and must always search for more. This fortress, however, is the home of the lord of the Land of Promise. I am the one who brought you the branch at Tara and asked for the three gifts. I am Manannán son of Ler."

Then the pig was cooked.

A portion of the animal was set before Cormac to eat, but he said he would not eat of it until fifty others joined him. Then Manannán sang a song to him and he fell asleep. When he awoke, there were fifty others at the table, including his daughter, son, and wife. He rejoiced greatly to see them.

A cup was brought to him made of refined red gold.

"That cup," said Cormac, "is the one treasure I desire most in the world, but it seems very easy to break."

Manannán gave the cup a blow so that it fell into three pieces.

"It is a great shame," Cormac said, "that the cup is now broken."

"It is a cup of truth," said Manannán. "If I speak the truth, it will be restored. And so I say to you that from the day I took them, your wife and daughter have not been touched."

And the cup became whole again.

Then Manannán gave the cup to Cormac and sent him and his family to bed. When they awoke the next morning, they were back in Tara and the Land of Promise had vanished.

THE ADVENTURE OF CONLA

Conla of the Red Hair, son of Conn of a Hundred Battles, was with his father and his men at Uisnech in the center of Ireland one day, when he saw a woman in strange clothing coming toward him.

"Woman, where have you come from?" asked Conla.

"I have come from the Land of the Living," said the woman, "where there is neither death nor evil. We enjoy everlasting feasts there and have joy without strife. We live in a great *síd* and thus are called the people of the *síd*."

"Who are you talking to?" Conn asked his son. For no one except Conla could see the woman.

"He speaks," said the woman, "to a beautiful young noblewoman who will face neither age nor death. I have fallen in love with Conla of the Red Hair and I invite him to the Plains of Delight, where the triumphant Boadach rules forever in a land without weeping or sorrow. Come away with me, Conla, and you will never die."

When he heard what the woman said, Conn turned to his druid, Corann.

"I beg you, Corann, stop this deceitful woman from stealing away my son with the magic of women."

The druid then sang a charm against the woman so that no one could hear her voice and Conla could see her no longer. But as the woman was fading away, she threw an apple to Conla.

For the next month, Conla wanted no food except the apple, which grew no smaller no matter how much he ate of it.

Then a great longing seized Conla to see the woman again.

A month later, as he was walking with his father by the sea, he saw the same woman coming toward him.

"Conla sits on the high throne of the ghostly dead," she said to him. "He waits fearfully for death. But those who dwell in the Land of the Living bid you come to us."

When Conn heard the woman's voice, he called for the druid.

"Conn of the Hundred Battles," said the woman, "do not rely on the magic of druids. For soon a man named Patrick will come to this island who will prove their teachings false."

"Conla, my son," said Conn, "do not listen to this woman."

"I love my people, father," said Conla, "but longing for her has seized me."

"Come away with me, Conla," said the woman. "Leave behind your struggles and cares. Away we will go in my crystal boat. There is another world, more beautiful than this land of shadows. It is far, but we can reach it by nightfall."

Then Conla ran away from his father and went with the woman into the crystal boat on the shore. Conn could only watch in sorrow as his son sailed away across the sea, never to be seen again.

THE ADVENTURES OF THE SONS OF EOCHAID MUGMEDÓN

There was once a king of Ireland at Tara known as Eochaid Mugmedón who frequently raided Britain and brought back captives to serve as his slaves. One of these slaves was Cairenn, daughter of the Saxon king Saxall Balb. Cairenn bore Eochaid a son named Niall. Both the child and his mother were hated by Mongfhind, the wife of Eochaid and mother of his other four sons, Brian, Ailill, Fiachra, and Fergus.

When Cairenn was pregnant with Niall, Mongfhind forced her to draw heavy buckets of water from the well in hope that she would miscarry. Even when she was in labor, Mongfhind forced her to do this, so that she gave birth on the grass of Tara next to her bucket. Because of Mongfhind, Cairenn could not touch the baby and was forced to leave him on the ground, exposed to the birds. Even the bravest warriors would not help the child, for they greatly feared Mongfhind.

Torna the poet happened to pass by that day and saw the birds attacking the baby on the ground. He took the boy into his arms and rescued him, foretelling in song that he would become a great king. Torna then raised the child as his own foster son.

One day years later, Niall saw his mother drawing water. He urged her to stop, but she could not because of the anger of Mongfhind. He then took his mother to the palace and clothed her in purple.

Mongfhind was furious at this and at the warriors of Eochaid who whispered that Niall would one day be king. She told her husband to declare publicly which of his sons would become king.

"I will not," said Eochaid, "but I will let Sithchenn the druid decide."

Sithchenn gathered the five sons of Eochaid inside a blacksmith's house and set it on fire, to judge what the boys would bring out.

Brian came out bearing the blacksmith's hammers with him.

"Brian shall be a warrior on battlefields," said Sithchenn.

Fiachra brought out a bucket of ale and the bellows.

"Fiachra shall be known for his beauty and skills," said Sithchenn.

Ailill came forth with a box of weapons.

"Ailill shall be a force of vengeance," said Sithchenn.

Fergus came out with a bundle of withered sticks.

"Fergus will wither away," said Sithchenn.

And last, Niall came out with the blacksmith's anvil.

"Niall shall be firm like an anvil and shall rule them all," said Sithchenn.

Mongfhind could not accept the judgment of the druid, so she ordered her sons to take Niall hunting and kill him deep in the woods.

The boys all went hunting and feasted that night on what they had killed. But they were terribly thirsty and sent Fergus to find them water. He came upon a well, but there was an old woman there who was hideous to look upon. Her eyes were black, her nose crooked, her teeth green, her bowels runny, and her feet twisted.

"Let me draw water from the well," Fergus said to the hag.

"Only if you kiss me first," she replied.

"I would rather die of thirst," said Fergus. Then he went back and told his brothers what had happened. Each of them in turn went to the well, but none would dare to kiss the hideous old woman.

"I will go," said Niall. And so he went and found the well.

"Give me a kiss and you shall drink," said the hag to Niall.

"Not only will I kiss you," he said, "but I will make love with you as well."

He lowered himself on the ground with her and kissed her passionately—but as he looked at her, she became the most beautiful woman he had ever seen, clad from head to toe in purple clothes.

"Who are you?" asked Niall in amazement.

"I am the sovereignty of Ireland," she replied. "And that sovereignty will belong to you and your descendants because you were willing to kiss me."

Niall then drew water from the well and returned to his brothers, but he would not let them drink until they had pledged their loyalty to him. They then returned and told Eochaid and the rest of the court all that had happened.

"My decision is confirmed," said Sithchenn the druid. "The kingship of Ireland will belong to Niall and his descendants from this day forward."

THE VOYAGE OF BRAN

Once when Bran the son of Febal was alone near his stronghold, he heard strange music behind him. He turned to see where it was coming from, but wherever he turned the music was always to his back. The sounds were so sweet that at last he fell asleep.

When he awoke, Bran found beside him a silver branch with white blossoms. He picked up the branch and took it inside his royal hall. There he and his men saw a woman in strange clothing standing suddenly in the middle of the room. She began to sing:

I bring a branch of an apple tree to you
from a distant land.
Branches of silver are on it
and crystal blossoms.

There is a distant island,
a delight to the eyes.
Let Bran hear and begin a voyage.
Perhaps he may reach that land.

The silver branch sprang from the hand of Bran, for he could not hold it. It flew into the hand of the woman—and then she disappeared.

Bran gathered together three companies of nine men each and set out upon the sea in search of the land the woman had spoken of. When he had been on the water for two days and two nights, he saw a man in a chariot coming toward him over the waves. The man said he was Manannán son of Ler. Then he began to sing:

Bran thinks he sails the clear sea,
a beautiful place, in his little coracle,
but to me in my chariot
it seems like he traverses a flowery plain.

Let Bran row steadily onward.
He is not far from the Island of Women,
a place with many hues of hospitality.
He will be there before the setting of the sun.

Bran soon came to an island, but it was not the Island of Women. On the shore was a crowd of people laughing as they looked at him and his men in their boat. They would not speak to Bran, but only laughed without ceasing. He sent one of his men to the island, but as soon as he landed on the shore he too began to laugh. Bran called to him to come back to the boat, though it was no use. His companion had lost all interest in them, so they left him there on the island and sailed away. The name of this place is the Island of Joy.

It wasn't long after this that they came to the Island of Women. The leader of the women called out to him from the shore: "Bran son of Febal, your coming is most welcome."

But Bran was reluctant to land on the island. Then the woman threw a ball of yarn at Bran while holding the end of the thread in her hand. The yarn stuck to his hand and could not be removed. Then the woman pulled his coracle to shore.

The women of the island welcomed Bran and his men to their home. They took them to a large house where there were three times nine beds ready, one for each of the men to share with one of the women of the island. A feast was made ready and placed before them. But as much as the men ate, the food and drink never diminished.

They stayed there for what seemed to them only a year, but in fact many years had passed. They had everything they might desire there and wanted for nothing.

At last a longing for home seized one of them, a man named Nechtan. He begged Bran many times to return to Ireland with him. After countless pleadings, Bran agreed and the men prepared to leave. The women of the island warned them, however, that they would regret returning home. When Bran wouldn't listen, they warned him to at least not touch the land with his feet when he came to Ireland.

Bran and his men left the Island of Women and sailed to the Island of Joy to bring their companion back with them. Then they sailed from there and came at last to Ireland. They saw a gathering of men there on the shore.

"I am Bran son of Febal," he shouted to the men on the beach.

"That's impossible," shouted back one of the men. "The voyage of Bran who left this land is one of our ancient tales."

Nechtan, the companion of Bran, could not wait any longer. He leapt from the boat and swam to shore. But as soon as he stepped onto the land, he turned into a pile of dust, as if he had been buried in the ground for many centuries.

When Bran saw what had happened, he stayed in the boat with his men and told those on the shore all of his adventures. Then he bade them all farewell and sailed away, never to be seen again.

FINN THE OUTLAW

IN EARLY IRELAND, LIFE CENTERED on the *tuath* or tribe to which a person belonged. Outside the civilized world of the tribe lay the wild and dangerous realm of the outlaws who lived by their own means and rules. This was the land of the famous outlaw leader Finn, who was a matchless warrior, a gifted poet, and a celebrated lover. Finn has much in common with other Irish heroes, especially Cú Chulainn, but he always lives on the margins of society rather than as part of the normal social structure. His tales, two of which are presented here, were among the most popular in medieval Ireland and survived in the folklore tradition until modern times.

THE BOYHOOD DEEDS OF FINN

Once there was a war between Cumall son of Trénmór and Uirgriu son of Lugach Corr over who should rule the outlaw bands of Ireland. One of Uirgriu's allies was Morna, whose son Goll killed Cumall in battle, taking his head and weapons as trophies. Thus, for ever after there was conflict between the family of Cumall and the sons of Morna.

Cumall died with his wife Muirne pregnant. She then gave birth to a son she named Demne, and gave him to two druid warrior-women to be raised, for the sons of Morna and their allies sought to kill the child. The names of the women who raised Demne were Bodbmall and Gray. They took him deep into the forests near Slieve Bloom and reared him there in secret, training him in the arts of war and magic until he was ready to become a warrior.

One day while Demne was still a young boy, he was hunting by himself and saw some ducks on a nearby lake. He cast his spear at one of the ducks so that it shaved all the feathers off the bird and made it faint. Then he took the limp bird back with him to the hut of the two druidesses where he lived. That was the first hunt of Demne.

Another time Demne went away with a group of poets who were fleeing from the sons of Morna. While he was with them, he developed scurvy and his hair fell out, so that they called him Demne the Bald. An outlaw named Fiacal attacked them and killed them all except Demne. The two druidesses who were raising Demne came looking for him and found him in Fiacal's house. They asked for the boy and he was returned safely to them.

On another day Demne was wandering as far as the plain near the Liffey River when he saw a group of boys playing hurley in front of a fort there. He joined in the game, but the boys were not pleased. When he returned the next day they sent a quarter of their number to attack him, but he defeated them all. The next day they sent a third, but he beat them as well. The following day they all went against him, but he fought and won against the whole band.

"What is your name?" they asked him at last.

"Demne," he replied. The boys then went in to the lord of the fort and told him what had happened.

"Kill him," said the man.

"We can't," they cried. "He is too strong and fast."

"What is he like?" asked the lord.

"He is handsome and fair [*finn*]," they replied.

"Then let him be called Finn from now on," said the man.

A week later the lad went back to the same fort and saw the boys swimming in a nearby lake. The boys dared him to try and dunk them, so he jumped in and held nine of them under the water until they begged for mercy. Then he returned to the forest.

"Who dunked these boys?" the people asked.

"Finn!" they all cried. And so that was his name from that day forward.

One time Finn was hunting in the forests of Slieve Bloom with his foster mothers when they saw a herd of red deer on the hillside.

"It's a shame we can't capture one of those," they said.

"I can!" yelled Finn. And so he ran after the herd and caught two deer by the horns. He brought them back to the hunt and did all the hunting for them thereafter.

One day the two women who had raised him told him that it was time for him to leave. The sons of Morna were drawing near to kill him, and they could not protect him any longer. He therefore went to the king of Bantry and offered him his services as a hunter, but he did not tell the king his name. Finn was the greatest hunter they had ever seen.

"If Cumall had a son," said the king to Finn, "he would be you."

Finn left the king of Bantry then, and went to Kerry to serve the king there. The king taught the boy to play *fidchell* and Finn promptly won seven games in a row.

"Who are you?" asked the king.

"I am nobody," said Finn, "just a boy from the woods."

"No, you're not," said the king. "Someone with your skill must be the son of Cumall. Get out of here before the sons of Morna kill you in front of my eyes."

Finn left there and went to Cullen, where he stayed with Lochan the blacksmith. Lochan had a beautiful daughter named Cruithne who fell madly in love with Finn.

"Even though I don't know who you are," said Lochan to Finn, "I'll give you my daughter to sleep with."

And so Finn and the girl slept together.

Lochan made Finn a spear and bade him farewell, with a warning to beware of a terrible pig near his lands.

"Don't follow the path of the sow," warned Lochan. "She is called the Live One and is a monstrous beast who laid waste to all of Munster."

But of course that's the path that Finn followed. When he found the sow, he cast his spear through her so that she died. He brought the head back to Lochan the smith as a bride price for his daughter Cruithne. From that day forward the mountain there was called Slieve Mucc, or Sow Mountain.

Finn left there and went to Connacht, where he came upon a lone woman crying in the woods. Her eyes were full of blood that dripped down her face so that her mouth was red.

"Why are you crying?" Finn asked.

"Because my son was killed," said the woman, "by a huge and ugly warrior."

"I will avenge you," said Finn.

The lad then tracked the warrior and killed him. Among the warrior's possessions was a bag of treasures taken from Finn's own father, Cumall, in battle. Finn went on and found some of his father's old outlaw band hiding in the woods of

Connacht. He gave them the bag of treasures and told them all that had happened to him.

Finn then left Connacht and went to the Boyne River to earn poetry from Finnéces the poet, for he did not dare to remain in Ireland to face the sons of Morna without the power of poetry.

Finnéces was an old man who had been sitting on the banks of the Boyne for seven years trying to catch a salmon at Féc's Pool. For it had been foretold that whoever could eat the salmon of Féc would know all things.

Finnéces caught the salmon at last and gave it to Finn to cook for him, warning the young man not to eat any of it. After it was cooked, he brought the fish to the poet.

"Did you eat any of the salmon, boy?" asked Finnéces.

"No," he replied, "but I burned my thumb on the fish and put it in my mouth without thinking."

"What is your name?" asked Finnéces.

"Demne," said the boy.

"No longer," the poet declared. "From now on it is Finn, for it was for you the fish was intended. You are the true Finn."

From that day on, whenever Finn needed to know something, he stuck his thumb in his mouth and chanted magic spells. When he did this, what he needed to know was revealed to him.

After this Finn went to Cethern son of Fintan to continue his study of poetry with him. Cethern would leave Finn every Samain to go off to the *síd* mound of Éle, the most beautiful of the fairy women of Ireland. Men went to her mound every Samain to woo her, for it was only on that day that the *síd* mounds of Ireland were open and the Otherworld touched our own. But every year when men would go to her, one of each company would be killed, for none could win the heart of Éle.

Finn left Cethern and traveled to the house of Fiacail the warrior. He told Fiacail about all that had happened and the deaths that took place at the fairy mound each year. Fiacail told him to go and hide himself on the next Samain between the two mountains of Munster, known as the breasts of the goddess Anu.

"At the Paps of Anu," said Cethern to Finn, "you will see a wonder."

On Samain, Finn hid himself in the valley between the Paps of Anu and waited. When the sun had set, he saw the blazing fires inside the doorways of the two fairy mounds there, for on that night they lay open to our world.

Finn saw a man coming out of one of the mounds carrying a tray of food to the other mound. On the tray was a live pig, a cooked calf, and wild garlic. As he passed, Finn threw his spear at the man in the darkness in revenge for his friends slain at the fairy mound of Éle.

Finn heard wailing and lamentation from the women of the fairy mounds. He rushed at one of them and captured her. He made her promise to return his spear before he let her go back to her mound, which she did. And after this, Finn was honored by the people of the fairy mounds of Ireland.

THE PURSUIT OF DIARMUID AND GRÁINNE

Early one morning when Finn was an old man, his son Oisín and his friend Diorruing found him sitting on a grassy hillside.

"Why are you up so early?" asked Oisín.

"I haven't slept well since my wife Maignis died," said Finn. "A man without a woman beside him tosses and turns all night."

"I know the perfect woman for you," said Diorruing. "Her name is Gráinne, the daughter of Cormac mac Airt, the high king at Tara. She is the most beautiful woman in all the world."

"Diorruing," said Finn, "you know Cormac and I have never been friends. I won't ask him for his daughter's hand just so he can turn me down."

"Leave that to us," said Oisín.

Oisín and Diorruing traveled to Tara while Cormac was holding a grand feast. They were welcomed by the king, who took them aside, for he could see they had come on important business.

"What can I do for you, my friends?" said Cormac. "If it is in my power, it is yours."

"We have come," said Oisín, "on behalf of Finn to ask for the hand of your daughter in marriage."

"Not likely," answered Cormac. "Finn and I have had our quarrels, but that isn't the problem. My daughter has rejected every proposal I have brought to her, offers from the finest men in the land. Ask Gráinne herself if she will go with Finn, then he won't blame me when she says no."

The king called for his daughter and Oisín presented to her the offer from Finn.

"Father," she said, "if you think Finn would make a good husband, then that is good enough for me."

Cormac was surprised at her answer, but he sent Oisín and Diorruing back to Finn with word for him to come to Tara on a certain day to celebrate his wedding to Gráinne.

The weeks passed until at last the day of the marriage arrived. Finn and his men arrived at Tara and were welcomed by Cormac and Gráinne. They all sat down for a grand feast at Cormac's hall, with Gráinne placed next to a druid named Dáire.

"Who is that man next to Oisín?" Gráinne asked the druid.

"That is Oscar," he replied, "the son of Oisín and the grandson of Finn."

"And beside him?"

"Caoilte, the fastest runner in Ireland."

"And beside him?"

"Goll mac Morna, a fierce warrior."

"And who is that handsome man at Oisín's left hand?" she asked.

"That is Diarmuid son of Duibne, the most skilled lover of women in Ireland. He is a friend of Óengus of the Tuatha Dé Danann."

"Is that so?" said Gráinne. "I would like to meet this man alone."

Gráinne sent one of her women to her room for a special goblet of gold studded with jewels. Gráinne filled it with wine and handed it to Finn, bidding him and the rest of the company there to drink deeply. As the cup made the rounds of all the guests, they began to fall asleep at the table. Only Oisín and Diarmuid had not yet drunk when the cup ran empty. Gráinne went to sit between them.

"Oisín," said Gráinne, "I'm surprised you asked for my hand for an old man like your father. Wouldn't you rather have me for yourself?"

"My lady, I cannot!" exclaimed Oisín. "I would never dishonor my father so."

She turned to face Diarmuid.

"What about you, Diarmuid?" she asked. "Would you like to marry me?"

"Never!" he proclaimed. "You are beautiful beyond measure, but I cannot take a wife from her husband on her wedding night."

"Is that so?" said Gráinne. "Then I place a *geis* on your head as a curse, Diarmuid. Unless you take me away as your wife this very moment, disgrace and destruction shall follow you."

Diarmuid cried aloud in anguish and asked Oisín what he should do. His friend told him the *geis* was unfair, but since it had been placed on him it would be best to take Gráinne away. But he warned Diarmuid to beware of the deceits of Finn, who would never stop pursuing him.

The couple ran from the feasting hall and found horses in a nearby field. They rode as fast as they could away from Tara and didn't stop until they came to the Shannon River.

"These horses make it easy for Finn to track us," said Diarmuid.

"Then we'll go on foot from here," answered Gráinne.

They waded across a ford on the Shannon and came at last to a forest of oak in Connacht, where Diarmuid made a bed of birch boughs for Gráinne to sleep on.

Finn arose from his stupor the next morning and discovered what had happened. He sent out men to track Diarmuid, but Oisín sent his best hound ahead of them to find Diarmuid and warn him that Finn was on his trail. The dog found him and Gráinne in the woods, and pushed his muzzle into Diarmuid's neck to wake him.

"This is a warning from Oisín," Gráinne said to Diarmuid. "We must flee."

"I will not run," declared Diarmuid. "It is better to face Finn here."

Finn meanwhile had led his band of outlaws to Connacht, where he surrounded the woods and trapped the couple with no way of escape.

A cold wind suddenly blew through the trees around Finn and his men. It reached the center of the woods where Diarmuid stood holding Gráinne.

Then out of the wind appeared Óengus of the Tuatha Dé.

"You are in trouble again, my friend?" said Óengus to Diarmuid. "Why is it always a woman?"

"Óengus," said Diarmuid, "please take Gráinne to safety. I will stay and fight Finn."

Óengus put Gráinne beneath his cloak and flew through the air, leaving Diarmuid to face Finn and his men. The young warrior rushed the old outlaw and jumped above his head, running onward through the plains and hills until he found Óengus and Gráinne roasting a pig in a hut. He told them all that had passed as they ate their fill. Then he took Gráinne and went to bed.

Finn was furious, but none of his men were eager to pursue Diarmuid.

"It is best to let him go," Oisín said to his father. "Let him have the girl. There are other women."

"Never!" declared Finn. "Diarmuid has insulted my honor. I will not let him live."

Over mountains and through caves, across lakes and rivers, for years Finn chased Diarmuid and Gráinne across Ireland without ceasing. Finn hired mercenaries from across the sea to help him, since his own men were reluctant to find their friend Diarmuid. Always on the run, Diarmuid guarded Gráinne with his life and lay with her in love every night. Even when she became pregnant, they could not cease from running.

At last, after many seasons had passed, the men of Ireland persuaded Finn to cease the pursuit of Diarmuid and Gráinne. Finn grumbled and cursed, but finally agreed. The lovers then made a home for themselves and lived in peace and happiness, raising four sons and a daughter.

One day when their children were almost grown, Gráinne asked Diarmuid if she could invite Finn to their home for a feast, hoping to make peace between him and Diarmuid. Her husband was wary, but agreed at last.

When Finn came, he and Diarmuid went together to hunt a great boar that was terrorizing the countryside around Ben Bulben. But during the hunt the beast gored Diarmuid and left him for dead.

Finn and his men found him on the ground still breathing.

"I wish Gráinne and the women of Ireland could see you now," said Finn with a smile. "You're not the handsome man you were."

"You can heal me, Finn," gasped Diarmuid. "When you tasted the salmon at the Boyne as a boy, you were given the gift of healing along with your poetry. If you bring water to an injured person in the palm of your hands, the person will recover."

"Grandfather," said Oscar to Finn, "you must heal him. Diarmuid is one of us and a man of honor."

Finn was silent for a long time, then walked to a nearby well and scooped up the water in his hands. But as he walked back to Diarmuid, he thought of Gráinne and let the water slip through his fingers.

Twice more his grandson sent him back for more water, but each time he let the water pass through his hands. By the third time, Diarmuid was dead.

When Gráinne heard of her husband's death, she told their grown sons that Finn had let their father die. A bloody war of vengeance between the families followed, until at last Gráinne made a pact with Finn and married him to spare the lives of her children. Then Gráinne and Finn lived together in peace for the rest of their days.

WELSH MYTHOLOGY—THE *MABINOGI*

THE FOUR LOOSELY CONNECTED MEDIEVAL tales that make up the *Mabinogi* are fascinating and sophisticated stories that stand on their own as part of the broader European tradition of the time, but their roots stretch back into ancient Celtic traditions and have much in common with early Irish literature.

PWYLL PRINCE OF DYFED

A prince named Pwyll once ruled over the kingdom of Dyfed in Wales. One day when he was in his court at Arberth, he decided to go hunting in a part of his realm called Glyn Cuch. He set off on horseback with his hounds and companions and came to that place, but while he was there he became separated from his friends and dogs. He heard the barking of his hounds in the distance, but he also heard the sounds of another pack coming toward his own. He soon came to a clearing and found his pack, but saw there the other pack dogs chasing a stag to the ground.

Never had he seen dogs like these before. They were shining white in color with red ears that stood out against the paleness of their bodies. He drove away the strange pack that had killed the stag and fed his own hounds upon it.

While his dogs were feeding, a horseman wearing gray hunting clothes came into the meadow on a large gray horse.

"I know who you are, but I will not greet you," said the man to Pwyll.

"Perhaps," said Pwyll, "you are of such high rank that you need not greet me."

"That isn't it," said the man. "It is because you have been so discourteous to me. My hounds killed this stag, yet you drove them off to feed your own. I will not take revenge on you now, but I will have my poets satirize you to the worth of a hundred stags."

"My lord," answered Pwyll, "I beg your pardon. What I did was wrong. Will you make peace with me?"

"You may if you do me a service," said the horseman. "I am Arawn, king of Annwfn. There is a king named Hafgan in my land who makes war on me continually. If you deliver me from this man, I will pardon your transgression today."

"I will gladly do so," said Pwyll, "but how can this be done?"

"I will trade places with you," said Arawn, "and give you my appearance and manner. You shall become king of Annwfn in my place for a year and have my queen to sleep with you every night. I have arranged with Hafgan to meet him in battle a year from tonight, but you shall be there in my place. Give him only a single blow and he shall not survive. Though he beg you to give him another and finish him off, do not do it. A single blow will kill him, but many blows will make him stronger."

"But what shall I do with my own kingdom for a year?" asked Pwyll.

"I shall rule there in your form," said Arawn. "No man or woman there will know I am not you."

"Agreed," said Pwyll.

Arawn then changed the appearance of Pwyll and sent him to his court in Annwfn. Pwyll entered the magnificent halls and chambers of Arawn and was greeted there as if he had always been lord over the place. The queen was the fairest woman he had ever seen. They conversed over a sumptuous dinner, then went to bed. But as soon as they had crawled beneath the covers, Pwyll turned his back to the queen and did not speak a word to her until morning. He was pleasant and kind to her every day, but every night for the next year he did the same as he had done the first night.

When a year had passed, Pwyll went to the appointed place to challenge Hafgan to single combat. They met in the middle of a ford and with the first blow Pwyll sent the king tumbling to the ground, wounded with a mortal blow.

"Kill me now," demanded Hafgan, "you have defeated me."

"Find someone else to slay you," answered Pwyll. "I will not do it."

"My death is at hand, then," said Hafgan. "There is now no king in Annwfn but you."

Pwyll received the homage of Hafgan's nobles, then rode away to the meadow where he had first met Arawn.

"Greetings, Pwyll," said Arawn. "How do you fare?"

"Well, my lord," he answered. "I have done as you asked of me."

"You have my thanks," said Arawn, "and my friendship forevermore."

Arawn changed Pwyll back to his previous form, then returned to his palace in Annwfn. He embraced his queen and took her to bed at once, making love with her through the night. When she asked him the next day why he had waited a year to take pleasure with her, he was amazed at the continence and friendship Pwyll had shown. He then told his queen of the whole adventure.

Pwyll meanwhile returned to Arberth in his own kingdom in Dyfed and learned that it had been ruled in justice and honor while he was gone. He revealed to his nobles what had happened during the last year and who had ruled over them in his place.

From that day forward Pwyll and Arawn were the best of friends. Because of his excellent rule over Arawn's realm for a year, Pwyll came to be known thenceforth not as Pwyll Prince of Dyfed, but as Pwyll King of Annwfn.

One time after this, Pwyll was in his court at Arberth holding a grand feast with his men. When dinner was over, Pwyll went forth to a nearby place called the Mound of Arberth.

"My lord," said one of his nobles, "it is well known that whoever sits on this mound will either suffer a grave injury or see a marvel."

"I am not afraid," said Pwyll.

As he sat there, he suddenly saw a woman in a golden silk brocade riding past on the road below him on a majestic pale white horse. To all who watched her, the horse seemed to have a slow and gentle gait.

Pwyll was struck by the beauty of the woman.

"Go down and find out who she is," said Pwyll.

One of his nobles did as he said and ran to meet her on the road, though somehow she passed him before he arrived there. He ran after her as quickly as he could, but the more he hastened, the farther away she was, even though she looked for all the world as if she were barely moving. The man returned to Pwyll and told him it was impossible to catch up to the woman.

Pwyll then sent one of his men to chase her on a horse, but again no matter how fast the man rode, he could not reach her. The woman then disappeared and Pwyll went back to his court with his men.

Pwyll returned to sit on the Mound of Arberth the next day with the swiftest horse in the kingdom. The woman on the white horse appeared again on the road, so Pwyll sent his best young rider after her on his horse. She rode at the same slow and steady pace as the day before, but the lad could not catch her, no matter how fast he pressed his mount.

Pwyll and his men returned again to his feasting hall to spend the night in song and drink, but the next day the prince returned to the mound with his own horse and saddle. He had scarcely been there a moment when the same woman appeared again riding her horse slowly on the road below him. Pwyll mounted his horse and set out after her, but he had no more success in catching her than did his two men.

At last in desperation he called out to the woman: "Madam, for the sake of the man you love most in the world, please wait for me."

She stopped then and looked at him.

"I will gladly wait for you," she said, "but it would have been easier on your horses if you had asked me earlier."

"Your pardon, my lady," said Pwyll, "but who are you and why do you travel this road?"

"I am Rhiannon daughter of Hyfaidd Hen," she replied. "I travel this road to see you. I have watched you for my whole life and love only you. I come to you to ask a favor."

"If it is in my power," Pwyll said, "I will do anything in the world for you. For I swear that of all the women in the world I have ever seen, none do I desire to be with more than you."

"My favor, then," said Rhiannon, "is that you set a date to marry me."

"The sooner, the better," said Pwyll, "and let it be wherever you like."

"Good, my lord," she answered. "Let it be a year from tonight in the court of my father Hyfaidd Hen. I will arrange a feast to be ready when you arrive. Remember to keep your promise."

"I pledge with all my heart that I will," he answered, and then they parted.

A year later, Pwyll set out from his court with a hundred horsemen for the palace of Hyfaidd Hen. The king and his daughter welcomed him warmly and sat down on either side of him for the wedding feast.

When dinner was over, a large nobleman in silk brocade came into the hall and greeted Pwyll.

"I would ask a favor of you, my lord," said the man to Pwyll.

"I will gladly do you anything you ask," he replied.

"You fool," said Rhiannon to Pwyll. "Why did you give him that answer?"

"Ah, but he did so, my lady," said the suppliant, "in the presence of the whole court."

"But what is it you want?" said Pwyll.

"Not too much," said the man, "only that you give me Rhiannon as my bride."

Pwyll sat in silence, unable to speak.

"Never has a man been more feeble-witted than you," said Rhiannon to Pwyll. "That man is Gwawl son of Clud, who has long sought to marry me. Now you must give me to him or face dishonor."

"But how can I do that?" asked Pwyll.

"Just agree," she said. "I will see that he never has me."

Pwyll agreed to give Rhiannon to Gwawl to sleep with a year from that day. But Rhiannon gave Pwyll a small bag and told him to return in a year dressed as a beggar. He was then to ask Gwawl to fill the bag with food. After this she sent Pwyll back to Dyfed.

A year later, Pwyll and his warriors returned to the court of Hyfaidd Hen for the wedding banquet of Gwawl and Rhiannon. He wore rags on his body and torn boots on his feet. After the dinner was finished and Gwawl was about to take Rhiannon to bed, Pwyll came alone before him and asked if he would fill his small bag with food.

"Of course, my good man," answered Gwawl, "that is a modest request."

He ordered the servants to fill the bag with the best food in the hall. But no matter how much they put into the bag, it was never full.

"That is a wondrous bag," said Gwawl. "Will it ever be filled?"

"No, my lord," answered Pwyll, "unless a great nobleman such as yourself stands on top of it and pushes the food down."

Gwawl rose and put his feet in the bag, but he immediately fell deep inside it. Pwyll quickly tied the bag at the top and called his men from hiding. He ordered them to beat the bag with sticks. Gwawl shouted and cried for mercy, but Pwyll and his men did not stop until he agreed not to marry Rhiannon nor seek vengeance against Pwyll. He was then released and left the court of Hyfaidd Hen forever.

Pwyll took the place of the bridegroom at the table next to Rhiannon. Afterward he went to bed with her and spent the night in pleasure and love. In the morning Pwyll arose and took his new queen back to his court at Arberth.

Pwyll and Rhiannon ruled the land of Dyfed together in happiness for the next three years, but the nobles of the kingdom began to grumble that it was not fitting for their lord to be without an heir. They urged him to take another wife so that he might have a son to rule after him. Pwyll urged them to be patient and give Rhiannon another year to become pregnant, to which they finally agreed.

Just before the year was done, Rhiannon gave birth to a son and the land was filled with great joy. Six women were brought to the palace to help the queen care for the boy. But one night while they were watching over the child, all six fell asleep. When they awoke, there was no sign of Pwyll's son.

"We will be slain by the king for neglecting our duty," they said.

"No," said one of the women. "There were puppies born in the court last night. Let us kill them and spread the blood over the queen while she still sleeps and say she killed her own son. That way we will escape punishment."

They all agreed and did so. When Rhiannon awoke she asked for her son, but the women in tears said she had killed him in the night. The queen knew this was not true, but the tale of the women spread throughout the kingdom so that Pwyll was forced to punish his wife. She was tried by the elders of the land and condemned to sit on the mounting block beside the gate of Arberth for seven years, and tell all that passed that she had murdered her own child. Moreover, she was forced to offer to carry visitors on her back like a horse from the gate to the great hall of the palace, though only rarely did a man allow himself to be carried.

At that time Teyrnon Twrf Liant ruled over the eastern Welsh kingdom of Gwent Is Coed, but he and his wife were childless. He had a beautiful mare in his household that gave birth to a foal on the eve of every May Day, but the foal would always disappear without anyone knowing what happened to it. That year, Teyrnon himself guarded the mare to discover why her foals disappeared. When the horse brought forth the foal, immediately Teyrnon saw a giant claw reaching for it from the nearby window. Teyrnon drew his sword and cut off the arm with the claw with a roar and wailing from the creature outside. He chased the monster, but when he returned because of the darkness he found a baby boy with yellow hair wrapped in silk inside the house next to the foal. Teyrnon took the child to his wife and they named him Gwri Golden-Hair. They gave him the colt born on the same night as a gift.

Teyrnon and his wife meanwhile heard the news of Rhiannon and her son. They looked closely at their child and saw that he was the very image of Pwyll, so they reluctantly took Gwri to Dyfed to return him to his parents and spare Rhiannon the shame of her punishment.

They went to the court of Pwyll and were welcomed there. Teyrnon told the king and queen all that had happened and the boy was received with great joy.

"You have greatly relieved my *pryder*, my anxiety," said Rhiannon.

"Lady," said Pwyll, "that shall be the name of our son—Pryderi son of Pwyll."

After this Pwyll swore friendship and alliance with Teyrnon and his kingdom. Pryderi grew into a fine man and in time he became lord of the seven cantrefs of Dyfed and ruled the kingdom thereafter.

BRANWEN DAUGHTER OF LLYR

When Bendigeidfran, the largest of all men, was king of Britain, one day he was sitting on the shore along with his brother Manawydan and his half-brothers Nisien and Efnisien. Nisien was a fine fellow who could bring peace between the worst of enemies, but Efnisien could make the most loving of brothers turn on each other.

As they were sitting on the shore, they saw thirteen ships on the western sea sailing swiftly toward them from Ireland.

"Tell the men of my court to arm themselves," said Bendigeidfran. "We don't know what the business is of the men on those ships."

The warriors of Bendigeidfran gathered with him on the shore to wait for the ships to draw near. They had never seen such splendid craft as these, with silk pennants streaming from their masts. They also saw a man on the lead ship turn his shield up as a sign of peace.

"May God prosper you," said Bendigeidfran when he drew up to the shore. "Whose ships are these and who rules over them?"

"My lord," their herald replied, "these are the ships of Matholwch, king of Ireland, and he is here with us. He seeks an alliance with you and the hand of your sister Branwen, the fairest lady in the world, in marriage so that our lands might be united."

"Well," said Bendigeidfran, "let him come ashore and we shall take counsel together."

There was a great feast that night in the halls of Bendigeidfran, and it was decided by the king to give Branwen to Matholwch. They set a date to meet at his castle at Aberffraw so that Matholwch might sleep with his bride.

The next day Efnisien, who had not been at the feast, saw the horses of the guests outside the hall and asked whose they were. When he was told they belonged to Matholwch king of Ireland and that his sister Branwen had been given to Matholwch as his bride, Efnisien was furious.

"He gave away my own sister without my permission? This is a great insult to me which shall not stand."

Efnisien then took his blade and cut the lips of the king's horses to the teeth and their eyelids to the bones. He also cut off their ears and tails so that they would be disfigured and no use could be made of them.

When word of this mutilation came to Matholwch, the king of Ireland was angry and disgraced. He gathered his nobles and made for their ships to sail back to their island. Bendigeidfran heard what had happened and raced to meet him before he could board.

"Why have you done this?" asked Matholwch.

"It was not my doing," swore Bendigeidfran. "My half-brother Efnisien did this foul deed. I would punish him gravely for it, but he is my own blood. However, I shall make all right by you and give you fine new horses along with your honor-price in silver and gold. I will also give you a cauldron of rare property, so that if you cast a dead warrior into it, the next day he shall live again, except that he shall not be able to speak. I acquired it in your own land from Llassar Llaes Gyfnewid and his giantess wife Cymidei Cymeinfoll."

"I know them," said Matholwch, "I drove them out of my land. But I welcome the gifts and would make peace with you on your terms."

When the gifts had been given to Matholwch, he took his bride Branwen and returned home with the blessings of Bendigeidfran.

In Ireland there was great rejoicing and a warm welcome was made for Branwen. All the nobles of the island came to pay their respects and none went away without a gift of a brooch or a ring from Branwen. After a proper time a son was born to her and the name he was given was Gwern son of Matholwch.

But in the second year a murmuring arose among the men of Ireland over the humiliation Matholwch had received in Britain with the disfiguring of his horses. The warriors and brothers of Matholwch reproached him until he could have no peace without taking action. The vengeance he took was to drive his wife Branwen from his chamber and force her to cook as a lowly servant for his court. He also had his butcher come with bloody hands each day and give her a blow on the ears.

Matholwch gave orders that no one from Ireland was to go to Britain lest the kinsmen of Branwen discover what shame had befallen her.

During that year of punishment, Branwen raised a starling chick at her kneading trough. She taught the bird speech and told it what to look for to recognize her brother Bendigeidfran. Then she wrote a note describing her dishonor and attached it to the bird's wing, after which she sent it across the sea to Britain.

The starling came at last to the court of Bendigeidfran and landed on his shoulder. He recognized that this was no ordinary bird and saw the note on its wing. He read it and immediately mustered all his warriors from throughout Britain, including his brothers and half-brothers, along with Pryderi the son of Pwyll and Rhiannon.

In those ancient days the sea between Ireland and Britain was not deep, so Bendigeidfran walked across the bottom with his head just above the waves as his ships followed him.

The swineherds of Matholwch were standing on a hill in Ireland when they saw a strange sight coming toward them from across the sea. They rushed to their king and described what they had seen: "My lord, we saw a large mountain next to a forest moving across the sea. There was a high ridge on the mountain with two lakes beside it on either side."

Matholwch sent for Branwen and asked her what might be coming to them from Britain.

"It is the men of my land coming to rescue me," she said. "The forest is the masts of their ships and the mountain is my brother, whom no ship could ever hold. The ridge they saw was his nose and the two lakes his eyes."

Matholwch was in a panic at this news and ordered his men to retreat west across the great River Shannon. He destroyed every bridge over the river so that Bendigeidfran and his warriors might not reach him.

When Bendigeidfran came to the banks of the Shannon, his men told him there was no way across, for all the bridges had been destroyed.

"Then I myself will be a bridge," he answered.

After he had lain down across the river, planks were put on his back so that his men could cross. Then the messengers of Matholwch came swiftly to him to ask for peace.

"My lord," they said, "Matholwch regrets his actions against your sister and will make amends. He abdicates his throne immediately in favor of his son, your nephew Gwern, son of your sister Branwen. The king moreover places himself in your hands."

Bendigeidfran sent the messengers back to Matholwch while he considered the king's offer. But the counselors of Matholwch urged the king to prepare a trap for Bendigeidfran. They told him to build a special house for Bendigeidfran, for up till then no building had been able to hold him. They would then hide warriors there to slay him when he came into the house.

The Irish built the house, but Bendigeidfran's half-brother Efnisien entered it first to make sure all was ready. He saw along the walls a hundred hide bags each hanging on a peg. Inside each one, the Irish lords had hidden an armed warrior to burst forth and kill Bendigeidfran at the right moment.

"What is in these bags?" Efnisien asked his hosts.

"Only flour," they answered.

Efnisien then went to each bag and squeezed it in turn so that the heads and brains of the Irish warriors were crushed.

When he had finished, the Irish king and noblemen entered on one side of the house while Bendigeidfran and the British warriors came in the other side with a roaring fire between them. Peace was declared and the kingship of Ireland was given to Gwern, son of Branwen and nephew of Bendigeidfran.

Then Efnisien arose and stood next to his nephew Gwern.

"I swear," he said, "that what I am about to do will seem an outrage, even to my own family."

He then grabbed Gwern by the feet and before anyone could stop him he thrust him into the fire. Branwen leapt up and tried to save him, but it was too late. The warriors of Ireland shouted for blood and seized their weapons. The men of Britain likewise took up arms, so that a great slaughter began which lasted for days.

During the battle the Irishmen kindled a fire beneath the magical cauldron of rebirth they had received as a gift from Bendigeidfran. Whenever a man on their side was slain, they threw his corpse into the cauldron so that the next day he was alive again, though unable to speak.

Efnisien saw what the Irish were doing and hid himself among their corpses. Then when he was thrown into the cauldron, he stretched out his limbs and shattered the vessel, though it meant his death as well.

Bendigeidfran was wounded in the battle by a poisoned spear. He fled from the house with his sister Branwen, his brother Manawydan, Pryderi the son of Pwyll, and five other of his men who were still alive.

Mortally wounded, Bendigeidfran told his men to cut off his head, then carry it to the white mount in London to be buried so that it might protect the island from invasion. His men did as he asked and decapitated their king, then crossed the sea back to Britain.

When they landed on the shore, the heart of Branwen broke and she died. They made a grave for her there and traveled on to Harlech, the court of Bendigeidfran. In their grief and weariness they began to feast and drink, so that they forgot their sorrow. The head of Bendigeidfran spoke and laughed and was as good a companion as when he had been alive. The magical birds of Rhiannon also came to them there and sang, so that they forgot their sorrows and lost all sense of time, though seven years passed.

At the end of seven years, they set out again to go to Gwales, a great castle that looked out across the water to Cornwall. But the door that faced Cornwall was kept closed. They feasted and drank with the head of Bendigeidfran until they lost track of the passing of time, though eighty years passed by.

One day, however, one of the men opened the door of the hall facing Cornwall—and all the memories of sorrow and loss returned to the company. They immediately set out for London and buried the head of Bendigeidfran as he had instructed, so that he might serve his land as a protector even in death.

MANAWYDAN SON OF LLYR

After the companions of Bendigeidfran buried the head of their king in London, Manawydan, the brother of the king, despaired because his brother was dead and another king now ruled Britain in his place.

Pryderi son of Pwyll spoke to him: "Lord, I hold in my possession the seven cantrefs of Dyfed, the finest land in all of Britain. My wife Cigfa is there with my mother Rhiannon, who is still beautiful. Come with me and I will give her to you to be your wife."

This seemed good to Manawydan, so they went to Arberth, the chief court of Dyfed. Rhiannon welcomed them and prepared a feast for all. Pryderi told her of his plan to give her to Manawydan in marriage, and she was well pleased with the idea. When the wedding was over and

Rhiannon had slept with Manawydan, Pryderi and his wife Cigfa joined them on a circuit of Dyfed to see their kingdom and take their pleasure in hunting.

When they returned home, they went one evening to the Mound of Arberth with their lords and ladies. As they sat there, a thick mist arose so that they could not see each other. When the mist lifted, there was no one the four could see except each other. All the members of the court along with all the people, cattle, and homes of the land had vanished. Only the buildings of the palace of Arberth remained, but those were empty.

"Dear Lord God," said Manawydan, "where has everyone gone? Let us go and search the land for them."

And so the four companions searched the land of Dyfed far and wide but could not find a single soul.

The two couples ate and drank in the court of Arberth for many days until there was nothing left, then they took to hunting and fishing to feed themselves. They passed a year in this way until one day Manawydan called them together.

"We cannot live like this," he said. "Let us go to England and take up a craft."

So they traveled to England and found a town named Henffordd filled with people. They took up the craft of making saddles there. Manawydan had never done such work before, but he was soon making the best saddles in all the land and driving the other saddlers out of business. The craftsmen of the town then met together and decided to kill Manawydan and his companions. When Pryderi heard of this, he advised his friends to fight.

"I swear to God," he said, "we should kill these peasants who plot against us."

"No," said Manawydan, "it will only cause trouble. Let us go to another town and take up a different trade."

The four of them then went to a different town and became makers of shields. But their shields were the best anyone had ever seen so that no one would any longer buy from the other armorers. These craftsmen thus plotted to kill them as well.

"I will not take this from such villains," declared Pryderi. "We should fight."

"No," said Manawydan, "I don't want to upset anyone. Let us move on and begin a different trade."

And so they went to yet another English town and became shoemakers. But in a short time no one would buy shoes from the other shoemakers of the town since those of Manawydan and his companions were so much better than the rest. These men also decided to kill the newcomers.

"This is too much," said Pryderi. "Now we must stand up against these thieving churls."

"No," said Manawydan. "Let us leave England and return to Dyfed. Perhaps the people of the land have returned by now."

The four companions journeyed back to Dyfed, but when they arrived they saw that nothing had changed. There were no people or cattle or houses in the whole land. Thus the four stayed again in the palace at Arberth and hunted every day for their food.

One morning as Manawydan and Pryderi were hunting with their hounds, the dogs ran ahead of them and went into a thicket of trees. Soon, however, they ran out in a panic. A great white wild boar followed them and led the men on a chase to a lofty fortress they had never seen before. Pryderi was determined to explore this great structure, but Manawydan urged him not to enter for he feared the power of magic. Pryderi nonetheless entered the gates and found at the center of the courtyard a marble slab and golden basin secured by four chains that reached up to the sky. As soon as Pryderi stood on the marble slab and touched the basin, his hands and feet were stuck and he could not speak.

Manawydan waited for him outside the fortress until evening, then returned to the castle at Arberth.

"Where is my son?" Rhiannon asked.

Manawydan told her all that had happened.

"God knows," said Rhiannon, "that you have been a poor friend."

She then rushed through the woods to the lofty fortress and found Pryderi stuck to the basin and mute. She tried to free him, but she too became trapped and stricken with silence. Then a mist descended on the whole fortress and it disappeared.

When Manawydan learned what had happened, he despaired. He swore to Pryderi's wife Cigfa that he would watch over her and would never take advantage of her.

He began to hunt again and planted a field of wheat nearby so that they might have bread. But one day he saw that the stalks of grain had been broken and eaten by a hoard of mice. He thus devised a trap for the mice and caught one of their number who was too large to escape. He brought the creature to Cigfa.

"I caught this thief stealing our grain," he said. "Tomorrow I will hang the villain."

"That hardly seems worth the trouble," Cigfa answered.

"Still, this thief will pay," he said.

The next day he went to the Mound of Arberth and built a small gallows. He was getting ready to hang the mouse when he saw a scholar approaching on the road. It had been seven years since he had seen anyone besides the four of them in the land of Dyfed.

"Greetings, lord," said the scholar. "May I ask what you're doing?"

"Hanging a mouse who is a thief," said Manawydan.

"That hardly seems like a business worthy of a nobleman," the man said. "For the sake of your honor, let me ransom the creature for a pound."

"No," said Manawydan. "This mouse must pay for the crimes of its fellows."

The scholar then rode away, but soon Manawydan saw a priest approaching.

"Greetings, my lord," said the priest. "You seem very busy with the small vermin I see before you. What are you doing?"

"Hanging someone who stole from me," said Manawydan.

"This is beneath you," said the priest. "I will give you three pounds for the mouse to save your honor."

"No," he said. "This thief must die."

The priest rode away, but soon Manawydan saw a bishop and his entourage approaching on the road.

"May God bless you," said the bishop. "What sort of work are you doing here?"

"Hanging a thief," said Manawydan.

"It's a good thing I came along, then," said the bishop. "I would not see a lord such as yourself gain a reputation for foolishness. I will pay you seven pounds in ransom for the fat little mouse."

"No," said Manawydan.

"Twenty-four pounds, then," said the bishop.

"That is not enough," said Manawydan.

"What is it you will accept, then," asked the bishop, "to let this poor creature go?"

"You must free Rhiannon and Pryderi," answered Manawydan. "Then you must lift the curse from this land."

The bishop was silent for a time, then he spoke: "It will be done. Now, for the love of God, please free this mouse."

"First," said Manawydan, "tell me who you are and why you did this."

"I am Llwyd son of Cil Coed, brother of Gwawl," he said, "whom Pryderi's father Pwyll trapped in a bag and beat in Annwfn. I have done all this for the honor of my family and to avenge my brother. That mouse is my pregnant wife. We came in the form of mice to destroy your crops. But everything will be restored as it was and we will leave you in peace forevermore."

Manawydan then gave the mouse to the bishop.

Pryderi and Rhiannon suddenly appeared before them, while all the people, cattle, and houses of the land were restored. Pryderi embraced Manawydan and told him he had been kept as a servant by Llwyd and his mother Rhiannon had been forced to wear the collar of an ass around her neck and carry hay for his court. But all was made right in the end and the four companions lived in peace thereafter in the castle of Arberth in Dyfed.

MATH SON OF MATHONWY

When Pryderi son of Pwyll ruled over Dyfed, the lord of Gwynedd in the north of Wales was Math son of Mathonwy. Unless he was engaged in a war, this king could only live while his feet rested in the lap of a maiden. The virgin who held his feet at that time was Goewin daughter of Pebin, and she was the most beautiful young woman in all the land. The two nephews of Math, Gilfaethwy and Gwydion the sons of Dôn, were valued advisers in the retinue of their uncle the king.

Gilfaethwy fell in love with the maiden Goewin, but as she was always with his uncle he could never be alone with her. His health began to fail and he grew more pale each day as his love consumed him. His brother Gwydion realized what was wrong and vowed to help him get the virgin alone. To do so he knew he must start a war.

Gwydion went to Math and told him that Pwyll, the lord of Dyfed, had brought a new kind of creature to their land called a pig, the flesh of which was sweeter than beef. He had received these pigs as a gift from his friend Arawn the king of Annwfn. Gwydion told his uncle that they should get the pigs for themselves.

"How can we do this without starting a war?" asked Math.

"Leave it to me," said Gwydion.

He and his brother Gilfaethwy disguised themselves as bards and went with ten other men to the court of Pryderi. This lord welcomed them and Gwydion entertained them with songs, for he was a great poet. When he was done, Pryderi was pleased and asked what reward he might like. Gwydion asked for his pigs.

"I cannot give them to you," said Pryderi, "for they are of great value to my people."

"Then let us strike a bargain," said Gwydion. "I will trade you twelve horses with golden saddles and twelve fine hunting dogs with golden collars in exchange for the pigs. You may then tell your people that you exchanged them for something even better."

Pryderi agreed to this arrangement, so that night Gwydion took wild mushrooms from the forest and transformed them through his magic into the horses and hounds he had promised. The next day they gave the animals to Pryderi and rode swiftly from the court with the pigs.

"My friends," said Gwydion to his companions, "we must make haste. The enchantment I placed on the mushrooms will last only for a day."

They drove the pigs quickly back to their court in Gwynedd with the army of Pryderi close behind them. Math was angry at what they had done, but he received them and mustered his own troops to face the forces of Pryderi. He rose from the throne and took his feet away from the lap of the maiden Goewin, for he was now at war.

When Math had led his troops out of the castle in Gwynedd, Gwydion and his brother Gilfaethwy went to his chamber. Gilfaethwy took the virgin Goewin by force and raped her there.

A great massacre befell the armies of both Math and Pryderi so that countless men from both sides perished in battle. At last Gwydion came to the king and proposed to meet Pryderi as his champion in single combat, as he was the man who had wronged him. Pryderi agreed, but Gwydion used his magic and enchantments against the good king so that Pryderi son of Pwyll was slain.

Peace was made and the armies of the south returned home without their lord. Math also returned to his own court and called Goewin so that he might rest his feet in the maiden's lap.

"My lord," she said, "you must seek a new virgin to hold your feet, for I have been shamed. Your nephews Gwydion and Gilfaethwy forced their way into your chamber and Gilfaethwy raped me there in your bed."

Math consoled the girl and declared that she would be his lawful wife and queen from that day forward. Then he sent for his nephews.

Gwydion and Gilfaethwy came before the king to submit themselves for punishment. Math arose and struck them with his staff of enchantment. At once Gwydion became a stag and Gilfaethwy a female deer.

"Since you two have been beasts," Math said to them, "I curse you with the punishment of being in the shapes and manners of animals for a cycle of the seasons. You shall be driven in shame to mate with each other and bear an offspring. Return to me here in one year."

At the end of that year, the hounds of the court were heard barking at something outside. The king looked from his window and saw a stag and a hind with a fawn between them. He rose and went down to them with his staff of enchantment.

"The one of you that has been a female this year," he told them, "shall now become a male for the year ahead. In the manner of the pigs you are you shall breed again and produce an offspring. Return here again in a year."

He struck them with his staff so that Gwydion, who had been a stag, became a sow, and Gilfaethwy, who had been a hind, became a boar. The two them ran off into the forest. Math took their fawn and changed him into a little boy, named him Hyddwn, and had him baptized. He was raised after that in the court of the king.

At the end of the year the hounds of Math's court began to bark. The king went forth outside the gate and found a wild boar there with a sow and a good-sized piglet. He took his magic staff and struck the boar, changing it into a wolf bitch, and the sow he changed into a wolf.

"Let your nature once again match your spirits," said the king. "You shall go out into the wild and breed with each other again. In one year, return here."

The two animals that were Gilfaethwy and his brother Gwydion then ran off into the woods. Math touched the piglet they left behind with his staff and changed him into a boy, then gave him the name Hychdwn. He had him baptized and raised him in his own household.

At the end of the year the dogs of court began to howl again. Math went to the gate and saw there a wolf, his mate, and a young cub. The king touched the cub with his staff and changed him into a handsome young boy, to whom he gave the name Bleiddwn. He then struck the two wolves with his staff and changed them back into their human shape.

"Men," said the king, "you have been punished enough. You have borne the shame of bearing each other's child. Go now, bathe and put on clothing, then join me in my hall."

When Gilfaethwy and Gwydion were properly arrayed, they came to the king.

"Advise me," he said to them. "I need a new maiden to hold my feet. Who should it be?"

"Lord," said Gwydion, "the choice is easy. It should be Arianrhod your niece, daughter of your sister."

The king called for the girl.

"Are you a virgin?" he asked.

"I do not know that I may not be," she said.

Then he took his magic staff and laid it on the floor.

"Step over this," he told the girl. "If you are not a maiden, I will know."

The girl stepped over the rod and suddenly a fine, yellow-haired baby boy fell from her womb. The girl was ashamed and ran toward the door, but as she went another small thing fell from her womb onto the floor. Before anyone could see, Gwydion took it and wrapped it in a bundle of brocaded silk, then hid it away in a chest at the foot of his bed.

The king picked up the yellow-haired boy.

"Well," he said, "I will have this one baptized and his name shall be Dylan."

As soon as the boy was baptized, he made for the nearby sea and leapt into the waves. His form changed and he began to swim better than any creature of the ocean. There he remained.

One day after this, Gwydion was lying in his bed when he heard a cry from the chest at his feet. He opened it and unwrapped the silk brocade. There he saw a baby boy crying and flailing his arms. Gwydion found a woman to nurse the child and he raised the boy himself, loving him as his own son, though the child did not have a name.

Gwydion and the boy went together on a journey to the home of the child's mother, Arianrhod. She was happy to see Gwydion but was filled with shame when she saw the boy.

"Why did you bring him here?" she asked.

"You have no reason to be ashamed of such a fine lad," he replied.

"You disgrace me nonetheless," she said. "I therefore put a curse on him that he shall not have a name until I give him one, though I never will."

Still," said Gwydion, "the boy will have a name and it will be you who gives it to him."

Gwydion went away from the home of Arianrhod in anger. The next day he went down to the shore and began to gather seaweed. With his magic he turned the seaweed into a small boat and conjured excellent leather, which he sewed into fine shoes. He put the boy in the ship and they sailed to the home of Arianrhod. While they were in the ship, he changed their appearance so that they became shoemakers.

From a window at her home Arianrhod asked one of her servants who the men were who had arrived by sea.

"They are shoemakers," said the maid.

"Go and see what sort of work they do," said Arianrhod. "Take the measurements of my feet. If their work is good, have them make me a pair of shoes."

The maid came and was impressed by the quality of their craftsmanship. She asked Gwydion to make a pair of shoes for her mistress, but he deliberately made them too large.

"These do not fit," said Arianrhod to her maid. "Have him make me another pair."

Gwydion did so, but this time he made them too small. When the maid returned to Gwydion to demand another pair, he told her that her mistress must come herself so that he could measure her feet himself. When she arrived, she greeted the shoemaker but did not know who he really was.

At that moment a wren perched on the deck of Gwydion's little boat. The boy cast a stone at it and struck it on the leg.

"That was a fine cast," said Arianrhod. "It is with a skillful hand (*llaw gyffes*) that the fair-haired one (*lleu*) has hit the bird."

"Well," said Gwydion. "you have given him a name. From now on he shall be called Lleu Llaw Gyffes."

At that moment the boat and all its belongings changed back into seaweed.

"That was an evil trick, Gwydion," said Arianrhod. "But you shall not defeat me. I now curse the boy so that he shall never take up arms until I give him weapons myself—and I never will."

"I swear by God himself," declared Gwydion, "that you will give him arms."

Gwydion returned home and trained the boy in every type of horsemanship. When the lad was ready to be a warrior, Gwydion took him back to the stronghold of his mother. Before they arrived, however, he changed their shape and appearance so that they seemed to be bards on a circuit around the country.

Arianrhod welcomed them and hosted them that night at a feast in which they entertained the guests with song and story. The next morning Gwydion used his magic to create the sound of trumpets and turmoil, as if the castle were being attacked by an army.

Arianrhod rushed to their chamber and asked them to help defend her palace. She gave them arms and helped the boy dress for war. It was then that Gwydion smiled.

"Lady," he said, "have your men stand down and put away their weapons. There is no army storming your gates."

At that he caused the roar of battle to cease and changed their appearance. Arianrhod was furious.

"You have made a fool of me twice," she exclaimed, "but I will have my revenge. I curse him and swear he will never have a wife from any race of women on this earth."

Gwydion and the lad left her then and went to the hall of Math the king. They told him all that had happened.

"Well," said Math, "we will find a wife for this young man in any case."

Math and Gwydion then took flowers and formed the fairest and most beautiful woman anyone had ever seen. They baptized her and named her Blodeuedd, then gave her to Lleu to sleep with. Math also gave him a fine piece of land to rule over with his bride.

One day Blodeuedd was visiting the castle of Math with her husband Lleu when she saw a handsome man hunting with his retinue. She asked who he was and was told he was Gronw Pebyr, the lord of Penllyn. Blodeuedd invited him to dine with her that night. When she gazed at him her whole body was filled with longing and love. After all the household was asleep that evening, she went to his chamber and the two made love together until the morning.

The same thing happened the next two nights, then Blodeuedd told Gronw Pebyr that they must kill her husband Lleu so that they could be together.

"My lady," he said, "how can that be done? He is protected by great enchantments."

"I will discover his weakness," she said, "so that you can slay him."

Blodeuedd went to her husband in tears the next day.

"My lord," she cried, "I am so afraid that you might die before me. I could not bear to lose you."

"Do not fear, my dear," he consoled her. "It is not easy to kill me."

"But I cannot be at peace unless I am sure you are safe," she said. "Tell me how hard it would be for someone to slay you."

He then assured her that to kill him a man would have to spend a year working on a poison spear that could only be shaped while people were at prayers on Sunday. He then revealed that he could not be hurt in a house or outside, on a horse or on foot. To kill him a man would have to make a bath for him on the riverbank and construct a wood frame above the tub. Then he himself would have to stand with one foot on a billy goat and the other on the edge of the tub while a man cast the poisoned spear at him.

"Well, thank God for that," she said. "That is not likely to happen."

She sent word to Gronw Pebyr telling him everything her husband Lleu had said. When the year had passed, Blodeuedd spoke to her husband again: "My lord, I was thinking about what you told me a year ago concerning the manner in which you could be killed. I cannot conceive of what you have said. Would you show me what you meant?"

Lleu was gracious to his wife and built a structure on the riverbank above a tub. Then he found a billy goat to stand near as he bathed in the tub. When he was finished, he stood with one foot on the tub and another on the goat.

Blodeuedd had sent word to Gronw to hide nearby with the spear. Just as Lleu mounted the tub, Gronw cast his spear at him so that he was struck through his side. Lleu let forth a horrible scream and took to the air in the form of an eagle, flying away until he was no longer seen. Gronw then took possession of his kingdom and shared the bed of Blodeuedd.

The news of what had befallen Lleu reached Math and Gwydion.

"Lord," Gwydion said to Math, "I will never rest until I find Lleu."

Gwydion set forth and searched all the land, but he could not find Lleu. At last he came to the home of a peasant in the forest and stayed the night there. The man kept a fine sow that he let out into the woods every morning to forage for food. Gwydion was struck by the eagerness of the sow to leave her pen, and so followed her the next morning into the forest. He found her under an oak tree feeding on rotten flesh and maggots.

When he looked up into the tree, he saw a gravely wounded eagle in the branches. When the eagle stirred, the rotten flesh would fall from its body onto the ground and the sow would eat it. He knew then that the eagle was Lleu.

Then Gwydion began to sing:

There's an oak that grows in the woods
that holds a prince in its branches.
If I sing the truth,
Lleu will come down to me.

The eagle flew down from the branches and rested its head in Gwydion's lap. He touched the bird with his magic rod and the eagle changed back into Lleu. But never had anyone seen a man in more wretched shape, with scarcely any flesh remaining on his body.

Gwydion took him to the palace of Math where they cared for Lleu and restored him to strength.

At the end of a year, Gwydion mustered his men and went to the castle of Blodeuedd. The woman made from flowers fled, but Gwydion caught her at last. He did not kill her, but turned her into an owl, a bird hated by all others, whose face is in the form of a flower.

As for her lover Gronw Pebyr, he sent a message to Lleu suing for peace. Instead of land or gold, Lleu demanded the man face him on the shore of the same river where he had struck him with a spear. There Lleu said he would cast a spear at Gronw Pebyr in return.

"My lord," said Gronw, "the evil I did was the fault of a woman. I will face your spear, but let me place a stone between me and the blow."

Lleu granted his request, but when he cast the spear at Gronw, it broke through the stone and pierced his body so that he died.

Lleu then took possession of his lands and ruled thereafter in justice and peace.

WELSH STORIES AND SAGAS

THERE ARE MANY OTHER EARLY Welsh stories that continue the themes found in the *Mabinogi*. Like those stories, these are set in the sophisticated life of the medieval Welsh courts, but they also draw on elements that stretch into the distant past of Celtic mythology. The tale of *Culhwch and Olwen* also stands out as one of the earliest stories of King Arthur.

LLUDD AND LLEUELYS

Once there was a king of all Britain, Beli Mawr, who had four sons, named Lludd, Caswallawn, Ninniaw, and Lleuelys. When Beli died, his kingdom passed to Lludd as the eldest son. Lludd was a worthy ruler who rebuilt the walls of his capital city with countless towers and filled it with excellent homes for his people. He loved this city more than all others in his kingdom. It was named for him as Caer Lludd, and then Caer Llundein, but in time the people began to call it London.

The favorite brother of Lludd was Lleuelys, who was a wise and thoughtful man. When Lleuelys heard that the king of France had died without an heir save for a daughter, he went to that land to ask for the crown and was given it along with the king's daughter in marriage.

After a number of years, the island of Britain suffered three terrible oppressions. The first was the coming of an evil people known as the Coraniaid, who could hear every word and whisper spoken throughout the land so that no one could ever do them harm. The second oppression was a cry that came on the eve of every May Day that terrified every creature and left all the women and cattle of the island barren. The third oppression was that once a year all the food of the king's court would mysteriously vanish except for what his nobles could eat on that single night.

Lludd did not know what to do to save his kingdom, so he took a ship and went to his brother Lleuelys to seek his advice. His brother met him on the sea and the two took counsel on what they might do to save Britain. They spoke through a long brass horn so that the Coraniaid could not hear them, but their words were confused by a demon who lived in the horn so that they could not understand each other. Lleuelys then took wine and poured it through the horn so that the demon was driven away.

The wise Lleuelys then advised his brother on how to drive away the oppressions that plagued his land. Lleuelys said to invite all his people and the Coraniaid to a great assembly. He should then mix into everyone's drink a powder made from mice which Lleuelys would give him to breed. The powder would not harm his own people, but it would poison the Coraniaid so that they all would die.

Lleuelys told his brother that the second oppression was a British dragon uttering a horrible scream as it fought a foreign dragon. The way to stop the terrible sound was to measure the length and breadth of Britain to find the exact center of the country, then dig a hole there and fill it with mead covered by a silk brocade. He would then see the two dragons fighting in the forms of various animals. When they assumed the shape of dragons and were tired of fighting in the air, they would fall in the shape of pigs onto the silk covering and sink to the bottom of the hole. They would then drink all the mead and fall asleep, so that they could be put in a stone chest and hidden in the ground. As long as they remained there, no oppression would come to Britain from beyond its borders.

The third oppression was a powerful magician who put everyone to sleep with music and stole all the food from the court. Lludd was to wait for him on the appointed day in a vat of cold water to keep himself awake, then defeat the magician in a fight with swords.

Lludd returned to his kingdom and did all his brother had said. The Coraniaid came to the feast and drank the poisoned water so that they all died. The center of the country was found and the dragons were captured, so that they were held in a stone chest ever after. Finally the magician was defeated when Lludd alone kept awake in the vat of cold water, and was forced to restore all that he had taken.

Thus did Lludd ward off the three oppressions from the Isle of Britain and ruled the land in peace for the rest of his life.

GWION BACH AND TALIESIN

In the days when Arthur ruled over Britain, there was a nobleman of the land named Tegid Foel, who had a wife named Ceridwen who was skilled in magic, enchantment, and divination. She and Tegid had a son who was terribly ugly. They named him Morfran, the Great Crow, but also called him Afagddu, or Utter Darkness.

Ceridwen loved and pitied her son, so she determined to give him the gift of prophecy to counter his hideous looks. She discovered that by certain herbs and cunning she could make a potion that would give him this special knowledge. The mixture had to be cooked in a great cauldron of water for a year and a day. At the end of that time, three drops containing the virtue of prophecy would spring forth from the cauldron.

Ceridwen found an old blind man to stir the cauldron for her. This man was led about by a small boy named Gwion Bach, who also fed kindling into the fire beneath the cauldron.

As the time neared at last, Ceridwen placed her son beside the cauldron so that the three drops would land on him when the potion was done. Then, exhausted from her labor, she sat down to rest.

She was asleep at the moment the three drops sprung from the cauldron. When they did, Gwion Bach shoved Morfran out of the way so that the drops landed on him instead. Then the cauldron uttered a terrible cry and shattered. Ceridwen awoke from her sleep and saw that little Gwion had received the gift of the drops instead of her son. She determined to destroy the boy and took out after him as he fled from her house. Through the power of magic he had received, Gwion turned himself into a hare to escape Ceridwen, but she changed into a greyhound and chased him. From place to place they ran across the country, each turning into different creatures along the way. At last Gwion ran into a barn and changed himself into a grain of wheat to hide. But Ceridwen knew what he had done and changed herself into a black hen and swallowed the lad.

She carried him nine months inside of her until she gave birth to him as a baby boy. When she saw him, she could not bring herself to harm him, so she wrapped the child in swaddling clothes and placed him into a hide-covered basket, then put him out to sea.

Forty years later, there was a wealthy lord named Gwyddno Garanhir who had a kind but spendthrift son named Elphin. When Gwyddno's money at last ran out, his son was forced to end his days of lavish spending. But his father did grant that he could have all the salmon caught in his fishing weir on All Hallows' Eve. When that day came, Elphin went to the weir and saw only a single salmon there. Elphin was in despair, but he saw in the weir also a small basket covered in hide. He took his knife and cut open the hide only to see the shining forehead of a baby boy.

"Behold, such a radiant forehead" (*tal iesin*), said Elphin. And thus the boy's name became Taliesin.

Elphin took the basket with the child and put it on his horse. Then the baby began to sing:

Fair Elphin, do not weep.
No fish caught in Gwyddno's weir
was ever as good as tonight.
Though I am small, I am gifted.

When Elphin reached his home, he gave the boy to his wife to care for. She raised him with great love and affection.

From the day that Taliesin came into his home, the fortunes of Elphin increased and he prospered greatly. He was honored by the nobles of the land and invited to the court of the king Maelgwn to celebrate the feast of Christmas. While he was their, the men of the king curried his royal favor by extolling Maelgwn and saying he was more blessed in every way—his power, his warriors, his virtuous wife, his poets—than any man of the land.

Elphin joined in praising the king, but then he boasted: "Indeed, Maelgwn in blessed in every way more than all, except regarding his wife and his poets. My wife is more chaste than any woman of the land and no poet can compare to my bard Taliesin."

The king was angry when he heard what Elphin said and was determined to prove him wrong. Maelgwn threw Elphin into prison and sent his son Rhun to test the faithfulness of Elphin's wife. For it was said that no man in the world was more lusty or charming than Rhun. No woman or maiden ever came away from an evening with him with her virtue intact.

But as Rhun was hastening to Elphin's home to despoil his wife, Taliesin already knew what was coming to pass. He told the lady what was planned for her and urged her to switch clothes and places with a fair young housekeeper of their manor. The wife did this and even gave her finest ring to the serving girl to wear. Then she placed the girl in her own chamber and waited on her.

When Rhun arrived and was welcomed for supper in the lady's chamber, Rhun greeted her pleasantly and beguiled the maid with his charm and seductive talk. Rhun made sure the young woman drank too much, even giving her a powder to make sure she didn't wait. He cut off her finger with the ring and wrapped it in his handkerchief. Then he had his way with the young woman and left.

Rhun returned to his father the king and told him all that had happened, while Elphin was forced to stand nearby to listen. Maelgwn declared that Elphin was a fool to think his wife was chaste when the proof of her infidelity was the ring in front of them.

"With your permission, my lord," said Elphin, "I think I can prove you wrong. This finger is rough from kneading dough and the nail is untrimmed—not like my wife's fingers at all. In addition, this finger is so large that the ring was forced over the knuckle, unlike my wife's fingers, which are fine and dainty. The woman your son seduced was not my wife."

The king was so angry at Elphin that he threw him back in prison until he at least made good on his second boast—that his poet was the greatest bard in the land.

Taliesin knew all that had passed, so he made his way to Maelgwn's court. When he arrived in the busy hall, he found a quiet place in the corner by the door to sit without attracting attention. When the chief bards of the kingdom filed into the hall, Taliesin put his finger to his puckered lips and whispered a sound like *blerum blerum* as they passed.

The poets all approached the king on his throne and bowed before him, but when they tried to sing his praise, the only sound that came from their mouths was *blerum blerum*. The king thought they had been drinking and ordered one of his nobles to strike the chief bard over the head with a silver platter so that he fell on his backside before the whole court.

"My lord, it is not our fault!" cried the chief bard. "We sound like fools because some evil spirit in the guise of a man is sitting in the corner there and has confounded us."

The king ordered Taliesin brought before him to be questioned.

"Who are you?" asked Maelgwn.

And Taliesin answered in song:

Chief poet to Elphin am I.
My home is the land of the angels.
I was with the Lord in the heavens
when Lucifer fell.
I was in the ark with Noah
and survived the fall of Troy.
I was atop the cross
of the merciful son of God.
Johannes the prophet called me Merlin,
but now kings call me Taliesin.
I am the chief poet of the West.
Now release Elphin from his chains.

A mighty rushing wind then swept into the court so that the king and the people feared the walls would fall down on them. Maelgwn therefore ordered that Elphin be released from prison immediately.

Taliesin then told Elphin to wager with the king that he had the fastest horse in the land, which his master did. When the day of the race came, Taliesin came there with twenty-four sticks of holly, one for each of the horses in the race save for Elphin's. He told the lad riding his master's horse to take the sticks and strike each of the horses on the rump with a single stick as he overtook them, then throw it on the ground. Taliesin also told him to throw his cap on the ground when he finished the race. The boy did as he was told, threw his cap on the ground, and won the race for Elphin, with the king and his nobles conceding defeat.

When everyone had gone, Taliesin told Elphin to dig where the cap lay on the ground. When he did, he found a huge cauldron of gold there.

"Elphin," said Taliesin, "here is your payment for saving me from the sea and raising me to this day."

After this, Elphin was highly honored among the nobility of the land, while Taliesin was celebrated ever after as the greatest bard in Britain.

CULHWCH AND OLWEN

Cilydd son of Celyddon Wledig wanted to marry a woman as noble as himself. He set his heart on Goleuddydd daughter of Anlawdd Wledig, and she agreed to marry him. After their wedding she became pregnant, but at the time of the conception she went insane and wandered the country avoiding people. When it was time to deliver the child, her senses returned and she found that she was near a pigsty with a swineherd and his pigs. Goleuddydd was so frightened of the pigs that she immediately gave birth. The swineherd took the woman and the baby to the court of her husband Cilydd. The child was named Culhwch the pig boy because of where he had been born. But he was of noble blood and a cousin to King Arthur himself. The boy was then given out to a noble couple in fosterage, as was the custom.

After the birth of Culhwch, his mother Goleuddydd became ill and knew that she would die. She called her husband Cilydd to her and told him that he should remarry when she was gone, but to wait until a briar was growing on her grave. When he left, Goleuddydd summoned her tutor and told him to tend her grave so that nothing would ever grow on it. Then she died.

Every morning after his wife's death, the king sent a boy to examine her grave to see if anything was growing there. However, the queen's tutor faithfully tended the grave and cleared it of all growth, until one day he forgot. The king was out hunting then and went to visit his wife's grave. He saw a briar growing there and decided to marry right away.

"I know a woman who would suit you well," said one of his men. "She is the wife of King Doged."

Cilydd and his men therefore killed King Doged and he took the woman for himself in marriage, along with his land.

One day this woman was out walking when she met a toothless old hag. The wife of Cilydd asked the hag where his children were.

"Cilydd has no children," she said, "except one son named Culhwch who is away in fosterage."

She returned to Cilydd and asked to meet his son Culhwch, so he was sent for and came to his home. When she met Culhwch, she decided to take vengeance on Cilydd for killing her husband and taking her, so she cursed the boy: "I swear that you shall not touch the flesh of a woman until you get for your wife Olwen the daughter of Ysbaddaden lord of the giants. And I curse you to fall in love with her."

The boy blushed and suddenly felt a love for the girl enter every limb of his body, though he had never seen her. He was determined to have Olwen for his wife, so he asked his father how he might win her.

"Go to your cousin Arthur," Cilydd said, "Ask him to help you make the girl your own."

Culhwch rode off on his steed to the court of Arthur, but the porter stopped him at the gate.

"Knife has gone into food and drink into horn," the porter told him. "No one except the son of a king or a craftsman is allowed inside."

"If you don't let me in," said Culhwch, "I will satirize both you and your Lord Arthur. I will also raise a shout that will make pregnant women miscarry and all other women barren for the rest of their lives."

"Let me talk with Arthur," said the porter.

He went inside the gate and told his lord that there was a man at the gate more noble than he had ever seen. Arthur ordered him to be allowed inside, though it was against his custom.

Culhwch rode into the feasting hall on his horse and demanded a gift from the king. If he did not receive it, he said, he would satirize him throughout the land.

"By my sword Caledfwlch and my wife Gwenhwyfar," said Arthur, "you shall have whatever you wish. But tell me who you are."

"I am Culhwch son of Cilydd and I am your cousin."

"I welcome and bless you, boy," said Arthur. "Now tell me what it is you desire."

"Your help," answered Culhwch, "so that I may have Olwen daughter of Ysbaddaden the chief of all the giants as my wife."

"Well," said Arthur, "I have never heard of this maiden or her father, but I will send messengers to seek her out."

For a year the heralds of Arthur roamed the land in search of news about Olwen, but they could learn nothing. Arthur then summoned all his knights with all their skills to join him on a quest with Culhwch for the maiden Olwen.

Culhwch and the band of Arthur's knights road forth from his castle with Arthur's man Cei and traveled the land in search of Ysbaddaden's daughter. At last they came to an open plain and saw the most splendid fort in the world before them. There was a large flock of sheep in the field before the castle and a shepherd clad in skins with them.

"Whose sheep do you guard?" asked one of Arthur's men.

"Those of the lord of yonder castle," answered the shepherd, "Ysbaddaden chief of the giants."

"We are here with Arthur to ask for Olwen, his daughter."

"God help you!" said the shepherd. "No man who has made that request of my master has ever come away alive."

Culhwch and Arthur's men went back with the shepherd to his hut and the man's wife welcomed them. She told them the girl they were seeking came there every Saturday to wash her hair and would come if she were sent for, which she did.

When Olwen arrived she was wearing a silk robe as red as flame and a gold torque studded with jewels. Her hair was as yellow as flowers of the field and her skin and breasts were whiter than the foam of the ocean. No hawk that ever flew had brighter eyes than the girl. Her cheeks were as red as rubies and wherever she walked white clover would spring up in her path.

She came into the house and sat beside Culhwch.

"Maiden," he said, "I have loved you and sought you throughout the land. Leave with me and be my wife, so that no one can accuse me of doing wrong."

"I cannot," said Olwen. "I have pledged to my father that I would never leave him without his blessing, for he can only live until I take a man as my husband. But if you truly love me, go to him and ask for my hand. Do whatever he asks of you and you shall have me. But if you hesitate, I will never be yours and you will not escape with your life."

"I will do so," said Culhwch, "and I will win you as my bride."

Olwen left before them, then Culhwch and his companions made their way to the castle of Ysbaddaden. The king of the giants was seated on an enormous throne at the front of his hall. He was so large that his eyelids had to be lifted by his servants with giant forks.

"Greetings, my lord," said Culhwch. "I come to seek your blessing to marry your daughter Olwen."

"Hmph," muttered Ysbaddaden. "We shall see about that. If you want to marry my daughter you must accomplish the tasks I set before you."

"I shall do whatever you ask," said Culhwch.

"Don't be so sure," said the giant. "The tasks are many and not easily done."

Ysbaddaden then laid out an endless list of impossible labors for Culhwch, from fetching the birds of Rhiannon to entertain him to hunting the great and terrible boar Twrch Trwyth. To each demand, Culhwch answered that he would accomplish it, with the help of his cousin Arthur.

His first task was to seek out Mabon son of Modron, who had been stolen from his mother when he was only three nights old. No one had seen him since.

To find out where Mabon was, Arthur and the men sought out the aged Blackbird of Cilgwri to ask for his help.

"When I first came here," said the blackbird, "there was a smith's anvil in this place. No work was ever done on it, but I only rested my beak on it at night. That was so long ago that today there is only a piece of the anvil the size of a nut that hasn't worn away. I am old, but I know nothing of Mabon. Seek out the Stag of Rhedynfre."

They came then to the ancient Stag of Rhedynfre and asked if he knew where Mabon was.

"When I first came here," said the stag, "there was a sapling oak. It grew over the ages into a mighty tree with a hundred branches. Today nothing is left of it but a stump.

I know nothing of the man you seek. But search out the Owl of Cwm Cawlwyd who is older than me. Perhaps he knows."

Arthur and his companions came then to the Owl of Cwm Cawlwyd and asked for his help.

"If I knew where Mabon was," said the owl, "I would tell you. When I came here this valley was empty. Then a forest grew here over the centuries, then men finally came and cut it down. A second forest grew, then a third, yet in all that time I have heard nothing of the man you seek. You should go to the oldest of all the creatures on the earth and the one who has wandered farthest, the Eagle of Gwernabwy."

The men finally found the Eagle of Gwernabwy and asked if he knew of Mabon.

"When I first came here," said the eagle, "I rested on a mountain so high I could touch the stars at night. Today that mountain is only the size of a fist. Yet in all that time I have heard nothing of Mabon. The only creature that may know something is the Salmon of Llyn Llyw."

Arthur at last found the Salmon of Llyn Llyw and asked if he knew of Mabon.

"As much as I know," said the salmon, "I will tell. With every tide I go up the river to Caer Loyw. There I have heard weeping and grieving the likes of which you have never heard."

The men went up the river to Caer Loyw and there heard weeping from behind the castle walls. They came to the sound and called out to the man on the other side.

"What man cries out in this stone prison?" they asked.

"I am Mabon the son of Modron," the voice said.

"We will rescue you," they cried.

Then Arthur and his men stormed the castle and freed Mabon from his prison. They took him back to the hall of

Ysbaddaden and showed him to the giant to prove they had done the deed.

With the help of Arthur and his men, Culhwch rode across the land and beyond the sea, doing all that Ysbaddaden asked of him, impossible though the tasks were.

At last only one labor remained. They must bring to Ysbaddaden the blood of the pitch-black witch, daughter of the white witch, who lived in a cave in the northern lands in the darkest part of the earth.

Arthur sent two men into the witch's cave, but they barely escaped with their lives. He sent more men into the darkness, but they too were driven away. At last Arthur himself entered into the cave and slew the witch with his own blade. They took the witch's blood as they had been told.

When all was done, Culhwch, Arthur, and his men returned to the castle of Ysbaddaden to claim Olwen.

"Is your daughter mine now?" asked Culhwch.

"She is," said the giant, "but you should thank Arthur for that. Now the time has come to end my life."

Then Culhwch's companion Goreu seized the giant by the hair and cut off his head. They stuck it on a post in the courtyard of the castle and Culhwch took possession of Ysbaddaden's kingdom. Culhwch slept that night with Olwen as his wife, then the next day Arthur and his men returned home.

CHRISTIAN MYTHOLOGY

THE COMING OF CHRISTIANITY TO Ireland did not mean the end of mythological stories, as the ancient themes of Celtic mythology were blended with Christian traditions, especially in the lives of the famous Irish saints Patrick, Brigid, and Brendan.

Two short letters written by Patrick himself in the fifth century survive in the manuscript tradition. They are remarkable documents that reveal a very human figure working to spread the Christian gospel in the face of opposition from both the non-Christian Irish and his Christian superiors in Britain. The mythic and imaginative life of Patrick by the Irish churchman Muirchú on which this section is based was composed two centuries after Patrick's death.

We know almost nothing about the historical Saint Brigid except that she probably lived in the generation after Patrick and founded a monastic church for both men and women at Kildare west of Dublin. There are three early lives of Brigid in Latin and Old Irish, but the story in this chapter is based on that composed by the Irish churchman Cogitosus, who lived in the seventh century.

The historical Brendan, about whom we know very little, lived in southwest Ireland and was probably a contemporary of Saint Brigid. The tale of his voyage, dating to perhaps the late seventh century, was a medieval bestseller copied and read throughout Europe. Although it is a metaphor for the journey of the Christian life, it may contain elements of real voyages across the North Atlantic by Irish sailors.

SAINT PATRICK

Patrick was born in Britain, across the sea from the shores of Ireland. When he was sixteen years old, he was kidnapped from his family's villa by Irish pirates and taken to Ireland to be sold as a slave. He was bought by a druid named Miliucc and set to work tending his sheep in hunger, cold, and rain. When he had nowhere else to turn, he found again his childhood faith and the spirit burned inside him. He prayed a hundred times each day and the same again each night asking God to save him.

One night after six years of captivity, Patrick heard a voice telling him to flee from his master and make his way to a ship that was waiting for him. Patrick listened to the voice and ran away. They sailed for three days and three nights on the sea and landed in a wilderness with nothing to eat or drink. Like the children of Israel, Patrick and the crew wandered through the deserted land. Finally, Patrick prayed to God for deliverance—and the Lord heard his prayer. A herd of wild pigs came near them and the crew killed and ate them.

Patrick returned at last to his family in Britain and was received with joy. While he was back in his home, he had many visions telling him to return to Ireland and preach the gospel. Thus, he determined to train as a priest and return to the land where he had been enslaved.

Patrick crossed the sea to Gaul on his way to Rome, but in the city of Auxerre he discovered a holy bishop named Germanus, and stayed with him a long time training in the ministry of God.

When the time was right, God sent an angel named Victoricus to Patrick to tell him it was time for him to return to Ireland. With the blessing of Germanus and ordination as a bishop, he traveled back to Britain and then on to the island of his enslavement accompanied by his companions Auxilius, Iserninus, and other helpers.

Now at this time in Ireland a great and mighty pagan king named Lóegaire ruled at Tara. He surrounded himself with druids and sorcerers who were masters of every sort of evil. There were two druids among his counselors named Lochru and Lucet Máel, who were able to see the future by the dark arts of the devil. They had predicted to the king that one day a man would arrive from across the sea who would destroy his kingdom and the gods themselves if he allowed it. Many times they proclaimed:

There will come a man with a shaved head
and a stick curved at the top.
He will chant evil words
from a table at the front of his house.
And his people will say: "Amen, let it be so."

This Lóegaire was ruling at Tara as king when Patrick arrived on the shore of Ireland at Inber Dee in Leinster. He then sailed north along the coast to Inber Sláne near the Boyne River and hid his boat there. He wanted to find his former master Miliucc and buy his freedom, for under Irish law he was still a slave.

A swineherd found Patrick and his men near their boat and went to tell his master Díchu. This man thought they were thieves or pirates and set out to kill them, but he was a man of natural goodness and the Lord turned his heart when he saw Patrick. The new bishop of Ireland preached to Díchu and won him to the faith, the first of his many converts in Ireland.

Patrick then traveled across the land to the mountain of Sliab Mis, where he had once been a slave. But when Miliucc heard that Patrick was on his way, he was prompted by the devil to kill himself lest he be ruled by a man who had once served him. Miliucc gathered together all his possessions in his house and set the structure on fire with himself inside.

Patrick saw the smoke in the distance and knew what Miliucc had done. He stood there for hours watching in silence while he wept.

"Why did you do this, Miliucc?" asked Patrick. "You submitted yourself to fire rather than to God. Therefore none of your sons will rule after you and your descendants will serve others."

Patrick left the lands of Miliucc and traveled around the nearby plain preaching the gospel. It was there the faith began to grow.

Now at that time Easter was drawing near and Patrick talked with his companions about where they might celebrate the holy festival in that land for the first time. He decided at last that they should celebrate Easter on the Plain of Brega near Tara, for this place was the center of paganism and idolatry in Ireland.

At the same time the heathens of the island were celebrating their own pagan festival with incantations, demonic rites, and idolatrous superstitions. Nobles and druids of the land had gathered at Tara to light a sacred fire. For it was an unbreakable law that no one could kindle a fire before the king had lit the holy fire on that night. But that evening Patrick kindled his fire before the king in full view of the Hill of Tara.

The king called his druids together and demanded to know who had lit a fire before him. He ordered that the man be hunted down and killed at once. The druids declared that they did not know whose fire it was, but they warned the king that unless he extinguished the fire that very night it would grow and outshine all the fires of Ireland, driving away the gods of the land and seducing all the people of his realm forever.

When Lóegaire heard these things he was greatly troubled and all of Tara with him. He declared that he would find the man responsible for the forbidden fire and slay him. He ordered his warriors to prepare their chariots for battle and follow him out of his fortress.

They found Patrick nearby and summoned him before the king. His chief druid Lochru mocked the holy man and the faith he taught, but Patrick looked him in the eye and prayed to heaven that he might pay for his impiety. The druid was then lifted up into the air and cast down on a rock, splitting his skull into pieces.

The pagans were all angry and afraid, so that the king ordered his men to seize Patrick. But darkness suddenly fell on them all and an earthquake struck the warriors. The horses were driven onto the plain and all the men died except for the king, his wife, and two of his men.

"I beseech you," said the queen to Patrick, "do not kill my husband. He will fall before you on bended knee."

Lóegaire was furious and still planned to kill Patrick, but he knelt before him to save his life. Patrick, however, knew what was in the heart of Lóegaire. Before Lóegaire could gather more warriors, Patrick turned himself into a deer and went into the forest. The king then returned to Tara with his few followers who had survived.

The next day King Lóegaire and his men were in his feasting hall at Tara brooding about what had happened the evening before. Suddenly holy Patrick and his followers appeared in the midst of them, even though the doors were closed. The king and his men were astonished. Lóegaire invited Patrick to sit and eat with them so that he might test him. Patrick, knowing what was about to happen, did not refuse.

While they were eating, the druid Lucet Máel placed a drop of poison in Patrick's cup while the holy man's eyes were turned. Patrick took the cup and blessed it, so that the liquid froze like ice. He then turned the cup upside down and the drop of poison fell out. Patrick blessed the cup again and the wine turned to liquid once more.

After dinner, the druid challenged Patrick to a duel of miracles on the plain before Tara.

"What kind of miracle would you like me to do?" asked Patrick.

"Let us call down snow on the land," the sorcerer replied.

"I do not wish to do anything contrary to God and nature," said Patrick.

"You are afraid you will fail," exclaimed Lucet Máel. "But I can do it."

The druid uttered magic spells and called down snow from the sky so that it covered the whole plain up to the depth of a man's waist.

"We have seen what harm you can do," said Patrick. "Now make the snow disappear."

"I do not have the power to remove it until tomorrow," said Lucet Máel.

Patrick then raised his hands and blessed the whole plain so that the snow disappeared in an instant. The crowd was amazed and cheered for the holy man. But the druids were very angry.

Next, the druid invoked his evil gods and called down darkness on the whole land. The people were frightened and begged him to bring back the light, but he could not. But Patrick prayed to God and straightaway the sun shone forth and all the people shouted with joy.

After these contests the king told both Patrick and the druids to throw their books into the water to test whether they would be damaged. Patrick agreed to do this, but the chief of the druids said he did not want to be judged by water, for water was sacred to the holy man—for he had heard that Patrick baptized in water.

"Then throw your books into fire," the king said.

Patrick agreed, but again the druid said he would not, for fire was also sacred to the Christian.

"This is not true," said Patrick to the druid. "I challenge you to go into an enclosed house along with one of my young followers. You wear my robe while my boy wears yours. Then set the house on fire and be judged by the Most High."

The druid agreed to this, so that a house was filled wet and dry wood. Holy Patrick sent his young disciple Benignus into the part of the house with dry wood wearing the robe of the druid. The druid entered the half with wet wood wearing Patrick's robe. The building was then sealed and set on fire while all the people watched.

Through the prayers of Patrick, the flames completely consumed the druid and the house, but left Benignus untouched.

The robe of Patrick, however, was not harmed, while the garment of the druid burned away.

The king was very angry, but Patrick spoke to him: "Unless you believe now, you will die. For the fury of the Lord has fallen upon your head."

King Lóegaire then called together his counselors to ask what he should do.

"It is better to believe than die," they told him.

So the king came reluctantly to Patrick to be baptized.

"You come to me now," said Patrick to Lóegaire, "but it would have been better for you if you had believed me right away. You shall remain as king, but because of your disbelief your descendants will not rule after you."

Patrick then went forth and preached the gospel across Ireland, baptizing all who believed in the name of the Father, Son, and Holy Spirit, and confirming the power of the Lord with miracles and wonders.

At this time there was across the sea in the pagan land of Britain a young woman named Monesan who was the daughter of a king. She was inspired by the Holy Spirit to refuse all offers of marriage. Even though her parents frequently beat her and drenched her in water to persuade her to change her mind, she would not yield. She would always ask who it was who had made the world and the lights of the heavens, for she was seeking through nature the creator of all creation.

Her parents did not know what to do with her, so when they heard of Patrick and his wondrous work in Ireland, they journeyed there with her to speak with him.

"Do you believe in God?" Patrick asked Monesan.

"I do with all my heart," she said.

Then Patrick baptized her with water and the Holy Spirit.

Immediately she fell down dead.

She was buried there in Ireland where she died. Twenty years later her remains were carried with honor to a nearby chapel, where her relics are adored to this day.

During these days there was a wicked British king named Corotic who was a great persecutor and murderer of Christians. Patrick wrote to him to urge him to follow the way of truth, but Corotic only laughed at him.

When this was told to Patrick, the holy man asked the Lord to expel the king from his presence, then and forevermore.

One day not long after this, Corotic heard the sound of music and a voice singing to him that it was time for him to leave his throne. Then all his family and followers burst into the same song. Suddenly, in the midst of them all, Corotic was changed into a fox and ran out of his palace. After that he was never seen again.

In these days there lived in Ulster a wicked, murderous pagan named Macc Cuill moccu Graccae who was so savage he was called the Cyclops. One day he was sitting on a hill looking for travelers to rob and kill when he saw Patrick coming down the road. Macc Cuill recognized the holy man and decided to test him before slaying him. He had one of his men pretend to be gravely ill and brought the man before Patrick to be healed.

"If he had truly been sick," Patrick said, "then you wouldn't be surprised by his current condition."

Macc Cuill pulled back the sheet covering the man and saw that he was dead. The outlaw was struck with sorrow and guilt over what he had done.

"Forgive me, Patrick," he said. "I confess my wickedness and submit myself to the judgment of your God."

Patrick baptized him and told him that to be forgiven by the Lord he must go down to the sea and cast himself from shore in a small boat with no food, water, or oars. He must let God take him where he would, whether to death or to life.

"I will do as you have said," replied Macc Cuill.

He went down to the sea and fettered his feet in chains and threw away the key. Then he set out to sea as he had been told. The north wind blew him for days until he came to an island. There he found two righteous priests who trained him in the way of the faith. He spent the rest of his life on that island, and in time became a bishop famous for his holiness and wisdom.

One day Patrick was preaching by the sea on a Sunday when he was troubled by the noise of some pagans digging a ditch around a fort. He ordered them not to work on the Lord's day, but they ignored him.

"*Mudebroth*!" he shouted. "You will gain nothing from your labor."

The next day a great storm arose and destroyed all the work the pagans had done, just as Patrick had said.

Once there was a wealthy and honored pagan in Ulster named Dáire. Patrick asked him if he would grant him some land for a church on a hill, but Dáire gave him a piece of low ground instead, which Patrick graciously accepted.

One day Dáire sent one of his horses to graze on Patrick's land, so that the holy man was offended. The next day Dáire's servants found the horse dead. Dáire then told his men to kill Patrick.

But as they were leaving Dáire's house, the wealthy man fell down dead. Two of his servants went to Patrick and begged him to give them something to help Dáire. Patrick blessed a cup of water and told them to sprinkle it on the dead horse. The servants did this and revived the horse, but they also sprinkled the water on Dáire as Patrick knew they would and brought their master back to life.

Dáire went to Patrick and thanked him, granting him the hill that he had first asked for, where now stands the holy city of Armagh.

On another day Patrick passed by a cross at a grave on the side of the road, but he didn't see it. When he found out later from his charioteer that he had passed it by, he was troubled, for it was his custom to always pray at whatever cross he came near.

Patrick immediately left the house where he was staying and made his way through the night to the grave. Through his miraculous powers granted by God, he asked the dead man buried there how he had died and whether he was a Christian.

"I was a pagan when I was buried here," said the dead man. "But a Christian man from another province died here. When his mother came to erect a cross for him, she mistook my grave for his and so placed the cross above my body."

Patrick said he had not seen the cross at first because it marked the grave of a pagan. He then ordered the cross to be moved to the burial place of the dead Christian and returned to the house where he was staying.

It was the custom of Patrick not to travel on Sunday. He was spending the night in a field one Lord's day when a great rain came upon the land and soaked all the ground except where Patrick was sleeping.

Patrick's charioteer told him in tears that the storm had driven away their horses and he could not find them in the darkness.

"God always hears us in our time of need," Patrick told the man.

Then Patrick rolled up his sleeve and drew out his hand. He raised his five fingers into the dark sky and they suddenly shone with a bright light. The charioteer ceased from weeping and found the horses with the help of Patrick's miraculous light.

When the time came for Patrick to die, an angel came to him and told him that God would grant him four petitions that he had sought.

The first was that his authority would ever after be in the city of Armagh. The second was that whoever sang his hymn would have the penance for their sins decided by him. The third was that the descendants of Díchu, who had first welcomed him to Ireland, would be granted mercy and would not perish. And the final petition was that all of the Irish would be judged by him at the end of the world.

And so on the seventeenth of March, in the one hundred and twentieth year of his life, Patrick passed from this life into the hands of God.

SAINT BRIGID

Holy Brigid was born in Ireland to noble Christian parents. Her father was named Dubthach and her mother Broicsech. From childhood she was full of self-restraint and modesty, and always desired to do good.

One day when Brigid was old enough, her mother told her to churn milk to turn it into butter. But being a kind girl wishing to obey God, she gave away all that she had made to the poor and homeless. When her mother came at the end of the day to collect the butter, the girl was very much afraid of her anger. God, however, heard the prayers of Brigid and miraculously restored the butter she needed. Everyone saw the great wonder God had done and praised the great faith in the heart of this virtuous maiden.

Not long after this her parents decided it was time to marry her to a man, as was the custom. But Brigid was determined to remain a chaste virgin and so went to a holy priest named Mac Caille to receive the veil of a nun. When he placed the veil on her head, she fell to her knees before the altar of the church and touched the wood at the base of the altar with her hand. Even today the place where she touched the wood remains green and heals the sickness of the faithful who touch it.

Once when Brigid was cooking bacon in a cauldron for visitors, she felt sorry for a begging dog and gave him some. But when the meat was taken from the cauldron and divided among the guests, there was no less to eat than when she had started. The guests marveled at this woman so blessed by God and unmatched in faith.

One day when Brigid was harvesting grain in her fields, the clouds began to gather and threatened a torrent of rain. Indeed, throughout the province floods of water fell from the sky and overflowed the glens and gullies of the land. Only Brigid's fields remained dry, by the power of God, so that she and her laborers were able to harvest from sunrise to sunset.

On a day when Brigid was tending her sheep and grazing them in a grassy field, she was soaked by a fierce downpour of rain from the heavens. She went inside a nearby house wearing her wet clothes. As she entered the dark home, she was blinded by a single ray of sunlight shining into the hut through a small opening. Thinking the light was a slanting beam built into the house, she hung her wet clothes on it and they remained there as if it were a solid piece of wood. When the owners of the home saw this miracle, they praised God and the woman so blessed by him.

When Brigid was in the field on another day tending her sheep, a young outlaw came to her to test her generosity. He sought her out seven times that day wearing different clothes each time and asking for a sheep to feed his family, which Brigid gladly gave him. But when the flock was driven back to the fold that night and counted, the sheep were no less in number than they had been that morning.

The lad who saw all this was struck by the power of God working through this woman and he returned the seven sheep she had given him. But when the sheep were counted again, there were still the same number as she had started with that morning.

One day lepers came to Brigid asking her for beer, but she had none to give them. But seeing water prepared for a bath, she blessed it and by the power of faith turned it into beer. She then drew out the drink in abundance and gave it to the thirsty lepers.

There was a certain young and beautiful nun who had taken a vow of virginity, but by human weakness had given in to youthful desire and slept with a man. She became pregnant and her womb began to swell. She came to Brigid to seek her forgiveness and help. Drawing on the potent strength of her matchless faith, holy Brigid blessed the young woman so that the fetus disappeared and she became a virgin again.

One day a twelve-year-old girl and her mother came to visit Brigid. The girl had not been able to speak a word since birth. Brigid welcomed them to her home and talked with the mother warmly, then asked the girl to come to her. The holy woman took her hand and asked what it was she wished to do with her life. The mother spoke up and said the girl could not answer, but Brigid replied that she would not let go of the girl's hand until she herself spoke. Then the girl opened her mouth and said that she wished to be a virgin of God like Brigid. From that day forward she was able to speak.

Evil men from another province who feared neither God nor man came one day and stole the cattle of Brigid from her field. But on their return journey they had to cross a shallow river. Suddenly the river rose like a towering wall and overwhelmed the thieves. It dragged them away and drowned them, but did not harm the cattle, who returned to their field by themselves.

One day when Brigid was in the forest with her pigs, a wild boar ran into the middle of the herd. The boar was terrified, but Brigid came to him and blessed him so that he lost his natural fear and was content to stay with the holy woman.

There was a certain foolish man who came once to the fort of a nearby king and saw a fox walking through the grounds. He thought it was a wild animal and killed it, but it was a tame fox valued highly by the king for its tricks.

The people of the king were horrified and brought him before their ruler. The king declared that he would kill the man and all his family unless he could produce another fox able to perform tricks as skillfully.

When holy Brigid heard of the man's plight, she was filled with compassion and came to the court of the king. There she prayed earnestly to the Lord, who sent a wild fox to her from the forest. The animal performed all the tricks the previous fox had done. When the king saw this he was overjoyed and released the condemned man from his chains and sent him away.

Brigid then returned home, but the clever fox ran away from the fort and back to his den in the forest, with the king's men chasing him all the way.

Once, when Brigid was preaching the gospel among the people of her province, she saw nine men in diabolical dress making noises as if they were filled with madness. They were part of an evil cult that served the devil. They swore they would commit murder and butchery in his dark service before the end of that month.

The most holy and kind Brigid talked with them and tried to turn them from their wicked ways, but they would not listen to her. When they left her, they seemed to see a man before them and they killed him, stabbing him repeatedly with their swords and cutting off his head. Then as if in a triumphal parade, they carried the head and their blood-covered weapons back through the fields for all to see.

But the Lord had worked a miracle. At the prayer of Brigid he had created a phantom for the men to kill and thus fulfill their evil vows. The men were filled then with shame at what they had done and turned their hearts in repentance to the Lord.

There was in the days of Brigid a lustful and wealthy layman who burned with desire for a beautiful young woman, but she would have nothing to do with him. He plotted how he might have sex with her by guile, and therefore entrusted to her a certain precious silver brooch for safekeeping, which she accepted.

The wicked man secretly stole the brooch from her and threw it into the sea, then demanded she return what he had entrusted to her. When she could not find it, he declared that he would take her as his slave so that he might satisfy his most disgraceful desires with her.

The chaste maiden went to Brigid and begged her for help. The holy woman listened to her story and before they had finished speaking, one of Brigid's men came into the house with a fish he had caught in the river. Brigid told him to cut the fish open. When he did, he found inside the entrails the same silver brooch the evil man had thrown into the sea.

Thus when the wicked man brought the young maiden to trial before the people and demanded she be given to him as his slave, she took the brooch from Brigid's hands in the presence of all and gave it back to him.

The man fell on his knees before Brigid and confessed his crime. The young maiden gave thanks to God for this great miracle and returned to her home.

One time the king of the country in which Brigid lived ordered all the clans of his people to come together to build a road through his kingdom. They were to lay a foundation of sturdy logs and rocks across his land, no matter if it were dry field or bogs, so that it could bear the weight of wagons and horsemen.

The most difficult section of the road by a swampy river was given by lot to Brigid's clan, which had fewer people than all the others. They asked a larger and more powerful clan to trade sections of the road with them, but the other clan only laughed and sent them away. The people of her own clan then came to holy Brigid for help, but she dismissed them, saying that the Lord himself had power over his creation.

The next morning when all the people of the clan arose, they found that the course of the river had moved from its ancient route away from their land and across the territory of the nearby tribe that had mocked them. Thus God exalted the meek and brought the mighty low.

Even after Brigid died, she still worked miracles through her divine power.

Once the abbot of her monastery asked his workers to cut a millstone from the summit of a nearby mountain and bring it to him. The laborers found and cut the stone from the quarry with no difficulty, but they had no way to bring such a heavy burden back down the steep slope of the mountain.

The abbot told them they could not give up after so much work and asked them to roll the stone down the mountain to the bottom. He then prayed to Brigid that the stone would not break on its way. The workers pushed the millstone to the edge of the slope and sent it crashing down the mountain. Sometimes it swerved away from other rocks and other times it jumped over them, but finally it made it to the bottom unharmed. From there the laborers were able to drag the stone to the mill with oxen.

Once the new millstone was in place, the people of the monastery were able to grind their grain to eat. But when a druid who lived nearby sent his grain with a Christian man to be ground at the mill, the stone refused to move. When the workers there discovered the grain was from a druid, they replaced it with wheat from the monastery fields and the stone moved again.

The mill later burned and destroyed all inside, but the millstone from the mountain remained unharmed. It was set up before the door of the church where people gathered to venerate the miracles of holy Brigid. To this day those who touch the stone are cured of disease and sickness through their faith and the miraculous power of most blessed Brigid.

SAINT BRENDAN

Holy Brendan the son of Findlug was born in Munster and was the spiritual father of countless monks.

Once he was praying in a meadow when a certain priest named Barrind came to him in the evening. This man began to cry and fell onto the ground until Brendan raised him from the earth and kissed him, asking him what troubled his soul.

Barrind told him of a hermit named Mernoc who had sailed out to sea and discovered a place called the Island of Delight. Barrind went to visit him there and found many monks living in individual huts and cells, but who all came together to eat and offer a sacrifice of praise to God. Barrind said while he was there he and Mernoc found a little boat on the shore and set off to search for the Land Promised to the Saints, a place God would give to his people at the end of the age. After a short time, they were surrounded by a fog and a great light shone all about them. They landed, then, on the shore of an island green and fruitful. They discovered a river on the island and found a man standing near it clothed in light. He told them to rejoice, for they had found the land for which they were searching. He welcomed them, but told them they could not stay and sent them back to the Island of Delight. The monks there rejoiced to see them return and marveled at the lingering odor of paradise on their clothing. Barrind told Brendan all this, then left him.

The next day Brendan called together fourteen brother monks from his community and proposed that they all seek out the Land Promised to the Saints. The brothers responded that they had left behind their families and fortunes to follow

Brendan and they would continue to do so to the ends of the earth.

Brendan and the brothers went down to the sea in the westernmost part of Munster to build a boat for the voyage. They made a frame of wood and covered this with cowhides tanned with oak bark, then greased all the seams with fat. They fixed a wooden mast in the center and placed food for forty days inside the boat.

Just as Brendan and his men were about to cast off into the sea, three monks arrived and begged to join them on the journey. Brendan, by the wisdom of God, knew that the latecomers would suffer judgment on the voyage, but he granted them leave to enter the boat. They then raised the sail and set off toward the setting sun.

After fifteen days the wind ceased, so the monks took up their oars and began to row. After a time Brendan spoke: "My brothers, bring in the oars and rudder. Roll up the sails and let God lead his servants and his ship where he wishes."

After forty days of sailing the ocean their food was gone. A high and rocky island then appeared before them to the north, and they drew near to it. From the tops of its soaring cliffs streams of fresh water poured down into the sea, but they could not reach the water nor were they able to find a place to land. The monks were tormented by hunger and thirst. Brendan then told them not to fear, for in three days the Lord would show them a place to bring their boat to shore.

Just as Brendan had said, three days later they found a landing place barely big enough for a single boat. They went onto the shore and found a dog there who ran up to them. He led Brendan and his men inland to a grand hall lined with beds and seats. In the hall was also a grand table with freshly baked bread, fish, and wine. On the walls were beautiful decorations, along with the bridles of horses covered with silver.

"Take care not to be tempted by these riches," Brendan said, "and pray for the soul of the man who gives in to Satan."

The brothers sat down in their chairs and gave thanks to God for the food and drink before them. When the meal was over and the worship of God complete, Brendan told the brothers to sleep and rest their weary bodies.

But when the monks were in bed, Brendan saw the devil at work. He was in the form of a small Ethiopian boy talking with one of the brothers who had come late to the voyage. Brendan could do nothing except fall to his knees in prayer for the brother.

After the morning service, the brothers began to go down to their boat, but a table suddenly appeared before them full of food and drink. So they stayed there for three days and three nights as God prepared a table before them each day for his servants.

When after three days they were ready to leave, Brendan warned them not to take anything of value from the island.

"We would never do such a thing," they all replied.

"One of you already has," said Brendan, turning his face to the brother who had been speaking with the devil.

The man fell on his knees before Brendan: "I have sinned, Father. Forgive me and pray for my soul lest I perish."

Holy Brendan raised the brother up and they all saw a little Ethiopian boy leap from his chest crying and flying away.

Brendan turned to the sinful brother and told him he would soon die. So after the man had received the Eucharist, his spirit left his body and was taken to heaven by the angels of light and his body was buried in that place.

As the monks were preparing to leave, a young man ran up to them carrying a basket of bread and a jar of water. He told Brendan that they had a long journey ahead of them, but they would not lack food or water before Easter. Holy Brendan accepted the gift with thanks and sailed away into the ocean. They ate every other day as their little boat was carried here and there across the sea.

One day they saw an island not far from them. A favorable wind arose and the boat found a landing place. Walking around the island, they saw many sheep, all shining white. There were so many animals they could scarcely see the ground. Brendan ordered them to take from the flock a spotless sheep, which they prepared for their meal.

Suddenly a man appeared before them with a basket of bread and everything else they needed. He fell flat on his face three times before Brendan. The holy man raised him to his feet and welcomed him among them. The man then told them they would celebrate Holy Saturday on that island, but they would sail to a nearby island for Easter. When Easter was over, they would then sail to another island called the Paradise of Birds, where they would remain until eight days after Pentecost.

Brendan asked the man how the sheep of his island grew so large, for they were as big as cattle. The man replied that there was no one on the island to milk them and that winter did not reach that land.

When Brendan and his monks set off in their boat toward the nearby island to celebrate Easter, they ran aground before it reached that place. The monks all climbed out of the boat and spent the night where they had landed, but Brendan remained aboard since he knew what kind of island it was. When morning came he told the men to sing the holy service, then build a fire to smoke some of the fish they had with them. But as soon as they built the fire, the ground began to shake. Brendan ordered them to hurry into the boat and push away. While they did this, the island began to move off deeper into the ocean.

Brendan spoke to the frightened brothers: "My friends, do not be afraid. This was not an island, but the greatest fish that lives in all the seas. His name is Jasconius and he is always trying to bring his tail to his head—but he cannot since he is so large."

They sailed then to the island called the Paradise of Birds and found at last on the southern side of that island a small river flowing from a spring where they could land. There was hanging above the spring an enormous tree with its branches covered by white birds.

Brendan sat down by the spring and gazed up at the birds. One of the creatures left the branches and flew down to stand beside him. The sound of its wings was like the chiming of bells. It stretched forth its wings as if making a sign of joy and spoke to the holy man.

"You wonder who we are and where we came from. We were angels once, but in the great rebellion of heaven we sided neither with Lucifer nor with God. For this reason God sent us here, unpunished but separated from those angels who stood with him. We wander through the firmament as spirits, but on holy days and each Sunday we take the form of the birds you see to sing and praise the creator. Holy father, you should know your voyage has just begun. You have six more years ahead of you. When that time is done, you will find the place you seek—the Land Promised to the Saints."

Brendan and his company stayed there until after Pentecost listening to the beautiful songs of the birds. Then they unfurled the sails and set off again into the ocean.

The little boat was blown across the wide sea for three months, so that the men inside saw nothing but water and sky. One day just as they were running out of food, an island appeared on the horizon, but a wind kept them from its shores. After three days of fasting and praying, they found a narrow inlet and landed the boat.

An old man with hair as white as snow met them there and embraced all of them. Brendan spoke to the man, but he indicated with signs that they should be silent for a time. When they came to a monastery, the abbot who had greeted them led them inside where his monks washed their feet and led them to a dining room with abundant loaves of bread.

The abbot then broke his silence and told Brendan they were an order of twenty-four monks cared for by the grace of the Lord. Each day twelve loaves of bread appeared on the table. For eighty years, since the days of holy Patrick, they had lived on the island, never growing old or weak.

Brendan and his brothers stayed there many days, then accepted provisions from the monks of the island and set out again into the ocean. They were blown in a circle for twenty days, then God sent to them again a favorable wind.

For years Brendan and his monks were blown across the sea to many islands. One of these was called the Island of Strong Men, where one of the monks who had come late to the boat remained. Another was a land of red grapes as big as apples. They also found in the middle of the ocean a towering column of crystal higher than the sky. They also found a place called the Island of Smiths populated by large and brutish men who threw molten chunks of metal at their boat.

One day a high mountain appeared before them on the sea covered with a great smoke coming from the summit.

The cliffs of this island were steep and the color of coal. The last of the monks who had come late to the boat suddenly jumped out and swam to shore, as if not by his own will. He cried out to Brendan and the monks in the boat, but they were not able to help him, since a multitude of demons appeared and set him on fire as punishment for his sins. Brendan and his brothers sadly sailed away from that island, looking back on that land as it glowed in the night like a mountain in flames.

When they had sailed away from the Island of Fire for seven days, they came upon a man sitting on a rock in the sea battered by the crashing waves.

Holy Brendan asked him who he was and how he came to be there.

"I am Judas," the man answered. "And I am here by the mercy of Jesus Christ. This is not a place of punishment for me but of relief in honor of his resurrection. After sunset apart from Sundays and holy days, I burn like molten lead in the mountain you saw as punishment for betraying my Lord. But by his mercy, I ask that you beseech God to let me stay here until sunrise tomorrow."

Brendan agreed, but that evening demons came to take Judas away.

"Go away, man of God," they said. "We cannot take this man until you leave."

"By the power of our master Jesus Christ," said Brendan, "you shall not touch him until sunrise."

"How can you invoke the name of the Lord to protect this wicked man?" they asked. "He is the very one who betrayed him."

"Nonetheless," warned Brendan, "you shall not touch him until the new day begins."

The demons cried out and gnashed their teeth, but they did not touch Judas until the sun rose. Then they carried him away, screaming and cursing, to the Island of Fire while Brendan and his brothers sailed away.

Three days later the boat came to a small island of bare rock that looked like flint. They found a landing place there and came ashore. A man named Paul was waiting for them there. He was a hermit clothed only in the white hair that fell over his entire body from his head and beard. Paul greeted them all by name and told them of how he had come to that island long ago from the monastery of holy Patrick. He lived there in a cave, nourished only by the water from a little spring. He told Brendan that his voyage was at last coming to an end and he would soon reach the Land Promised to the Saints.

Not long after, Brendan and his brothers left that island and sailed for forty days into a great fog. When the sky grew clear, Brendan saw that he was near a wide and beautiful land filled with a great light. They came ashore and wandered about the island, marveling at trees filled with fruit. Even though they passed much time there, the land never grew dark, for the Lord Jesus himself was the light of the place.

They came at last to a river swift and cold that flowed from the center of the island. A young man appeared to them there and told them they could not cross that river. He told Brendan that he must instead return to the land of his birth and sleep with his fathers, for that land was not yet for him.

Brendan and his brothers sadly left that island and sailed back through the fog in little time to the Island of

Delight from where they had begun their journey, for the Land Promised to the Saints had never been far from them.

From there they journeyed back to Munster and returned to the monastery where their brothers were still waiting for them. They were greeted with joy and wept when Brendan told them all he soon must die.

Thus after the holy man had settled his affairs and partaken of the divine sacraments, he passed into the hands of the Lord, to whom are honor and glory from ages past to ages yet to come.

NOTES

Introduction: Who Were the Celts?

Over two thousand years ago: The brief story of the twin gods from Timaeus is preserved in Diodorus Siculus *Geography* 4.56.

We first hear of a people called the Keltoi: Translations of many of the Greek and Roman passages on the ancient Celts along with some inscriptions translated from the early Celtic languages may be found in my *War, Women, and Druids: Eyewitness Reports and Early Accounts of the Ancient Celts.*

I, however, who have copied this history: From the end of the *Book of Leinster* version of the *Táin.*

Chapter 1: The Earliest Celtic Gods

The greatest of the gods of ancient Gaul was Mercury: Julius Caesar *Gallic War* 6.17–18. Excellent discussions of the ancient Celtic gods and their possible equivalents in Ireland and Wales are in Mac Cana, *Celtic Mythology*, 20–53; and Aldhouse-Green, *The Celtic Myths.*

The Roman poet Lucan: Civil War 1.444–446.

a practice mentioned by Caesar himself: Gallic War 6.16.

Maximus of Tyre: Sayings 8.8.

Pompeius Trogus: via the *Epitome* (43.4) of Justin.
Salvianus of Marseille: De Gubernatione Dei 6.60.
Gregory of Tours: De Miraculis 17.5.
Bishop Eligius: Vita Sancti Eligii 2.16.
Ogmios: Lucian *Hercules* 1–6.
Artemidorus: Strabo 4.4.6.
Andraste: Dio Cassius 62.7.1–3.
Posidonius: Strabo *Geography* 4.4.5.

Chapter 2: The Book of Invasions

The three stories of the *Book of Invasions*, the short tale of Tuán, and the war of the *Cath Maige Tuired* form a continuous tale and are combined in this chapter. The standard edition of the *Book of Invasions* is that of Macalister. The best version of the tale of Tuán is from Carey, "Scél Tuáin meic Chairill," 93–111; and Koch and Carey, *The Celtic Heroic Age*, 223–225. The story of the battle between the Formorians and the Tuatha Dé Danann is taken from Grey, *Cath Maige Tuired*.

Chapter 3: The Wooing of Étaín

The Wooing of Étaín is found at least in part in the late medieval manuscript collections known as the *Book of the Dun Cow* and the *Yellow Book of Lecan*, but the story dates from an earlier period, perhaps the eighth or ninth century. It was translated by Gantz, *Early Irish Myths and Sagas*, 37–59; and appears in Koch and Carey, *The Celtic Heroic Age*, 146–165.

for all of time is day and night: In another early Irish story called *De Gabail in t-Síde (The Taking of the Síd)* found in the twelfth-century *Book of Leinster* and translated in Koch and Carey, *The Celtic Heroic Age*, 145, it is the Dagda himself whom Óengus tricks in the same way into giving up possession of the Bruig na Bóinne. The Bruig na Bóinne is usually identified as the reconstructed tomb of Newgrange on the Boyne River north of Dublin which dates to c. 3000 B.C.E.

a purple butterfly: In some versions simply a fly.

Chapter 4: Cú Chulainn and the Táin Bó Cuailnge

The best Irish text of the *Táin* is O'Rahilly, *Táin Bó Cuailnge: Recension I.* Recent translations of the *Táin* with excellent introductions and notes include Kinsella, *The Táin*, and Carson, *The Táin*.

At last one night a young poet named Emine: There are other versions of the recovery of the *Táin*, including one in which Senchán goes for help to St. Colm Cille, who leads him to the grave of Fergus.

The story begins with a young woman named Nes: There is more than one version of this early story, called in Irish the *Compert Conchoboir*, including a later and more elaborate version in which Nes is a warrior princess who becomes pregnant after being forced to swallow two worms.

One of the noblemen of Conchobar was Cruinniuc mac Agnomain: The story of Macha is included here to explain why the Ulstermen are incapacitated during much of the Connacht attack in the *Táin*. There are actually three women named Macha in Irish legend, all of whom have supernatural qualities, and they may be seen as aspects of the same goddess.

Conchobar and the warriors of Ulster were gathered together for a feast: The story of the Exile of the Sons of Uisliu (*Longes mac n-Uislenn*) is a fore tale (*rémscel*) of the *Táin* and answers the question in the epic of why so many warriors of Ulster were fighting in the armies of Ailill and Medb of Connacht. The story survives in many versions and is the inspiration for modern Irish retellings such as Yeats's play *Deirdre* and Synge's *Deirdre of the Sorrows*.

The story of Cú Chulainn's birth: Taken from the tale known in Irish as *Compert ConCulainn*, in which the details of the story vary according to different versions. In one Deichtine is Conchobar's sister, in another his daughter.

to change in form and appearance: This is the first instance of the famous *ríastrad* or battle fury, also called a warp spasm, of Cú Chulainn which overtakes him before the heat of combat. This and the following stories are taken from the first recension of the *Táin*.

One night far away in Connacht, when the royal bed was prepared for Ailill and Medb: This introductory section to the *Táin* proper comes from the twelfth-century manuscript of the *Book of Leinster.* Medb—whose name means "one who intoxicates"—is seen by many scholars as the survival of an Irish goddess of sovereignty who bestows her blessing on rulers by means of her sexuality.

imbas forasnai: The *imbas* ("great knowledge") *forasnai* ("that illuminates") is described in the tenth-century *Cormac's Glossary* as a poetic and prophetic ritual in which a poet chews the raw flesh of a pig, dog, or cat, chants over a flagstone to the gods, then lies in bed undisturbed with his hands on his cheeks waiting for a supernatural vision.

Ogam script: An ancient Irish writing system of lines carved usually on the edge of a stone, representing consonants and vowels. Such writing is known from the end of Roman times until the medieval period and came to have magical associations, though in origin it was used primarily for names on memorial stones.

Chapter 5: Tales from the Ulster Cycle

The Story of Mac Da Thó's Pig: In Irish, *Scéla Muicce Meic Dá Thó.* The oldest version of the tale is preserved in the twelfth-century *Book of Leinster.* The standard edition is Thurneysen, *Scéla Muicce Meic Dá Thó*, with translations in Gantz, *Early Irish Myths and Sagas*, 179–187; and Koch and Carey, *The Celtic Heroic Age*, 68–75.

The Cattle Raid of Fróech: This eighth-century tale filled with common folklore motifs is an antecedent to the *Táin Bó Cuailnge*—in which Fróech is killed by Cú Chulainn in single combat—but stands on its own as a story of a handsome young man seeking his princess, the slaying of a monster, the recovery of a magic ring, and an unrelated journey to the Alps to recover his cattle and family. In the conclusion of the original tale—which in origin is certainly a separate story—the men who steal his cattle also take Fróech's previously unmentioned wife and three sons. The text of *The Cattle Raid of Fróech* was edited by Byrne and Dillon in 1933 and by Meid in 1974, and is translated by Gantz, *Early Irish Myths and Sagas*, 113–126.

The Destruction of Dá Derga's Hostel: In Irish, the *Togail Bruidne Dá Derga*, an odd name for a story in which the hostel is never actually destroyed. Composed in perhaps the eighth or ninth century, the text is preserved in the *Book of the Dun Cow* and the *Yellow Book of Lecan*. This story is traditionally part of the Ulster Cycle even though much of the action takes place in the southern province of Leinster. The story begins with a continuation of the *Wooing of Étaín* and focuses on the king Conaire Mór, a man who, like Oedipus of Greek myth, is pursued by relentless fate. The text was edited by Whitley Stokes in 1901 and by Eleanor Knott in 1936. Translations include Gantz, *Early Irish Myths and Sagas*, 60–106; and Koch and Carey, *The Celtic Heroic Age*, 166–184.

Athairne and Amairgen: This story is found in the *Book of Leinster* and is translated in Koch and Carey, *The Celtic Heroic Age*, 65–66.

Briccriu's Feast: The Irish *Fled Bricrenn* is a rambling story of heroic contests, Otherworld visitations, humor, and parody, with noticeable similarities in the final section to the English tale of *Sir Gawain and the Green Knight*. The text is presented in Koch and Carey, *The Celtic Heroic Age*, 76–105.

The Intoxication of the Ulstermen: The comic and loosely organized tale known in Irish as the *Mesca Ulad* is preserved in the *Book of Leinster* and the *Book of the Dun Cow*, but the stories in the two manuscripts are notably different from each other. The abridged story preserved here combines elements from both manuscripts, with the long passages of personal and place names omitted. The tale is published in Watson, *Mesca Ulad*; Gantz, *Early Irish Myths and Sagas*, 188–218; and Koch and Carey, *The Celtic Heroic Age*, 106–127.

The Wasting Sickness of Cú Chulainn and the Only Jealousy of Emer: Known in Irish as the *Serglige Con Culainn agus Óenét Emire*, this strange and beautiful story, found in the *Book of the Dun Cow*, is a combination of two earlier tales, causing some serious incongruities in the narrative. For example, in the first part of the text Cú Chulainn is married to Eithne Ingubai, who changes abruptly to Emer in the second half. (For the sake of narrative continuity I have made Emer his wife throughout.) The standard Irish text is Myles Dillon, *Serglige Con Culainn*. The story is translated in Gantz, *Early Irish Myths and Sagas*, 153–178.

The Death of Cú Chulainn. There are various stories of Cú Chulainn's death, some involving Queen Medb of Connacht and others the battle goddess Badb who is angry at Cú Chulainn for killing her father. This account is adapted from the *Book of Leinster* version. See Tymoczko, *Two Death Tales from the Ulster Cycle*, and Koch and Carey, *The Celtic Heroic Age*, 134–143.

Chapter 6: Stories of the Irish Otherworld

The Adventure of Nera: The *Echtra Nera* text is translated in Koch and Carey, *The Celtic Heroic Age*, 127–132. The cave at Cruachan features regularly in early Irish stories as a passage to the Otherworld. I have omitted from the story a secondary tale of Nera's bull calf, which he brings out of the *síd* and which loses a fight with the White Bull found in the *Táin Bó Cuailnge*.

The Adventure of Cormac: Texts of the *Echtra Cormaic* are found in several medieval manuscripts. It is translated by Koch and Carey, *The Celtic Heroic Age*, 184–187.

The Adventure of Conla: The *Echtrae Conli* is translated in Jackson, *A Celtic Miscellany*, 143–145.

The Adventures of the Sons of Eochaid Mugmedón: The *Echtra Mac nEchach Muigmedóin* is an eleventh-century tale found in the *Yellow Book of Lecan* and the *Book of Ballymote*. The story is translated in Koch and Carey, *The Celtic Heroic Age*, 203–208. The theme of an ugly woman transformed into beautiful sovereignty is a motif found in Chaucer's "Wife of Bath's Tale" in the *Canterbury Tales* and elsewhere in medieval literature.

The Voyage of Bran: The *Imram Brain* is an early story found in several manuscripts, including the *Book of the Dun Cow* and the *Book of Leinster*. The original story contains extensive verse segments, most of which I have omitted. The text was edited and translated by Meyer, *The Voyage of Bran*.

Chapter 7: Finn the Outlaw

The Boyhood Deeds of Finn: The *Macgnímartha Finn* is one early tale in the large and widespread corpus of stories about Finn. The best edition is Meyer, "Boyish Exploits of Finn." For Finn in general, the best study is Nagy, *The Wisdom of the Outlaw*.

The Pursuit of Diarmuid and Gráinne: The most famous narrative in the Fenian Cycle, the texts of the story date only from modern times, though parts of the tale are much older. The best edition and translation is Ní Sheaghdha, *Tóraidheacht Dhiarmada agus Gráinne.*

Chapter 8: Welsh Mythology—The *Mabinogi*

The Mabinogi: The sources of the *Mabinogi* are primarily two manuscripts written around the late 1300s to early 1400s and housed in the National Library of Wales and in Oxford's Bodleian Library. A standard Welsh edition is Williams, *Pedair Keinc y Mabinogi*, with recent translations by Davies, *The Mabinogion*, and Ford, *The Mabinogi and Other Medieval Welsh Tales.*

Chapter 9: Welsh Stories and Sagas

The tale of *Lludd and Lleuelys* (Welsh *Cyfranc Llud a Llefelys*) is translated in Ford, *The Mabinogi and Other Medieval Welsh Tales*, 111–117. *Gwion Bach and Taliesin* is translated in Ford, 159–181. The eleventh-century *Culhwch and Olwen* is edited by Bromwich, *Culhwch ac Olwen*, and translated by Ford, 119–157.

Chapter 10: Christian Mythology

Saint Patrick: The best scholarly edition in the original Latin of these is Ludwig Bieler, *Libri Epistolarum Sancti Patricii Episcopi*. The Latin text of Muirchú along with translation is found in Bieler, *The Patrician Texts in the Book of Armagh*, 62–123. Both Patrick's letters and Muirchú are translated in my *World of Saint Patrick*.

a wicked British king named Corotic: Patrick names this British king as Coroticus in his *Letter to the Soldiers of Coroticus*. In this document Patrick describes how Coroticus had kidnapped or killed some of his Irish converts, then ignored Patrick's pleas to release them.

Mudebroth: This is probably a corrupted phrase of Patrick's native language of British meaning "by the judgment of God."

Saint Brigid: There is not yet a proper scholarly edition of the life of Brigid by Cogitosus, but a complete translation can be found in my *World of Saint Patrick*, 95–128.

Saint Brendan: The Latin text and scholarly discussion is found in Selmer, *Navigatio Sancti Brendani Abbatis*. The story is translated in O'Meara, *The Voyage of Saint Brendan*, and in my *World of Saint Patrick*, 129–197.

GLOSSARY

Adsagsona A Gaulish goddess invoked by a cult of women in the first-century A.D. tablet from Larzac in southern France.
Áed Abrat The Otherworld father of Fand and Óengus.
Aericula Divine consort of Dis Pater in ancient Gaul.
Afagddu (Welsh, "utter darkness") An alternate name for Morfran.
Aife Along with her rival Scáthach, a skilled woman warrior of Britain. She sleeps with Cú Chulainn and is the mother of his only son, Conla.
Ailbe (1) Famous dog of Mac Dá Thó, sought by the kings of Ulster and Connacht. (2) Daughter of Cormac in the *Adventure of Cormac.*
Ailill (1) Husband of Medb and king of Connacht. (2) Son of Eochaid Mugmedón who yields authority to his half-brother Niall. (3) Father of Étaín. (4) Lovesick brother of Eochaid who longs for Étaín.
Albiorix Gaulish epithet for Mars.
Alisanos Gaulish god, perhaps associated with rock.
Amairgen (1) Son of Míl Espáine, poet who invokes the forces of nature against the Tuatha Dé Danann. (2) Born a hideously ugly son of Eccet Salach, he becomes chief poet of Ulster.
Andraste British goddess invoked by Boudicca with the sacrifice of a hare.

Annwfn Welsh name for the Celtic Otherworld.

Anu Irish mother goddess; the breast-shaped mountains called the Paps of Anu in Munster are named for her.

Apollo Greek and Roman god of healing, his name is given to a Gaulish god of similar function known by various epithets, such as Apollo Belenus.

Arawn King of Annwfn, the Welsh Otherworld, and friend of Pwyll.

Arberth Royal residence of Pwyll in the Welsh land of Dyfed.

Arianrhod Mother of Dylan and Lleu Llaw Gyffes, she fails a virginity test to be a foot-holder for Math.

Armagh Site in northern Ireland near the Ulster capital of Emain Macha; the church and town were traditionally founded by Saint Patrick.

Arthur Famous king of Britain and uncle of Culhwch.

Athairne Chief poet of Ulster until replaced by Amairgen.

Balor Evil-eyed king of the Formorians killed by Lug.

Banba Irish goddess whose name, along with those of Fódla and Ériu, is associated with Ireland.

bard A poet and singer of high status throughout the Celtic world.

Barrind Monk who tells Saint Brendan of the Land Promised to the Saints.

Bé Chuille Magical woman of the Tuatha Dé Danann.

Bé Find Magical woman of the Otherworld, mother of Fróech, sister of Bóand.

Belenus Ancient Celtic healing god known from Italy, Gaul, and Britain.

Beli Mawr King of Britain, father of Lludd and Lleuelys.

Belisama (Gallo-British, "brightest") Water goddess of Gaul and Britain equated with Minerva.

Beltaine Irish spring festival of May 1, associated with fire.

Bendigeidfran (Welsh, "The Blessed Crow") Son of the sea god Llyr, brother of Branwen and Manawydan.

Benignus Young apprentice of Saint Patrick.

Bith Son of Noah and father of Cesair in the *Book of Invasions*.

Blaí Briuga A foster father of Cú Chulainn and Ulster warrior known for his hospitality.

Blodeuedd (Welsh, "Flower Face") Woman created from flowers by Gwydion and Math, she betrayed Lleu Llaw Gyffes and later was transformed into an owl.

Boadach Ruler of the otherworldly Land of the Living.

Bóand (Irish, "White Cow") Goddess of the Boyne River, mother of Óengus by an affair with the Dagda.

Bodbmall Druidess and warrior who trains the young outlaw Finn.

Book of Invasions (Irish, *Lebor Gabála Érenn*) Mythological history of the conquests of Ireland.

Book of Leinster (Irish, *Lebor Laignech*) Manuscript compiled in the late twelfth century, a major source of Irish myth and legend.

Book of the Dun Cow (Irish, *Lebor na hUidre*) Manuscript of the early twelfth century containing early versions of many Irish myths and epics.

Borvo (Gaulish, "boiling") Gaulish god of healing springs.

Boudicca Historical queen of the Iceni tribe of eastern Britain who led a rebellion against the Romans.

Branwen Daughter of Llyr, sister of Bendigeidfran, given to Matholwch king of Ireland as his bride.

Brega Broad plain between the Boyne and Liffey rivers in eastern Ireland.

Brendan Irish saint who sails with his monks to the Land Promised to the Saints.

Breogon A leader of the Milesians in the *Book of Invasions* who built a tower on the northern coast of Spain from which his son Íth first saw Ireland.

Bres Beautiful son of the Tuatha Dé Danann woman Ériu and the Formorian king Elatha, he leads the Formorians against the Tuatha Dé in the second battle of Mag Tuired.

Bresal Druid and foster father of Fuamnach who gave her the spells to drive Étaín from Midir.

Briccriu Evil-tongued warrior among the Ulstermen who delights in making trouble.

Brigantia British goddess equated with Minerva.

Brigid (1) Triple goddess of fertility, medicine, and poetry among the Irish. (2) Early Christian saint who founded a monastery at Kildare.

Brixianus Epithet for Gaulish god Jupiter.

Brown Bull of Cuailnge (Irish, *Donn Cuailnge*) Ulster bull stolen by Medb in the *Táin Bó Cuailnge.*

Bruig na Bóinne Large Neolithic passage tomb of Newgrange in the Boyne River valley north of Dublin. It became in Irish mythology the Otherworld residence first of the Dagda, then of Óengus.

Bull Feast (Irish, *Feis Temro*) Also known as the Bull Sleep, a magical ritual in which a man drank the broth of a bull and dreamed of the proper choice for the new king.

Cailb Female seer who foretells the death of Conaire in the *Destruction of Dá Derga's Hostel.*

Cairenn Wife of Eochaid Mugmedón and mother of Niall of the Nine Hostages.

Caledfwlch Name for Arthur's sword, the later Excalibur.

Camall Doorkeeper of the Tuatha Dé in the *Second Battle of Mag Tuired.*

Caswallawn Son of Beli Mawr, he conquers Britain in Bendigeidfran's absence.

Cathbad Druid in the court of Conchobar mac Nessa featured frequently in the Ulster Cycle of tales.

Caturix (Gaulish, "battle king") Epithet of Gaulish Mars.

Ceridwen Mother of Morfran who brews the magical drops of poetry stolen by Gwion Bach.

Cernunnos (Gaulish, "horned") Gaulish god of nature and animals.

Cesair Granddaughter of Noah and leader of the first settlement of Ireland according to the *Book of Invasions.*

Cet Connacht warrior in the *Story of Mac Dá Thó's Pig* who is bested by the Ulsterman Conall Cernach.

Cethern Connacht warrior in the Ulster Cycle and teacher of Finn in the Fenian Cycle.

Cigfa Wife of Pryderi in the *Mabinogi.*

Cilydd Welsh king, husband of Goleuddydd and father of Culhwch.

Conaire King of Ireland beset by conflicting prohibitions in the *Destruction of Dá Derga's Hostel.*

Conall Cernach Leading warrior and hero in many tales of the Ulster Cycle.

Conchobar mac Nessa Ulster king who rules at Emain Macha and is prominent in many tales of the Ulster Cycle.

Condere Ulster warrior who is the first to face Cú Chulainn's son Conla.

Connacht Province of western Ireland ruled by Ailill and Medb in many Ulster Cycle tales.

Conn Cétchathach (Irish, "Conn of the Hundred Battles") Famed Irish king and father of Conla (2).

Conla (1) Son of Aife and Cú Chulainn, he is killed by his father. (2) Son of Conn of a Hundred Battles who follows a magical woman into the Otherworld never to return.

Coraniaid Evil, magical race who harass Britain in *Lludd and Lleuelys*.

Cormac (1) Cormac mac Airt, legendary king of Ireland at Tara. (2) Son of the Ulster king Conchobar.

Corotic British king who harasses Christians in the legendary story of Saint Patrick and is changed into a fox; he is based on the historical king Coroticus in Patrick's *Letter to the Soldiers of Coroticus*.

Cruachan Capital of the province of Connacht and site of a cave which serves as an entrance to the Otherworld.

Cruinniuc Wealthy but foolish farmer of Ulster who marries Macha.

Cú Chulainn Born Sétanta, the most famous of Irish warriors, hero of the *Táin Bó Cuailnge* and the Ulster Cycle tales.

Culann Owner of the hound slain by Cú Chulainn from which the hero took his name.

Culhwch Hero of the Welsh Arthurian tale of *Culhwch and Olwen* who wins as his bride Olwen, daughter of the giant Ysbaddaden.

Cumall Irish outlaw leader and father of Finn.

Cunomaglus Gaulish epithet of the god Apollo.

Cú Roí Magical hero and judge of Munster.

Cymidei Cymeinfoll Giantess and previous owner of a magical cauldron in *Branwen*, the second branch of the *Mabinogi*.

Dagda (Irish, "the good god") Also known as Eochaid Ollathair ("father of all"), a leader of the Tuatha Dé Danann.
Damona Gaulish goddess and consort of the god Borvo.
Deichtine Sister of King Conchobar of Ulster and mother of Cú Chulainn.
Deirdre Tragic heroine beloved by Noíse in the *Exile of the Sons of Uisnech.*
Demne Boyhood name of the outlaw Finn.
Dianann A woman weaver of magic among the Tuatha Dé Danann.
Dian Cécht Physician among the Tuatha Dé Danann.
Diarmuid Hero and lover of Gráinne in the Fenian Cycle.
Díchu First convert of Saint Patrick in Ireland.
Dis Pater Roman name for the god of the dead in Gaulish religion.
Dôn Mother of Gilfaethwy and Gwydion.
Donn Irish god of the dead, also identified with a son of Míl of the Milesians.
Donn Cuailnge Brown Bull of Ulster sought by Medb in the *Táin Bó Cuailnge.*
druid A member of the priestly class in pre-Christian Celtic religion.
Dubthach (1) Ulster warrior. (2) Father of Saint Brigid.
Dunatis Gaulish god of fortified places.
Dyfed Province in southwestern Wales ruled by Pwyll and later Pryderi.
Dylan Son of Arianrhod.
Éber Donn Son of Míl Espáine.
Eccet Salach Ulster blacksmith and father of poet Amairgen.
Efnisien Malevolent brother of Nisien and half-brother of Branwen.
Eithne (1) Mother of Óengus by an affair with the Dagda. (2) In some stories, a wife of Cú Chulainn. (3) Wife of Cormac, king of Ireland.
Elatha Formorian king who fathered Bres with Ériu.
Elcmar Original lord of the Bruig na Bóinne who is tricked out of his holding by Óengus.
Éle Most beautiful of the fairy women in the Fenian Cycle.
Elphin Spendthrift son who discovers baby Taliesin in a fish weir.

Emain Macha Capital of Ulster and seat of its kings.
Emer Wife of Cú Chulainn.
Eochaid (1) Eochaid Ollathair, alternate name for the Dagda. (2) Eochaid Mugmedón, father of Niall of the Nine Hostages. (3) Eochaid mac Eirc, king of the Fir Bolg. (4) Eochaid Airem, king of Ireland and husband of Étaín.
Eochu (1) Eochu Feidlech, king of Ireland and father of Medb. (2) Son of Erc, early ruler of Ireland.
Éogan Warrior who killed Noíse when he returned to Ireland.
Epona Gaulish horse goddess.
Ériu Tuatha Dé Danann mother of Bres, the poet Amairgen agreed to give her name to Ireland.
Esus Important Gaulish god depicted as a woodcutter.
Étaín (1) Beautiful woman who is beloved by Midir in the *Wooing of Étaín*. (2) Étaín Óg ("Étaín the Young"), daughter of Étaín (1).
Étar Ulster king whose wife gives birth to reborn Étaín (1).
Eterscél Father of Conaire Mór by his own daughter Étaín (2) or in the *Destruction of Dá Derga's Hostel*, by her stepdaughter.
Fand Wife of Manannán and Otherworld lover of Cú Chulainn.
Fedelm Prophetess of Connacht.
Fedlimid Chief storyteller of Ulster and father of Deirdre.
Fer Caille Deformed man with a hideous wife who greets Conaire in the *Destruction of Dá Derga's Hostel*.
Ferdia Foster brother of Cú Chulainn who is slain by him in the *Táin Bó Cuailnge*.
Fergus mac Roich Former king of Ulster, leader of the Ulster exiles in Connacht.
Fer Loga Charioteer of Ailill and Medb.
Fiacha Son of Conchobar slain while protecting Noíse.
fidchell Early Irish board game.
Finn Finn mac Cumhaill, outlaw leader and hero of the Fenian Cycle.
Finnabair Daughter of Ailill and Medb.
Finnbennach Medb's white bull in the *Táin Bó Cuailnge*.
Finnchaem Sister of Conchobar.
Finnéces Seer who unwittingly helps the boy Finn gain the power of divination.

Fintan mac Néill Ruler of one-third of Ulster.
Fir Bolg Early settlers of Ireland.
Fir Domnann Early settlers of Ireland.
Follamain Son of Conchobar who dies leading the boy troop against Connacht invaders.
Forgall Monach Father of Emer who opposes her marriage to Cú Chulainn.
Formorians Sometimes monstrous but powerful early race of Ireland who oppress and battle the Tuatha Dé Danann.
Fótla One of three goddesses who gave her name to Ireland.
Fróech Connacht warrior and hero of the *Cattle Raid of Fróech*.
Fuamnach First wife of Midir who seeks to destroy Étaín.
gae bolga Unstoppable spear of Cú Chulainn.
Gaels Name for the Irish, often associated with the Milesian invaders of the *Book of Invasions*.
Galatia Area of Asia Minor invaded and settle by Celts in the third century B.C.E.
Galeóin Mighty warriors of Leinster whom Medb sought to kill.
Gaul Ancient name for what is roughly modern-day France.
geis (plural, *gessa*) Irish word for a prohibition or taboo placed on a person.
Gilfaethwy Brother of Gwydion who rapes Goewin in the fourth branch of the *Mabinogi*.
Goewin Virgin foot-holder of Math raped by Gilfaethwy, later wife of Math.
Goibniu Smith of the Tuatha Dé Danann.
Goleuddydd Wife of Cilydd and mother of Culhwch in *Culhwch and Olwen*.
Gráinne Daughter of Cormac mac Airt who elopes with Diarmuid to escape marriage to Finn.
Grannus Epithet of Gaulish Apollo.
Greth Servant of the poet Athairne.
Gronw Pebyr Welsh hunter who has affair with Blodeuedd.
Gundestrup Cauldron Large and ornate silver cauldron from antiquity found in peat bog in Denmark, decorated with scenes that seem to depict Celtic mythology.
Gwawl Rival suitor for Rhiannon defeated by Pwyll.
Gwenhwyfar Wife of King Arthur.

Gwern Son of Branwen and Matholwch.

Gwion Bach Young servant who steals the gift of poetic inspiration from Ceridwen and becomes Taliesin.

Gwri Son of Rhiannon and Pwyll, later renamed Pryderi.

Gwydion Son of Dôn and brother of Gilfaethwy transformed by Math as punishment for raping Goewin.

Hafgan Otherworld rival of King Arawn of Annwfn.

Hercules Greek and Roman hero of supernatural strength equated with the Gaulish god Ogmios.

Ibor Charioteer of Conchobar.

imbas forasnai Irish magical ritual in which a poet chews the raw flesh of a pig, dog, or cat to gain prophetic knowledge.

Ír Son of Míl Espáine who drowns during the invasion of Ireland.

Island of Women Female-only island in the *Voyage of Bran*.

Íth Milesian leader who first sailed from Spain to Ireland, where he was killed.

Jasconius Enormous sea creature in the *Voyage of Brendan*.

Judas Betrayer of Christ found undergoing punishment in the *Voyage of Brendan*.

Jupiter Chief Roman deity, identified with a Gaulish god by Julius Caesar.

Kildare (Irish, "church of the oak") Monastic site west of modern Dublin founded by Saint Brigid.

Korneli Cornish saint whose cult may continue elements of the Gaulish god Cernunnos.

Labraid Lúathlám Otherworld Irish king who sends his wife Lí Ban to seek the help of Cú Chulainn.

Ladicus Epithet of Celtic god Jupiter found in Spain.

Land Promised to the Saints Christian island paradise with many elements of the Celtic Otherworld in the *Voyage of Saint Brendan*.

Leborcham Woman poet and satirist in the *Exile of the Sons of Uisliu*.

Leinster Province in southeast Ireland.

Lenus Epithet of Mars in Gaul and Britain.

Ler Irish sea god, father of Manannán.

Lia Fáil Magical stone on the Hill of Tara that proclaims a true king of Ireland.

Liath Macha Favorite horse of Cú Chulainn.

Lí Ban Otherworld woman, sister of Fand, who invites Cú Chulainn to her land to help her husband Laibraid Lúathlám.

Liffey River in eastern Ireland.

Llassar Llaes Gyfnewid Original owner of the magical cauldron of rebirth.

Lleu Llaw Gyffes Son of Arianrhod aided by Gwydion.

Lleuelys Wise brother of Lludd and king of France.

Lludd Son of Beli Mawr and brother of Lleuelys who delivers Britain from three plagues.

Llyr Father of Manawydan, probably related in origin to the Irish sea god Ler.

Llwyd Brother of Gwawl who yields to Manawydan and restores the land of Dyfed.

Lochan Blacksmith who gives his daughter to Finn.

Lochru Druid of King Lóegaire defeated by Saint Patrick.

Lóeg Charioteer of Cú Chulainn.

Lóegaire (1) Lóegaire Búadach, Ulster hero. (2) Lóegaire mac Néill, pagan king of Tara defeated and converted by Saint Patrick.

Lucet Máel Druid of King Lóegaire defeated by Saint Patrick.

Lug Tuatha Dé Danann hero and divine father of Cú Chulainn.

Lugaid mac Con Roí Slayer of Cú Chulainn.

Lughnasa Holiday on August 1 in celebration of the god Lug.

Lugus Ancient Celtic god probably identical with Caesar's Mercury.

Mabinogi Masterwork of medieval Welsh literature in four branches composed in perhaps the twelfth century but drawing on older traditions.

Mabon Son of mother Modron, rescued by Arthur in *Culhwch and Olwen.*

mac Irish "son"

Mac Dá Thó Keeper of a hostel and owner of the dog Ailbe fought over by the leaders of Connacht and Ulster.

Macha Otherworld woman who, after giving birth to twins after being forced to race by Conchobar, curses the Ulstermen with the debilitating pain of childbirth when attacked.

Mac Cécht Loyal companion of Conaire in the *Destruction of Dá Derga's Hostel.*

Macc Cuill moccu Graecae Murderous pagan converted by Saint Patrick.

Mac Óg (Irish, "the young son") Alternate name for Óengus.
Mac Roth Messenger of Queen Medb.
Madron Mother of Mabon, related to Gaulish mother goddess Matrona.
Maelgwn King of Gwynedd in northern Wales.
Mag Tuired Plain of uncertain location where multiple battles were fought in Irish mythology.
Manannán Son of Ler, sea god of the Irish.
Manawydan Son of Llyr, Welsh hero of the third branch of the *Mabinogi*, husband of Rhiannon.
Maponos Gaulish and British divine youth, often linked to Apollo.
Mars Roman god of war and healing, linked to the Gaulish god Teutates.
Math Lord of Gwynedd and uncle of Gwydion in the *Mabinogi*.
Matholwch King of Ireland in the second branch of the *Mabinogi*.
Matrona Gaulish mother goddess who gave her name to the Marne River.
Medb Wife of Ailill, queen of Connacht and foe of Ulster.
Mercury Roman name given by Julius Caesar to the chief Gaulish divinity, probably Lugus.
Mernoc Hermit who discovered the Island of Delight in the *Voyage of Brendan*.
Midir A king of the Tuatha Dé Danann and husband of Étaín.
Míl Eponymous ancestor of the Milesian people who invaded Ireland and defeated the Tuatha Dé Danann.
Milesians Descendants of Míl Espáine who were the final invaders of Ireland.
Miliucc Druid and owner of Saint Patrick when he was a young slave in Ireland.
Minerva Roman goddess and name given to the only female Gaulish divinity named by Julius Caesar.
Modron Mother of the abducted Mabon in *Culhwch and Olwen*.
Monesan British girl of natural inclination to God, converted by Saint Patrick.
Mongfhind Wife of Eochaid Mugmedón and jealous stepmother of Niall of the Nine Hostages.
Morann Druid adviser of Conchobar who predicts birth of Cú Chulainn.

Morfran Also known as Afagddu, ugly son of Ceridwen cheated out of his poetic gift by Gwion Bach.

Morna Clan who killed Finn's father and sought to kill Finn as well.

Mórrígan Irish goddess of war.

mudebroth Curse uttered by Saint Patrick which may be his native British for "by the God of judgment."

Mugain Wife of Conchobar.

Muirgen Poet to whom the phantom of Fergus mac Roich recites the *Táin Bó Cuailnge.*

Muirne Mother of Finn.

Munster Province in southwestern Ireland.

Nantosvelta Gaulish and British goddess associated with ravens.

Nechtan A companion of Bran in his voyage across the sea.

Nechta Scéne Father of the first three warriors to face and be slain by Cú Chulainn.

Nehalennia Gaulish goddess perhaps associated with seafarers.

Nemed Leader of the third group of invaders of Ireland in the *Book of Invasions.*

Nemedians Early invaders of Ireland led by Nemed.

Némglan Otherworld king of birds in the *Destruction of Dá Derga's Hostel.*

Nera Young Connacht warrior who dares to face the forces of the Otherworld on Samain.

Nes Mother of King Conchobar.

Niall Niall of the Nine Hostages (Niall Noígiallach), son of Eochaid Mugmedón and British slave Cairenn, he rises to become high king of Ireland.

Nisien Kindly brother of Efnisien.

Noíse Warrior and lover of Deirdre.

Nuadu Nuadu Airgetlám ("silverarm"), king of the Tuatha Dé Danann.

Óengus Also known as Mac Óg, son of the Dagda and god of youth among the Tuatha Dé Danann.

Ogam Early native form of Irish script of lines and notches used primarily for grave markers but also having magical associations.

Ogma God of poetry among the Tuatha Dé Danann.

Ogmios Gaulish god of eloquence associated with Hercules.

Oisín Son of Finn, warrior and poet.
Olwen Daughter of giant Ysbaddaden sought by Culhwch.
Oscar Son of Oisín, grandson of Finn.
Otherworld Supernatural Celtic world of gods and spirits often entered through an ancient *síd* burial mound, a cave, or a distant island.
Paradise of Birds Island encountered by Saint Brendan on his voyage.
Partholón Leader of the second mythic invasion of Ireland.
Partholonians Followers of Partholón who were early settlers of Ireland.
Patrick Historical saint of the fifth century who preached Christianity in Ireland.
Posidonius Greek philosopher who traveled to Gaul in the first century B.C.E. and recorded accounts of Gaulish culture.
Pryderi Son of Pwyll and Rhiannon, the only continuous character in the *Mabinogi*.
Pwyll Prince of Dyfed, husband of Rhiannon, and father of Pryderi.
Rhiannon Otherworld wife of Pwyll and Manawydan, mother of Pryderi.
Rhun Son of Maelgwn sent to seduce Elphin's wife.
Rosmerta Gaulish goddess of prosperity frequently paired with Gaulish Mercury.
Sainrith Father of Macha.
Samain Annual Irish harvest feast on November 1, when Otherworld encounters often take place.
Saxons Germanic people who invaded Celtic Britain beginning in the fifth century A.D.
Scáthach Woman warrior of Britain who trains Cú Chulainn.
Sémión Descendant of Nemedian invaders of Ireland who traveled to Greece and whose own descendants returned to Ireland.
Sencha Chief judge of Ulster under Conchobar.
Senchán Torpéist Chief bard of Ireland whose visit to King Gúaire of Connacht prompts the rediscovery of the *Táin Bó Cuailnge*.
Sequana Gaulish goddess of the River Seine.
Sétanta Boyhood name of Cú Chulainn.

síd (plural, *síde*) Ancient Irish burial mound and frequent entrance to the Otherworld.

Sithchenn Druid at the court of Eochaid Mugmedón.

Sliab Fúait Mountain in County Armagh.

Sliab Mis (1) Mountain on the Dingle peninsula where the Gaels first battled the Tuatha Dé Danann. (2) Mountain in County Antrim where young Patrick was traditionally held in slavery.

Sreng Fir Bolg warrior who cuts off the hand of Nuadu.

Sualdam Mortal father of Cú Chulainn.

Sucellus Gaulish god often depicted with long beard and hammer in his hands.

Sulis British goddess of healing.

Táin Bó Cuailnge Central Irish epic of a cattle raid by Connacht rulers Ailill and Medb on Ulster to obtain a prized bull.

Taliesin Born Gwion Bach, he is reborn as the greatest poet of Welsh tradition.

Tara Hill north of Dublin that was the traditional seat of the high king of Ireland.

Taranis Important Gaulish god associated with thunder.

Tarvos Trigaranus Gaulish god pictured in sculpture with bull and cranes.

Temair Luachra Royal residence of Munster kings.

Teutates Important Gaulish god whose victims were sacrificed by drowning.

Teyrnon Twrf Liant Lord of Gwent Is Coed who discovers child Pryderi.

Tír Tairngaire Otherworldly Land of Promise in Irish tradition associated with sea god Manannán.

Torna Poet who rescues baby Niall.

Triath Boy of the Fir Bolg who prompts Óengus to discover his true father.

Tuán mac Cairill Sole survivor of the Partholonian invaders of Ireland who is reborn in animal form repeatedly until the time of Saint Patrick.

tuath (plural, *tuatha*) Irish "tribe."

Tuatha Dé Danann Also known as the Tuatha Dé, magical invaders of Ireland defeated at last by the Milesians and driven underground to become the fairy people of Ireland.

Twrch Trwyth Ferocious boar hunted by Culhwch and his companions.

Uathach Daughter of Scáthach and lover of Cú Chulainn.

Uisliu Father of Noíse and his brothers.

Uisnech Hill in County Westmeath considered in Irish mythology to be the ritual center of the island.

Ulaid Ulster tribesmen of northern Ireland.

Ulster Northern province of Ireland.

Ulster Cycle Series of stories recounting the adventures of Ulster heroes.

Victoricus Angel who helps Saint Patrick.

Yellow Book of Lecan Important Irish manuscript collection compiled in late fourteenth century.

Ysbaddaden Welsh giant and father of Olwen.

BIBLIOGRAPHY

Aldhouse-Green, Miranda. *The Celtic Myths: A Guide to the Ancient Gods and Legends*. London: Thames and Hudson, 2015.

Bergin, Osborn, and R. I. Best. "Tomarc Étaíne." *Ériu* 12 (1938): 137–196.

Bieler, Ludwig. *Libri Epistolarum Sancti Patricii Episcopi*. Dublin: Royal Irish Academy, 1993.

Bieler, Ludwig. *The Patrician Texts in the Book of Armagh*. Dublin: Dublin Institute for Advanced Studies, 1979.

Bromwich, Rachel. *Culhwch ac Olwen*. Cardiff: University of Wales Press, 1992.

Byrne, Mary, and Miles Dillon. *Táin Bó Fraích*. Dublin: Dublin Institute for Advanced Study, 1933.

Carey, John. "Scél Tuáin meic Chairill." *Ériu* 35 (1984): 93–111.

Carson, Ciaran. *The Táin*. New York: Penguin, 2007.

Davies, Sioned. *The Mabinogion*. Oxford: Oxford University Press, 2007.

Dillon, Myles. *Serglige Con Culainn*. Dublin: Dublin Institute for Advanced Studies, 1953.

Ford, Patrick. *The Mabinogi and Other Medieval Welsh Tales*. Berkeley: University of California Press, 2008.

Freeman, Philip. *War, Women, and Druids: Eyewitness Reports and Early Accounts of the Ancient Celts*. Austin: University of Texas Press, 2002.

Freeman, Philip. *The World of Saint Patrick*. New York: Oxford University Press, 2014.

Gantz, Jeffery. *Early Irish Myths and Sagas*. New York: Penguin, 1981.

Grey, Elizabeth A. *Cath Maige Tuired*. Dublin: Irish Texts Society, 1982.

Jackson, Kenneth. *A Celtic Miscellany*. New York: Penguin, 1971.

Kinsella, Thomas. *The Táin*. Oxford: Oxford University Press, 1969.

Koch, John, and John Carey. *The Celtic Heroic Age*. Aberystwyth, Wales: Celtic Studies Publications, 2003.

Macalister, R. A. Stewart. *Book of Invasions*. London: Irish Texts Society, 1993.

Mac Cana, Proinsias. *Celtic Mythology*. New York: Peter Bedrick Books, 1983.

MacKillop, James. *Dictionary of Celtic Mythology*. Oxford: Oxford University Press, 1998.

Meid, Wolfgang. *Táin Bó Fraích*. Dublin: Dublin Institute for Advanced Studies, 1974.

Meyer, Kuno. "Boyish Exploits of Finn." *Ériu* 1 (1904): 180–190.

Meyer, Kuno. *The Voyage of Bran*. London: David Nutt, 1895.

Nagy, Joseph. *The Wisdom of the Outlaw*. Berkeley: University of California Press, 1985.

Ní Sheaghdha, Nessa. *Tóraidheacht Dhiarmada agus Gráinne*. Dublin: Irish Texts Society, 1967.

O'Meara, John. *The Voyage of Saint Brendan*. Buckinghamshire: Colin Smythe, 1991.

O'Rahilly, Cecile. *Táin Bó Cuailnge: Recension I*. Dublin: Dublin Institute for Advanced Studies, 1976.

Selmer, Carl. *Navigatio Sancti Brendani Abbatis*. Dublin: Four Courts Press, 1989.

Thurneysen, Rudolph. *Scéla Muicce Meic Dá Thó*. Dublin: Dublin Institute for Advanced Study, 1935.

Tymoczko, Maria. *Two Death Tales from the Ulster Cycle*. Dublin: Dolmen Press, 1981.

Watson, J. Carmichael. *Mesca Ulad*. Dublin: Dublin Institute for Advanced Studies, 1983.

Williams, Ifor. *Pedair Keinc y Mabinogi*. Caerdydd: Gwasg Prifysgol Cymru, 1996.

INDEX

Adam, 15
Adsagsona, 12
Aericula, 7
Afagddu, 200
Agnoman, 17
Aife, 73–74
Ailbe, 92
Ailbe, daughter of Cormac, 142
Ailill, king of Connacht, 57, 77, 84, 90–91, 92–94, 97, 98–103, 118, 125, 137–141
Ailill, king of Ulster, 33–34
Ailill Anguba, 38–40
Albiorix, 4
Alisanos, 12
Amairgen, chief poet of Ulster, 60, 115–116
Amairgen, son of Míl, 25–27, 123
Andraste, 12
Anluán, 96
Annwfn, 166
Apollo, 3–4
Aranrhod, 189–194
Arawn, 166–168
Aristotle, xi
Artemidorus, 10
Arthur, 206–211
Athairne, 115–116

Balor, 24
Banba, 26
bards, xii
Barrind, 231
Bé Chuille, 23
Bé Find, 98
Belenus, 4
Beli Mawr, 197
Belisama, 6
Beltaine, 4
Bendigeidfran, 174–180
birds, 7–8, 12, 58, 70, 75, 106–107, 127–128, 147, 154, 176, 179
Bith, 16
Blaí Briuga, 60
Bleiddwn, 189
Blodeuedd, 192–193
Boadach, 145
Bóand, 98

Bodbmall, 154
Borvo, 4
Boudicca, 12
Bran, 149–152
Branwen, 174–179
Brendan, St., xiv, 231–239
Breogan, 25
Bres, 19–20, 22–26
Bresal, 34–36
Briccriu, 58, 60, 75, 94, 116–120, 126
Brigantia, 12
Brigid, goddess, 12
Brigid, St., xiv, 12, 224–230
Brión, 140
Brixianus, 5
Bruig na Bóinne, 29–31, 34–35, 58
Buddha, 8
Bull Feast, 107
bulls, 78, 91
butterfly, 35–36

Caesar, Julius, xi, 1, 4–7, 10
Cailb, 112
Cairell, 28
Cairenn, 147
Cairpre, son of Cormac, 142
Camall mac Riagail, 21
Caswallawn, 197
Cathbad, 48, 52, 66–67, 75
Caturix, 4
Cei, 207
Celtchair, 95
Ceridwen, 199–200
Cerna, 108
Cernunnos, 8
Cesair, 14, 16
Cethern, 157
Cet mac Mágach, 94–96
Cichuil, 111
Cigfa, 180
Cilydd, 206
Cochar Cruibne, 73
Coipre, 23
Conaire, 106–113
Conall Cernach, 58, 68, 76, 96–97, 103–104, 114, 118–119, 121–122, 127, 136
Conchobar, 48–67, 71, 80, 89, 92, 116–117, 121, 123–124, 133
Condere, 75
Conla, son of Conn, 145–146
Conla, 74–76
Conn of the Hundred Battles, 146
Coraniaid, 198–199
Corann, 145
Cormac, king of Ulster, 105–106
Cormac, son of Art, 141–145, 159–160
Cormac, son of Conchobar, 56–57
Corotic, 221
Cruachain, 77, 91, 98, 101, 137, 139
Cruinniuc mac Agnomain, 50
Cruithne, 156
Cú Chulainn, 2, 46, 57–91, 118–123, 127–136, 153
Culann, 65–66
Culhwch, 205–211
Cumall, 153, 156
Cumscraid, 96
Cunomaglus, 4
Cú Roí, 120, 123, 125
curse, 51
Cymidei Cymeinfoll, 176

Dá Derga, 110–111
Dagda, 18, 20, 22–23, 29–35
Dáire, 222–223
Dáire mac Fiachna, 79–80
Damona, 4
Deichtine, 58–59
Deirdre, 53–57

Demeter, 10
Demne, 154, 157
Dianann, 23
Dian Cécht, 21, 23–24, 33
Diarmuid, 160–164
Díchu, 216, 224
Diodorus, x
Diorruing, 158–159
Dis, 7
Donn, 7
druids, xii, 13, 22, 28, 34, 60, 79, 125, 133, 145, 148–149, 154, 215–219
Dubthach, 56–57
Dunatis, 12
Dylan, 190

Éber Donn, 26
Eccet Salach, 115
Efnisien, 174–176, 178
Egypt, x
Eithne, 29–30
Eithne, wife of Cormac, 142
Elatha, 19–20
Elcmar, 29–32
Éle, 157
Elphin, 201–205
Emain Macha, 48, 51, 56–57, 61, 70, 91, 97, 116, 123, 133
Emer, 72, 74–76, 119–120, 127, 131–132, 136
Emine, 47
Eochaid Airem, 37–45
Eochaid Feidleach, 104–106
Eochaid mac Eirc, 18
Eochaid Mugmedón, 147
Eochaid Ollathair, 29–30
Eochaid Sálbuide, 48
Eochu, 18
Eogan mac Durthacht, 56–57, 63
Éogan Mór of Ulster, 95
Epona, 11
Ériu, 19, 26
Esus, 7
Étaín, 29–45, 105
Étar, 37, 105
Eterscél, 106–107
Eve, 15

fairies, 15
Fand, 129–133
Fannall, 68–69
Fedelm, seer of Connacht, 80–81
Fedelm, wife of Lóegaire, 119
Fedlimid mac Daill, 52
Fer Caille, 111
Ferdia, 73, 86–89
Fer Gar, 107
Fergus mac Roich, 47–48, 56, 60, 63, 75, 81–82, 90, 117, 120, 127
Fer Le, 107
Fer Loga, 97–98
Fer Rogain, 107
Fiacail, 158
Fiacha, son of Fergus, 56
Fiachal, 154
fidchell, 41–42, 155
Finn, 153–164
Finnabair, 98–99
Finnchaem, 60
Finnéces, 157
Fintain mac Néill, 123
Fir Bolg, 15, 17–19, 30
Fir Domnann, 17
flood, 14–16
Fóill, 68–69
Follomon, son of Conchobar, 61, 84
Forgall Monach, 72–73
Formorians, 15, 17, 19–20, 22–25
Fótla, 26

Fróech mac Fidaig, 82–83
Fróech son of Idath, 98–104
Fuamnach, 34–36, 39

gae bolga, 73, 76, 88
Gaels, 25–28
Gaile Dána, 86
Galatians, xi
Galeóin, 81
Gardens of Lug, 72
Gaul, xi, 1–13
geis, (plural *gessa*), 56, 107, 110–112, 134, 161
Germanus, 215
Gilfaethwy, 186–188
gods, xii, 1–13, 15
Goewin, 186–187
Goibniu, 23
Goleuddydd, 205
Goll, 153
Gráinne, 159–164
Grannus, 4
Gray, 154
Greth, 115–116
Gronw Pebyr, 193–195
Gúaire, 47
Gundestrup, 5
Gwawl, 171–172, 185
Gwern, 176, 178–179
Gwion Bach, 200–201
Gwri Golden-Hair, 173
Gwydion, 186–195

Hades, 7
Hafgan, 166–168
heads, xi, 49, 69, 121–123, 153, 179
Hercules, 9
horses, 11, 50–51, 58, 136, 168–169, 173

Ibor, 68–70
imbas forasnai, 80
Imbolc, 12
Ingcél Cáech, 109, 112–113
Ír, 25–26
Island of Delight, 231
Island of Joy, 151
Island of Smiths, 236
Island of Strong Men, 236
Island of Women, 150–151
Íth, 25

Jasconius, 235
Judas, 237–238
Jupiter, 3, 5

Keltoi, x
Korneli, 8

Labraid Lúathlám, 129–130
Ladicus, 5
Lám Gabuid, 95
Lámraige, 41–42
Land of Promise, 144
Land of the Living, 145
Land Promised to the Saints, 231, 235, 239
Larzac, 12
Leborcham, 53
Le Fer Flaith, 110
Lendabair, 119
Lenus, 4
Lewis, C. S., x
Lia Fáil, 18
Liath Macha, 136
Lí Ban, 129–130
Llassar Llaes Gyfnewid, 176
Lleuelys, 197–199
Lleu Llaw Gyffes, 3, 191–196
Llud, 197–199
Llwyd, 185
Lochan, 156
Lochru, 215–216
Lóeg, 130, 134
Lóegaire, king at Tara, 215–218

Lóegaire Buadach of Ulster, 94, 117–118, 121
Lomna Drúth, 113
Lucan, 5, 7
Lucet Máel, 215–219
Lucian, 9
Lucifer, 15, 18, 204, 235
Lug, 2–3, 21–25, 35, 59, 83–85
Lugaid mac Con Roí, 133–135
Lugaid Réoderg, 129
Lughnasa, 3

Mabinogi, xii, 165–196
Mabon, 4, 209–210
Macc Cuill moccu Graccae, 221–222
Mac Cécht, 110, 113–114
Mac Dá Thó, 92–98
Macha, 11, 50–51, 80
Mac Óg, 30
Mac Roth, 78–79
Maelgwn, 201–204
Mag Tuired, 18, 23–25
Maine, 109
Manandán, son of Ler, 130, 132–133, 144–145, 150
Manawydan, 174, 179–185
Maponos, 4
Marbán, 47
Mars, 3–4
Massalia, 6
Math, 185–196
Matholwch, 174–177
Matrona, 11
Maximus of Tyre, 5
Medb, 57, 77–91, 92–94, 97, 98–103, 125, 137–141
Mend, 95
Mercury, 1, 8
Merlin, 204
Mernoc, 231
Midir, 29–45
Míl, 15, 25, 123
Miliucc, 214–216
Minerva, 3, 6–7, 10
Monesan, 220–221
Mongfhind, 147
Morann, 60
Morfran, 200
Morna, 153
Mórrígan, 22, 90, 134
mother goddess, 10–11
Mugain, 71
Muirgen, 47–48
Muirne, 154
Muirthemne, 61
Munremar, 95

Nantosvelta, 8
Nechtan, 151–152
Nechta Scéne, 68
Nehalennia, 12
Nemedians, 15, 17
Némglan, 107
Nera, 138–141
Nes, 48–49
Niall, son of Eochaid Mugmedón, 147
Nimrod, 25
Ninniaw, 197
ninth wave, 27
Nisien, 174
Noah, 14–16, 25
Noíse, 53–57
Nuadu, 18–19, 21

oak, 5
ocean, ix
Odin, 7
Óengus, 30–35, 162
Óengus, son of Áed Abrat, 129
Óengus of Ulster, 94
Ogam, 8, 82
Ogma, 8, 10, 20, 22–23, 35
Ogmios, 8–10
Oisín, 158–161

Olwen, 206–211
Oscar, 163
Otherworld, xiii, 98, 101, 105, 110, 129, 131, 137–152, 157

Paps of Anu, 158
Paradise of Birds, 234–235
Partholonians, 15–16
Patrick, St., xiii, 28, 213–224, 238
Paul, St., xi
pigs, 17
Poeninus, 5
Pompeius Trogus, 6
Posidonius, xi–xii, 13
Pryderi, 174, 179–187
Pwyll, 165–174, 186–187

reincarnation, x
Rhiannon, 11–12, 170–174, 179–185, 209
Rhun, 202–203
ring, 20, 100
Rosmerta, 2

sacrifice, 5, 7, 12
Sainrith mac Imbaith, 51
salmon, 26, 100, 102, 157
Samain, 22, 31–32, 110, 123, 126–128, 137–138, 158
samildánach, 2
Scáthach, 72–74
Sémión, 17
Sencha, 52, 60, 117–118, 124
Senchán Torpéist, 47–48
Sequana, 12
Sétanta, 58–66
shape-shifting, 15, 17–18, 28, 35, 37, 43, 59, 188–189, 200
síd, 29, 31, 43, 58, 83, 98, 101, 105, 123, 137, 139, 145, 157, 168, 181
Sithchenn, 148–149
slavery, xiii, 33, 105, 116, 214
Sliab Fúait, 68
Sliab Mis, 26
Solinus, 6
Sreng mac Sengainn, 19
Sualdam, 59
Sucellus, 8
Sulis, 6

Taliesin, 201–205
Tara, 18, 21, 27, 37–40, 108, 141, 159, 215
Taranis, 5
Tarvos Trigaranus, 7
Teutates, 5
Teyrnon Twrf Liant, 173–174
Timaeus, ix
Tolkien, x
Torna the Poet, 147
Triath, 30
Túachell, 68–69
Tuán, 15–18, 25, 28
tuath, 153
Tuatha Dé Danann, 14–15, 18–28, 29, 33, 35, 123, 162
twins, ix, 51, 190
Twrch Trwyth, 209

Uathach, 73
Uirgriu, 153
Uisnech, 26, 31, 109, 145

Victoricus, 215

wolves, 114

Xenophon, xi

Ysbaddaden, 206–211

Zeus, 5